Astrid Noble

and the Dragon Watchers

by E. M. Ritter

Copyright 2016 by E. M. Ritter

The moral right of the author has been asserted. No part of this publication may be reproduced, stored in a retrieval system, or transmitted in any form or by any means without the prior permission in writing of the publisher. Nor be otherwise circulated in any form of binding or cover other than that in which it is published and without a similar condition including this condition being imposed on the subsequent purchaser.

All rights reserved.

All characters and events in this publication, other than those clearly in the public domain, are fictitious and any resemblance to real persons, living or dead, is purely coincidental.
ISBN-13: 978-1530517503

CHAPTER 1

This is the last time, I thought, knowing I made this same promise at least a dozen times before. The quaint English marketplace was bustling with people, some hired by the rich to purchase ingredients for their decadent meals. Others were looking to trade what little they had for a small roll of bread and a quart of milk, to last all of that night and the next day if lucky. Dried chilies hung above boxes overflowing with spices and dried herbs. Women with flowers wilting from the heat begged men to buy from them to no avail.

Out of sight, I crouched behind the barrels emanating the stench of salted herring. There was a leakage in one of the barrels, and the salty fish water drenched the tattered hem of my dress. The butcher was just across the way. It was the perfect spot for me to complete my mission, grab a ham hock and save the boy.

It was the same young boy, as usual, getting his hands whipped for stealing in the marketplace. I had bailed him out countless times before. He was about eight years old, half my age and too young to know the proper way to steal without being caught. I have to admit, I'm not entirely innocent either. Although my palms were filthy and coated in soot, my skin was never broken. Along with the boy, I lived in the same abandoned factory where all the other orphan children lived independently among each other. There were about forty of us all together, but no one was close enough to know me firsthand. Instead, they were aware of the stories shared about the things I'd done to protect them. I was the oldest of them all and there was no question why this was the way it was. I've survived longer than any orphan they ever knew. It was obvious I could to fend for myself like none of them ever could. The children admired my longevity and the protection I supplied them. They called me *The Watcher*, a nickname that made me cringe. It made me sound like some kind of spy or guard on patrol. I assure you I'm neither of those. Simply put, I just so happen to be at the right places at the right time. The right place always seemed to be the marketplace where there's plenty of food to be stolen and plenty of orphans looking for their next meal.

"You have to be quicker, kid," I said under my breath, "like me. You can't let them catch you."

Donned in a bloodied apron, the burly butcher towered over the young thief. He gripped the struggling boy with one arm and readied a hunting whip to lash him with the other.

"This will teach you to steal from me, boy," the butcher growled. "Open your hand!"

The butcher drew back his whip. Its length would strike more than the boy's palm, and I could instantly tell the man delighted in knowing this.

Prepared to feel the sting at any moment, the boy shielded his face in the crook of his arm. I bet he wished he had longer sleeves to wear that day. Too bad he didn't have a choice. Just like all of the orphans, the shirt on his back was the only one he owned. It was a risk to steal from the butcher, but the chunk of dried deer he was able to grab and stuff quickly into his mouth before his capture was probably worth it. The meat most likely sank into his empty stomach, and, although he was still starving, the feeling of something in his belly that wasn't a cricket or blades of grass was satisfying.

Time for intervention. If I didn't get a move on helping this kid out soon, he'd be reduced to a piece of meat himself. Eyeing his captor from above his shielding arm, the boy watched as the butcher's whip came down. He winced in anticipation. Before he could feel the thong slice through, the boy's arm was released and he fell to the ground. Wrapped around the butcher's arm was my bullwhip eight feet in length. His hunting whip had fallen to the ground, and he fought to release himself from me. The bottom of my dress dripped with water and in my other hand I held a ham hock.

"Run," I urged the boy.

"*The Watcher*," he breathed, eyes widening.

I furrowed my brows and shouted with greater urgency, "Run! Or I'll set him loose on you again."

It took him a moment before he fully understood I meant what I said and scurried from the marketplace. Anger rose in the butcher's face in the color of red as he watched the boy escape.

Gritting his teeth, he grabbed onto my bullwhip wrapped around his arm and swung it with great force. Off the ground I was lifted, flailing in the air until crashing onto the butcher's table among the dried meats. The butcher sneered, snapping the bullwhip on the ground as he got closer.

"So you're *the Watcher*, eh? Tell me, what gives you the right to stop us hard working shop owners from seeking justice from thieving, little criminals?"

"I'm no one's *watcher*," I stood and brushed my black hair from my eyes. "And perhaps you should show a little pity on hungry children once in a while. They didn't ask for their parents to die or abandon them."

With the ham hock still in my grip, I ripped a piece of dried meat off the bone with my teeth before throwing it to the ground.

"Bring it on, little girl," he scoffed, wiping the sweat collecting from his upper lip. "When I'm done with you, you'll wish you didn't care so much about those thieving orphans."

This man was huge, perhaps three times my size. I had a feeling what he just said was probably not too far from the truth. I thought quickly to avoid giving up my title of oldest surviving orphan. "You don't have to fight me. I'll work to repay for whatever was stolen this past year. And when that debt is done, I'll work to buy the scraps you'll throw out at the end of the day. That's extra money for you and food for the children."

"You'll be working your whole life repaying that debt. You'll never get the chance to buy any extras for anybody." He inched closer, and I could his feel warm breath panting on me.

"I'll work long hours, I promise. The debt will be paid."

The butcher towered over me. He was either considering my proposition and contemplating how much to trust this juvenile delinquent, or he was determining the best way to pound me into the ground. I stood still and confident as he glared into my cerulean blue eyes.

"Who are you?" he asked suspiciously.

I raised my chin slightly and straightened my shoulders. With an unfaltering voice, I answered, "I am Astrid Noble."

Taking a step back, the butcher's face softened. He held out my bullwhip for me to take.

"Noble, huh?" he said with raised eyebrows. "Since when did orphans have last names?"

"It's one I chose myself. From a book, *The Noble King*," I said.

"Ah... Well then, Astrid... *Noble.* I'll allow you to work to pay off the debt of the orphans, so long as they stop stealing from my shop. At the end of the day, you can take whatever scraps you like back to them." His tone softened a bit. "I'm not all that bad, you know. I have two small children of my own, so I can sympathize. You can start right now," he said and motioned towards the slanted table with spilled dried meats. "I've got a wreckage on my hands and no one else to help me."

Making my way to the mess, I let out a breath I didn't know I'd been holding. There's no doubt I was grateful for the peaceful ending and the promise of food for the children at the end of the day.

It was dark and the cobbled street was moist from a light but steady mist. The shops of the marketplace were all closed and the people had scattered long ago. Only a few individuals roamed the darkness, trying their best to blend into the shadows. Heads down, hats lowered, passing each other like ghosts afraid of ghosts.

Carrying a covered box filled with dried meat scraps, I hastened down the street and through musty alleys. The factory where I lived was not much further away. When I finally reached the end of the last alley, I tossed the box over the brick wall. With great ease that comes with years of practice, I hoisted myself to the top of the wall at least eight feet in height. It still remained a mystery to me how the other much younger orphans were able to jump this wall just as I did. Food is a powerful motivator. We'd been training to jump these walls at a very young age in order to reward our bellies with something from the marketplace.

Once on the other side, the abandoned factory was hard to miss. Scattered piles of cinder blocks and brick lined the path leading to its entrance. They were remnants of an industrialized city that no longer stood, crumbled to the ground after failure moved its people away. A brick wall was built around the perimeter to shield the town from the reminder of a past better left forgotten.

The orphaned children didn't mind the look of destruction outside the walls of their brown stone factory. They'd affectionately dubbed it *the castle*. Two smokestacks stood tall, relics of a time long ago when they would wave their smoky grey flags in the air, the symbol of success. The four-storied building was all they had for themselves. A home where the townspeople would never dare to enter or have anything to do with.

I gathered the meats that had escaped from the box and placed them back in before venturing to the castle entrance. The metal door was heavy, but, using my back, I pushed it open with ease. The castle was expansive and mainly vacant, except for rusty pipes along the ceiling and broken windows that decorated the walls. I set the food on the floor near the center of the room.

"There's meat for everyone," I announced to the empty space. "If you come out, you can eat. I've had my share, so I'll be on my way."

I took no more than three steps back before I heard the faint sound of timid footsteps resonating off the concrete walls. Although

I couldn't see them, I knew they were there lingering in the shadows. As I turned to leave, I collided into something soft against my stomach. I jumped back, startled for not quite a second when I realized what I had bumped into.

The younger girl was no more than four years old. Her stringy blonde hair, matted in oils and dirt, framed her round apple cheeks perfectly. There were streaks of dirt across her face, and her clothes that were once white were now brown and grey. The little girl beamed her brown, doe-eyes directly at me.

"Thank you," the little girl said simply.

I nodded and patted the girl on the head. Without warning, the arms of the child wrapped around my waist. Flustered, I thought of how warm the girl felt and wondered how one so starved could manage to have the strength to squeeze so hard.

When she finally released me from her grip, the little girl spoke again, "Today you saved my brother, John. And I'm Pike."

I cringed. In all the three years I lived in the castle, I tried my hardest not to learn any of the residents' names. Children would come and leave, or disappear, all too quickly. Keeping to myself made life simpler, made it easier to stay in one place for longer. I'd just secured work with the butcher and daily scraps for the orphans. There was no way I would let anyone compromise my stay at the castle, no one.

I loomed over Pike and glared at her, "Tell your brother to stay away from the butcher's table, or he and you will no longer be invited to eat the scraps I bring."

Pike bit her lower lip and nodded.

"Good," I said. "Now go eat."

I made my way to the door leading to the upper levels. I lingered behind the door as the orphans carefully stepped out of the shadows. Although their stomachs growled, calling out for food, they were impressively calm and organized. The children passed the meat around to each other, the youngest ones were served first. Whatever was left over, the oldest orphans divided amongst themselves.

This is why, I reminded myself, I can never leave. This is why this place is my home.

CHAPTER 2

It was a record of about three seconds to fall asleep. My belly was more full than it had ever been, and the adventure in the marketplace was more than enough to knock me out good. I slept in a room tucked in the far end of the second floor. Luckily for me, it was one of the few remaining rooms with a window still intact.

One of the benefits of being the eldest of all the orphans in the castle was that everyone else was too scared to sleep alone. Most of the children huddled together in rooms on the higher levels. Their greatest fear was being taken in the middle of the night by the men from the Agency. No one had ever seen them. Some even believed the Agency was make believe told by the older orphans to the younger ones to keep them close at night. The youngest children had a higher chance of abduction. They were easier to train and far easier to subdue in the middle of the night. Those taken would be separated and forced illegally to work in the coal mines or steel factories, the exact same places their parents once worked. Workplace accidents were all too common, and so were orphans. I relished in the privacy of my own room, no one to talk to meant no attachments. Just the way I wanted it to stay. The next time I have scraps to deliver for the orphans, it'd be best not to announce it. One of them will smell it and alert the others anyway. I'd like to avoid another "Pike incident" if I could.

"Astrid," the wind seemed to whisper my name as I slept.

"Astrid," it called to me again, but the voice was much louder, clearer.

I stirred, fighting to stay asleep. Something didn't feel right. I turned over on my dusty mattress, a luxury I discovered in the room of another child who disappeared from the castle two years before.

"Astrid!" This time the voice was speaking directly into my ear. My eyes shot open as I sat up. I scanned the room for anything or anyone that could've beckoned. No one was around, and there was no way someone could've fled so quickly after waking me. I decided there was no intruder, and the phantom voice was simply from a dream. My muscles were restless in my back and along my neck, like a worm inching just underneath my skin. Something wasn't quite right.

I stood up and stretched my arms. Nothing. I turned at the waist to remove some tension along my back. Still no luck. Eventually, I tried cracking my neck and turned it from side to side. Anxiety flooded me even more so. I slipped into my boots and began to jog in place. Once I'd had enough jogging, I bent over to touch my toes. The sound of glass shattering prompted me upright again. A rock the size of an adult fist had broken through my window, flew over my bent down body, and landed on the mattress behind me. The rock had been wrapped in cloth and set ablaze. My mattress began to burn.

"Holy smokes!" I called out and quickly stamped out the flames with my blanket.

I rushed to the window, hoping to catch the culprit before he ran away. There was no sign of anyone outside the castle. The night seemed still, eerily calm. I scanned the outside grounds again but found nothing unusual.

Unexpectedly, the entrance to the castle suddenly swung open. Two figures dressed in black exited, each carried a sleeping child over his shoulder. It was dark, but the moon was full. I could make out a boy of about six years old slung over one figure's shoulder. The other child was blonde with stringy hair and apple cheeks.

"Pike," I uttered in dismay. I grabbed my bullwhip and raced out the door.

The other orphans were still locked away in their rooms, unaware of the abductions that were taking place. I cracked the whip a few times to wake them as I headed towards the stairwell to the main floor.

"Wake up!" I hollered. "Wake everyone up! The Agency is here, and they've got two of us!"

At first, the children rubbed their droopy eyelids. It was apparent dreams of filling their bellies once again with meats from the butcher's block were fresh in their heads. The mention of the Agency changed all that. The younger children screamed and scrambled back into their rooms, their sweet dreams disrupted by the nightmarish reality. Some of the older children followed as I ran out of the castle, while others dispersed noisily to wake the others.

Once outside the castle doors, I could make out the figures hauling away the two children. They were walking at a steady pace up until they heard me crack my whip from behind them. I had to stop them before they got the children to the wall. I was certain they had a vehicle waiting for them on the other side. Then Pike and the boy would be gone forever.

A pack of eight older orphans were still far behind. The agents were one hundred feet from the wall, too close. I charged forward faster, ignoring the side stitch that threatened to slow me down. I managed to catch up close enough to see the figures were clothed from top to bottom in black. They wore ski masks over their heads and belts with holstered guns.

The taller of the two agents carried Pike. A red tranquilizer dart protruded from her neck. Her head bobbled against his back as he moved. The agent grabbed onto the top of the wall with one arm, while holding onto Pike with the other. With great ease, the shorter agent hauled himself and the boy still draped over his shoulder to the top of the wall. I snapped my whip back and then flung it towards the agent. It wrapped around his leg before he could swing it over the wall. I pulled him down to the ground, the boy falling from his grasp and into a patch of shrubbery. The fallen agent shuffled to his feet and quickly made his way over the wall, disappearing almost instantly. At the top of the wall, the taller agent struggled to pull himself up with Pike as quickly as his partner. Again I drew my bullwhip and wrapped it around one of the agent's legs as he sat at the very top of the wall.

The eight other orphans finally arrived, and few of them were able to take the boy to safety. The rest stood by me.

"Get ready to catch Pike when I pull her down," I instructed them. I yanked the agent hard. Before he tipped to the ground and fell, he threw Pike over on the other side of the wall. The children heard a loud thump, the sound of her body hitting the concrete.

"No!" I screamed. With little hesitation, I climbed the wall.

The orphans pounded their fists on the fallen agent, but he managed to push away and flee to another part of the wall to disappear over it.

Once I landed safely on the city-side of the wall, I made my way immediately to the lifeless body of the little girl. Falling to my knees, I scooped up Pike into my arms. A rush of emotion flooded my chest. Maybe it was what I felt for all the orphans I lived with, surfacing for the first time after a near lifetime of denial. But Pike was also very special. This little girl meant a lot to me, too. Pike was the first person to offer me a loving embrace since the day I lost my parents, a day I would never forget. Something inside me awakened when the little girl showed me warmth, a sense of family and belonging. I couldn't lose Pike now that I'd just found her. The lump in my throat was unfamiliar. I swallowed to get it down. I regretted my last words to her. My tone had been so cold. Why did I have to be so hardhearted?

"Pike," I soothed. "Hey, Pike. Wake up."

I brushed her Pike's hair from her eyes and caressed her apple cheeks. My vision began to blur as tears welled up. It felt so strange to cry. I couldn't remember a time before that I ever did. I blinked and one tear escaped. It landed onto Pike's cheek and rolled off her face. I gently laid the little girl on the ground and stood over her.

"I'm going to find those agents and make them pay for what they've done," I promised. Once the words escaped my mouth, the little girl groaned in obvious pain. I knelt down beside her.

"You're alive," I gasped, smiling through tears. I picked up Pike into my arms.

"Not so fast," the nasal voice of a man warned me from behind. "That girl belongs to the Agency now."

I had a feeling it was the short agent. The one that was quick on his feet and had ran away as fast as he could. Of course, a character like him would show up when his enemy was flooding with tears.

"If I don't bring a kid back, I don't get paid. So you'd be doing my own kids a great disservice because if I don't get paid, they don't eat. You got that, girl?" He cocked the hammer of his gun, cautioning me to follow his directions. "Put the girl down and turn around."

My tears quickly dried as heated adrenaline coursed through my body. I carefully placed Pike back onto the ground, feeling the handle of my whip tucked in the back of my pants. Everything had happened so suddenly that evening, I didn't have the chance to fasten my holster. I rose slowly.

"Turn around slowly," he ordered. "I want you to watch me when I kill you."

Obediently, I faced the short agent. My eyes were kept slightly lowered and timid. He stepped closer, pointing his gun at my forehead. Without warning, I bolted my eyes up to meet his. Before he could pull the trigger, I swiftly raised my arm and with the back of my hand, knocked the gun from his grasp. Lifting my knee, I struck him in the place I knew would cause the most pain, and he cowered low. Recovering almost straight away, the short agent rammed his head into my stomach, and I fell to the ground onto my back. I quickly rebounded to my feet. I noticed several arms reaching over from above the brick wall. The orphans were making their way over.

As the short agent made his way to Pike, I pulled my bullwhip from behind. I snapped the whip, and it wrapped around his waist. There was no way I'd let him take her again. I jerked him to the ground.

"Astrid," I heard someone call. Thinking it was one of the orphans, I spun around only to find myself not ten feet away from the other, taller agent. His head was still covered under the black ski mask, but his eyes showed through. They were a stormy grey, beautiful yet haunting.

"I'm glad I finally found you," he said, as he raised his gun with a unique ivory and wooden handgrip I've never seen before.

Before I could react, I watched the bullet as it traveled closer towards me. It was headed between my eyes, and there was no time to move. It was over. A white light flashed before my eyes. I felt a gentle tug at my wrist and then everything went black.

CHAPTER 3

"Astrid," it was the wind again, blowing in the distance.

"Astrid." This time it was louder, the muffled voice of a man.

My eyes fluttered as I fought to regain consciousness. How long was I out? It was daylight, but I couldn't see very well. My vision was blurred, and I felt slightly dizzy. Someone was hovering over me, watching me closely. I rubbed my eyes, but it only made my vision hazier.

"Astrid, it's time to start moving," the man urged. "They'll be here soon."

Unable to gauge distance with my compromised vision, I sat up quickly and knocked my forehead against the man's head.

"Sorry," the man apologized. "I didn't have enough time to warn you to close your eyes before we traveled through the portal."

I rubbed my head and winced. "Does this mean I'm not dead?"

Leaves crunched in the distance. Someone or something was approaching rapidly.

"No, you're not dead, but you will be if we don't get a move on," the man's voice was rough and deep. Even with blurred vision, I could tell he was much older, with a long, white beard and matching bushy eyebrows. He was dressed in a long, brown robe that reached the ground paired with a brown, Renaissance flat hat atop his head.

"Where are we going?" I asked.

The man took my hand and pulled me to my feet. "Less talking, more running. I'll answer all questions later, and I know you'll have plenty."

Who was this person, and how did I know he wasn't working for the Agency? Every adult is a greedy suspect right now. He took several steps before realizing I wasn't following him.

"How do I know I can trust you?" I crossed my arms.

As if to answer my question, an arrow came hurtling through the trees. I couldn't see it very well with my poor vision until it got dangerously close. From yards away, the man held his hand out as if pulling the end of the arrow to slow it down. The arrow came to a halt, barely touching the tip of my nose before it dropped to the ground. Stunned, I turned to the old man with bewildered eyes.

"Run," he ordered.

I ran and caught up quickly to the old man. We ducked to avoid a stream of arrows coming at us from their right. It was useless and only a matter of time before we'd both get struck if the man didn't pick up his pace. Before I could worry any further, the man's arms spread out, growing feathers over his skin. His legs pulled up, replaced by bird's legs and talons. Although I was regaining my eyesight quickly, I began to think my brain wasn't all in place. Before my eyes, the man swiftly transformed into a magnificent peregrine falcon. Instead of the pace being too slow now, I found myself having difficulty keeping up with the fleeting bird.

We fled through the forest, venturing deeper into its swampy center. I felt my heart pound in my chest as I pushed myself in order to keep up. Soon we came to a dead end. Tangled branches that looked like twisted fingers riddled with thorns threatened to stop us in our tracks. The falcon opened his wings, commanding the trees. The branches pulled apart like hands welcoming us in. A passageway for us to walk through was created. Once through, the branches closed behind us. Walking through the tunnel of branches felt almost everlasting, but I trudged on and followed the bird. When the last thorny branch parted, a clearing was exposed. The thorny branches grew in arches above. They intertwined and created a cover, shielding the area from intruders overhead. There stood a considerably giant boulder in the middle of the shaded clearing. It was huge and seemingly out of place. There were no mountains or hills in sight. Where the boulder came from was a mystery to me. A dense forest served as its backdrop, and I strolled ahead, ready to continue our journey.

When I realized the falcon wasn't leading the way, I turned around. There he was, but he was no longer a bird but a man again.

He stood before the boulder and held his palm out. Part of the rock glided open like a door. Then the man walked in, and I, less reluctantly this time, followed him.

I'd never been inside of a boulder before, much less one whose interior looked surprisingly like a real home. It was a real home, at least to this man.

Or is he a bird turned into a man? I contemplated.

Difficult to tell from the outside, but the home was more spacious than I expected. We stood in what I presumed to be the living area. There were all sorts of exotic stringed instruments lined against one wall. Among them was a lute, Hardanger fiddle, and a lute-like instrument that resembled a walking stick with a gourd on its end. A strange, large hazelnut-shaped contraption attached behind its neck. I fought the urge to pluck all their strings. If I'd broken anything from his collection, I wouldn't know where to find replacements. So I continued to look elsewhere. Books lined another wall with titles I didn't recognize because they were written in languages I'd never seen before. There were windows that looked out that I didn't see from outside the boulder, and even a fireplace, although I couldn't recall seeing a chimney. Nothing about the exterior of the boulder even hinted it was someone's home. Also, nothing about the interior suggested it was rock.

"Please," the man said in his scruffy, grandfatherly voice. "Make yourself at home and I'll prepare something for us to eat."

He held his hand out and, without touching it, dragged a wooden chair closer to where I stood. Dumbfounded, I obediently sat down. I wasn't quite sure when I would get used to seeing all this magic, *if* I'd get used to it.

The man took his hat off and threw it towards a coat rack.

"That's much better," he sighed. "Can't go around the forest saving fugitives looking like an accomplice wizard now, can I?"

The hat glided across the room, as if carried off by butterflies before finding its place on a hook. He lifted his hand and a hat that resembled more of a brown sorcerer's hat floated onto his head. He pulled a pair of silver rimmed spectacles from his pocket. Although they lacked temples, the spectacles rested easily on his nose without any sign of unsteadiness.

"I'm feeling like hairy turtle soup tonight. Sound good to you?" he asked casually, as he made his way to the stove in the adjacent room.

"Wait!" I called out. "I mean, who are you? You haven't told me who you are or why I'm here."

"Too many questions before we eat. Let's eat first, and then I'll explain everything," he grinned.

I buried my head into my hands. There was so much to take in, the burning rock in my room, the Agency abducting Pike, barely surviving a bullet between the eyes and an arrow through the nose. Perhaps there was still a chance I'd wake up from this dream. I needed answers, but I knew I needed to be patient. The wizard was obviously risking his life to protect me. But why? I hadn't a clue. Nevertheless, I decided to reciprocate the kindness and not push for any more information. Unfortunately, patience was never my forte.

A whimper escaped from my throat, unaware it was loud enough for the wizard to hear.

"You can call me Willox," he said, taking pity on me. "And there is much more you'll need to know, but not on an empty stomach."

I offered a grateful smile in return, "Thank you."

"Hairy turtle soup?" he added excitedly.

Hairy turtle what? That sounded so disgusting and hard to swallow.

"Hairy turtle soup sounds great," I lied.

# # #

I didn't know how I did it, but I cleaned my bowl out of every drop of the hairy turtle soup. Either it was truly delicious, like eating pork chunks wrapped in corn silk in a thick broth, or I was extremely hungry after all the running we'd done the night before.

I was filled to the brim with a home cooked meal. I couldn't even remember the last time someone had ever cooked anything for me. It was a comforting feeling to have someone who cared, a feeling I wished would last forever.

Pike, I thought. Did the Agency take her? Who'll look after her now?

I stood up abruptly from the dining table. What was I doing filling my belly and enjoying the comforts of a wizard's magical boulder home? I needed to get back to the castle and fast.

"I'm so sorry to have to leave so suddenly," I apologized. "But I have to get back home to Pike. She needs me, and so do the others."

"Nothing to worry about, Astrid," Willox said between sips. "The girl will be fine, and the butcher will bring the trimmings at the end of the day. He's a good man and won't forget the children."

"But the Agency," I began. "The agent had a gun."

"The smaller agent was outnumbered by the other orphans that came to help. They took Pike back to the factory. She should be awake by now."

"But how do you know?" I was still not convinced.

He simply tapped his wizard hat, "There are a lot of things I can do and see. Of course, there are many more I have no control over."

"What about the other agent? Did he hurt any of them?"

Willox placed his spoon on the table and smoothed out his robe. I could tell he was preparing me for something I wasn't sure I was quite ready to hear.

"The second agent," he spoke warily, "was sent to kill you and nobody else. The other children were of no interest to him. Pike was a mere decoy to lure you from the factory."

It was a lot to take in. I'd always hoped living as an orphan in an abandoned factory was the worst it would ever get. Never in my wildest dreams did I imagine being stalked by a stranger who wanted to end my life. Whose path did I cross that could have led to such malice against me? I couldn't think of a single person. Sliding back into my chair, I stared blankly at the table sorting through my past escapades.

My cheeks burned with rage when I finally figured it out, "It was Hendricks, wasn't it? He sent that man to take Pike and probably threw that burning rock through my window. It was him, wasn't it? I knew he was lying when he said he forgave me for burning down his stable."

Willox raised an eyebrow in wonderment.

"What?" I shrugged. "I was cold, and I didn't think hay would go up in flames so quickly. I was nine at the time, too, so I didn't know as much as I do now. I see it as a learning experience. I mean, it was because of that accident that I learned a lot about how fires work, what burns and what doesn't, and how to put one out. Sure, I had to learn the hard way, but... I did spend the rest of the year making up for it. Any other guilty kid would've run away. I stayed back and helped to rebuild."

"It wasn't Hendricks, or whoever you may think it is," he casually interjected.

"Okay," I said, embarrassed by my confession.

"You see," he said as he held his closed fist over the table. I leaned in closer to see what was inside. When he opened his hand, a ball of light danced before me. Every second it twirled, the larger it expanded until the image of a man and woman holding hands at the altar appeared from within.

"Astrid," he continued. "These are your parents."

Their faces were none I could remember. My father was hardly a couple inches taller than my mother. He had black, choppy hair and blue eyes like my own. My mother, on the other hand, wore her hair long. The blonde locks of hair flowed down her back like the mane of a unicorn. Her eyes were as blue and passionate as my father's.

"She's so beautiful, and he is, too," I breathed. Then I brought myself to ask, "What were they like?"

His face softened as he remembered. "Never have I had a negative thought about your parents. In fact, people couldn't get enough of being in their presence. Each of them possessed an essence of something special that couldn't be found anywhere else, within anyone else. But even more so, they were remarkable together. Your father never spoke more than he needed to. I suppose you can say he was the listener and your mother was the talker in their relationship. On the rare occasion he did have something to say, you knew you'd have to listen for it was going to be significant and mostly likely beneficial. Your mother, on the other hand, was extremely charismatic and a born leader. Honestly, I don't think I've ever witnessed anyone fall for someone as deeply as your father fell for her. Since the day he met her, not a day could he be without her."

Willox held his palm under the projection, and the light retreated into his hand. He closed his fist and then opened it again, revealing an amber stone.

"They wanted you to have this when the time was right. I've been holding onto this amulet for years. The image inside was captured by wizardry and melded into this stone with the help of a dragon's breath."

"It's beautiful," I acknowledged. "But don't you have cameras like we do in England?"

He shook his head, "The technologies of other worlds are strictly prohibited. At least, that was what was agreed upon to preserve our traditions and existence."

"You mean, we're not in England anymore?" I asked, feigning astonishment. I held out my hand and Willox dropped the amulet into it.

"No," he assured me. "I'm not even sure we're in the same reality that your England exists."

I shook my head in confusion, "I'm not following."

"Astrid, the important concept to understand right now is that you're in grave danger. King Haggin has creatures from all over looking for you to destroy you. The tall agent was working for Haggin."

"So who is this King Haggin, and why does he care about finding me?" I asked. "There are so many other people out there that know him personally and wish him ill will, I'm sure. He's a king. There's always someone in the inner circle who'd want to overthrow him, right? So why come after me?"

"There's a prophecy that tells of the near destruction of Alderek. The demise of the creatures that inhabit our world will follow after the rise of the darkness. He is suppressing cultures, wiping out colonies, and destroying food supplies. But the prophecy also speaks of hope in the form of a child. A child King Haggin never knew existed until now."

"So where is this kid?" I asked perplexed. "Can't we find him and get him to overthrow Haggin?"

Willox raised his eyebrows as if amused by my naiveté. I shifted in my seat.

"You're not suggesting," I began with a nervous chuckle. I gulped. By the look on his face, I already knew the answer but hung on to the hope I was seriously wrong. "The child in the prophecy, you think it's me."

"Before I continue, I think you should know something else," he said. It would be more serious stuff. I could tell because it was his turn to gulp. What he said next seemed like an eternity to deliver. He spoke ever-so deliberately, "You're not an orphan. And your parents are very much alive."

"Impossible," I gasped. "I saw the explosion. No one could've survived that. I watched them die."

"They escaped through a transport, much like the one I took you through to get here. They needed you to believe they were dead," he said.

"Why?" I said, agitated. "So I could grow up alone? So I could spend my days wondering why they sent me outside to play when they should've come with me?"

Resentment mounted in my head, at the same time I couldn't deny the sorrow of time lost in my heart. How could this happen? Why did they leave me? I could barely move, barely breathe. All I wanted to do was to get things sorted out, so I could get back home. Parents or no parents, I had an obligation to myself to take care of the orphans in the castle. Regardless of why my parents thought they needed to abandon me, I couldn't do the same to them.

Willox stood from the table and transformed into a peregrine falcon. "Follow me," his voice said in my ear. I looked to see if anyone was next to me, but only the falcon hovered in front.

"You can speak telepathically, too?" I asked, impressed.

"Only in my falcon form," he replied. Then he added, "I'm not a parrot."

"Of course. That would be silly if falcons could speak like parrots, wouldn't it?"

Dropping the amulet into my pocket, I followed Willox out the back door his boulder home.

"Prophecy or no prophecy, Willox, why would King Haggin think a nobody girl from a different world like me would be able to stop him from destroying Alderek? I mean, is he that insecure?" I wondered as I continued to spew out more questions. "What about my parents? Can you take me to see them? Where are we going?"

"To see Queen Pavia." Although he flew twenty feet ahead of me, I could hear him as if he was next to me. "She was a friend of your great, great grandfather's and all his descendants after him, even your parents. She can tell you what you'll need to know."

"She knew my great, great grandfather? How old is she?"

"It's hard to tell a fairy's age. They aren't born looking like babies, nor do they die looking like an aged wizard," he said. "Try to ask for one's age, and you'll discover it's even harder to get an answer."

"Fairy?" I said. "What doesn't this place have? Secret boulder homes, wizards that shape shift into falcons..."

"There are no *wizards* in Alderek," he said. "Only me."

"You mean, you're the only one?" I gasped.

"It's part of our long and very painful history, Astrid," he answered solemnly. "Our world has never been the same since King Haggin came to rule. Perhaps Queen Pavia can tell the story better than I can."

I couldn't imagine what it must have felt like to be the last of any kind. There was a lot, I was beginning to learn, that this King Haggin had deprived the creatures of Alderek. Why were there no more wizards besides Willox? What did he know about wizards that he forbade more than one in Alderek? What did he know about me that made him want to kill me? I was beginning to think Haggin's fear of the unknown, was fueling his need to destroy in order to control.

We ventured into the clearing beyond Willox's home. High above, the thick, thorny vines began to knit into the dense canopy of the woods that lay ahead. Under our feet, the soft green moss turned to trees damp grey leaves. It was dark in the forest. The sunshine ceased to travel beyond the wall of slender trunks. Only slivers of daylight made their way through the tops of the trees, which seemed impossibly tall. They were nestled extremely close together, naturally forming a protective enclosure hidden from unwanted intruders. The air became noticeably colder as we trekked deeper into the forest, and a faint silver frost started to show on the trunks. The ground beneath us was dusted in patches of white snow. I watched as my breath became visible and swirled, revealing the pattern of the chill air. There were noises I'd never heard before from animals I'd never seen before. Although it was dark and unfamiliar, I somehow felt safe. Something about the forest made me feel watched or, better put, looked after. We were about a mile into the forest when Willox perched onto a fallen log. I sat next to him, emulating his behavior of being still and quiet.

"Don't be afraid," he told me.

And then I saw them, hundreds of them, swarm me.

CHAPTER 4

Fairies gathered around. Some found resting spots next to me on the log, while others chose to land directly onto me. They got comfortable on my arms, legs, and even my shoulders and head.

"I love her hair," the fairy on top of my head sighed. "It's so silky smooth!"

"Her arms are like rocks," another said as he pinched my arm muscles.

"Ouch! Hey," I pulled the fairy from my arm and placed him on the ground.

There were at least two to three hundred of them, all between six to eight inches tall. Their wings were transparent like glass, each with intricate and unique opaque patterns. All the fairies were talking at once, and I could make out only fragments of what they were saying.

"She's too short," one complained.

"She's only a child. What did you expect?" another quickly chastised.

"Alderek will never be saved now. What can she do for us?" several others grumbled.

"I think she's lovely," a little voice managed to pipe up.

"Willox, are you crazy? All our lives are at risk now that you've brought her here!" shrieked another.

"We'll starve in this dastardly forest for sure if this is the one the Omaan spoke of," another griped.

"The Omaan is wrong!" shouted one of the larger fairies. Before I knew what was happening, fairies pushed me from the log on one side. They attempted to roll me away. Pygmy fairies, too small to intervene with either side, watched from the sidelines. Their eyes were large and their heads were round like bubbles. I tried to get to my feet. The force of the little hands was too great, and I stumbled repeatedly. Other fairies came to my rescue, coming in between the angry ones and me. My clothes and hair were pulled in every which way, as I tried my best to swat them off.

"Let her go," demanded a bold female voice.

Every fairy obeyed her command at once. Without the pull of the fairies on either side of me, I fell back to the ground.

"Forgive them, child," the female continued. "They are too young to understand the prophecies of the Omaan."

The once indignant fairies hid behind the tree trunks and among the leaves, the shame in their eyes obvious.

"The Omaan," I repeated. "What is it?"

A young fairy with cheeks that filled her face much like Pike's quickly answered, "It's not a *what* so much as a *who*. And, please, don't listen to the others. I really like you. They're just sore because we haven't been home for so long and we're all getting so hungry. There's not much left to eat that won't kill us." The fairy wrapped her hands around her neck as if she was choking, closed her eyes, and stuck her tongue out. There and then, I knew I liked this fairy and her dark sense of humor.

"Myrilla!" a portly male fairy scolded. "Let Queen Pavia do the explaining, or you'll just confuse her even more."

He turned to me, "Excuse my friend here. She doesn't mean to scare you off so soon. Myrilla's a bit morbid at times. I'm Ecson, by the way. And if you want to know more about the Omaan, I'm the fairy to ask. The Omaan's like the oldest guy in Alderek. No one's ever seen his face because he walks around with this brown cape and hood and cane like this..."

Ecson demonstrated the Omaan's walk, which was not much different than the walk of an elderly man.

Another fairy cut Ecson off. "Don't listen to him," he advised. "Neither Ecson nor any of the others here have ever seen the Omaan. Only Queen Pavia has. All we know is he carries that burden of foreseeing the future of all of Alderek."

The fairy held out his hand. I kindly offered mine, and he planted a gentle kiss on one of my fingers.

"The name is Maddux, my lady," he continued.

I blushed and felt slightly silly for being moved by an eight inch fairy. Despite his tiny exterior, Maddux was undeniably oozing with fairy charm and personality.

"That'll be enough. Thank you, Maddux," Willox interrupted, as he cleared his throat. He was returned to his wizard form, and offered me a hand from off of the forest floor.

The fairies and Willox lowered their heads as they stepped to the side to make room for the woman with the bold voice. A calming blue glow appeared to radiate from her skin and all around her body. Everything about her was long and slender, from her physique to her limbs and fingers. Her platinum blonde hair was chopped short and playful, unlike the pale blue gown she wore that teased to caress the ground. Although she surpassed the other fairies in size and perhaps was as tall as Willox, there was no doubt she too was a fairy. After all, it was hard not to notice her upwardly pointed-tipped ears and the magnificent translucent wings on her back.
This must be Queen Pavia, I thought. *But she's so young and so beautiful. She can't be any older than my mother's age, and certainly not old enough to have known my great, great grandfather.*

Then Queen Pavia spoke, and all the fairies, even those that hid behind the trees, came forth to listen and watch.

"There is no time to waste. The memories of your parents have been transferred to me, only the ones they've chosen to share," the queen began and laid her palm over my temple. "Just relax, Astrid. This won't hurt."

Before I could feel nervous, warmth radiated from the queen's hand. I was simultaneously overwhelmed by a deep calming trust and a sense of urgency that transferred from the queen. Images of my parents flooded before me, as Queen Pavia projected them into my mind. Memories shuffled through rapidly. At first they portrayed peaceful times when I was a child, such as the time my mother bought me my first popsicle which I ended up sharing with a puppy. There was even the memory of my father dancing with my mother. I couldn't make out the music that played, but I spied contently from underneath a table. I obviously thought they were aware of my presence, but their memory proved otherwise. Gradually, the memories grew darker as I watched my parents suffer the turmoil of having to abandon their only daughter in London only to return to Alderek to witness its destruction. Eventually, the images halted on a single vision. Confined in a dark cell, my parents together on the damp floor and chained to the wall. They did not look like the strong, young couple Willox had shown me through the amber amulet. Instead, they appeared fragile and defeated.

Queen Pavia released her touch from my temple. "Your parents are Tyrus and Amoldine Baker. Their lives are at risk but, even more so, is Alderek," she explained. "King Haggin has already endangered numerous populations of creatures in our world. He is threatening to annihilate the dragons and every single dragon watcher in order to claim the rest of the fairy population and more. The dragons and their watchers were the peacekeepers of our world. Once they're destroyed, the fairies will lack the protection we need against him. Haggin's created a potion that creates a dramatic change in the fairy physiology and mental state. If it was up to him, we'll all undergo the conversion after sipping his potion. It wipes our memories and transforms us into fenova, the dark fairies."

"Dark fairies?" I repeated.

"Part of the conversion, like I said, is physical. Fenovas grow as large as humans. Haggin uses the stronger ones in his army. The others he uses to collect creatures throughout the lands so they may slave on his fields. His kingdom is expanding rapidly and the fenova numbers are increasing as he takes over the remaining fairy colonies," Queen Pavia explained.

"How many colonies are left?"

The fairies exchanged looks of despair among each other. Ecson wrapped his arms around Myrilla, as she buried her face in her hands, taken by grief.

"We believe there are only two left." Willox finally spoke, an obvious despair in his voice. "This one and one more. With the dangers between travels, it's been difficult to keep in contact with the others."

"The dragon watchers. Who are they?" I asked. The questions kept flooding my head, and I didn't know how to make them stop. Everything was simply overwhelming. I continued, "And what does all this have to do with my parents? Why does this King Haggin have them locked away? What does he want from them?"

Queen Pavia made a scooping motion with her hand. It was as if she scooped some air into her palm and, like magic, appeared a frosty white amulet much like the amber one I had in my pocket. "Perhaps this will help you better understand the conflict Alderek is experiencing," she said.

The queen blew the amulet, and, with little effort, it drifted between us. It glowed and grew into a hazy, white cloud until it was twice the size of my head. Inside were the images that followed Queen Pavia's story.

"Long ago, before the Second Great Divide, which was created by King Haggin and is what we are experiencing right now, Alderek had no single ruler. Every creature that roamed our world lived and shared with each other. However, it wasn't always this way. Peace is never born from itself. So, let me take you to a time before this peace and a time before Haggin," Queen Pavia turned the cloud to reveal the images of this time of long ago. She continued, "The Omaan had predicted the First Great Divide of King Ganic, ruler of a small colony of humans at the edge of the Silk Forest. His prophecy proclaimed that a son would rise and bring peace amongst the turmoil that would pit every man against the dragons, causing great destruction. Naturally, Ganic, in his confusion felt threatened. There was no turmoil that existed between man and dragon yet, and his wife bore no children at the time. There was no timeline mentioned for when this prophecy would fall into place. Ganic lost much sleep over this prediction. When his wife came to him with the news of her pregnancy, he decided to take matters into his own hands. He assumed the "son" that would rise meant that his own flesh and blood would overthrow his crown. He feared this prophecy so much that when his only son was finally born, he decided he would kill him. When the Omaan learned of the king's plan, he stole the child and brought him to safety. Naturally, the dragons, being the largest and strongest of all of Alderek's creatures, were another fear of Ganic as they were also mentioned in the prophecy. But that fear only lasted so long. King Ganic wanted to do everything he could to annihilate them before they could destroy him. At this time, the dragons dwelled peacefully beneath the soil of Alderek. Before Ganic's wage of war against them, there was no history of bloodshed between dragon and man. They trusted the king and his people. Fueled by the fear created by the prophecy, the king discovered his people could mass produce weapons like spears and taught his army how to use them to bring the dragons down with a single spear through the heart. Little did King Ganic know, the son he sought to kill was brought to the dragons by the Omaan. He was raised, loved, and respected by the dragons, something rarely seen between man and beast. His name was Arturo. He was your great, great grandfather. It was he who became the first dragon watcher, the keepers of peace. Born with a rare ability to communicate with the dragons, Arturo found a way to live and work among them. They had an incredible amount of respect for each other, and, in due time, their friendship with Arturo helped them to bring peace back to Alderek and eventually overthrow his father, King Ganic.

"For generations under the guidance of your great, great grandfather, the dragons kept watch over the land and lived peacefully above the surface with all the creatures. Their mission was clear. Never again would they allow fear, greed, and selfishness to dominate and destroy. Arturo made certain the generations after him understood the need to respect each creature that shared the land and the world. Amoldine, your mother, is Arturo's great granddaughter, a dragon watcher by blood. Your mother, too, can communicate with the dragons. She's one of the last born into the dragon watchers. The others, about fifteen of them, are trusted and trained watchers. They can't speak directly to the dragons, but know enough to work with them."

"My mother can speak to dragons?" I asked in amazement. "Then why doesn't she call upon the dragons to set her free from wherever she is?"

"She's locked up on the top of the mountain beyond Kasus! She's been there for far too long," Myrilla blurted. "The dragons have no way of communicating with her when she's so far away, especially since they've been driven back below the ground. No one can tell them where she is because no one knows how to speak to dragons without getting their wings singed. Only you can do it, Astrid! Only you can speak to them!"

"Me?" I gasped, then shook my head. "No, I've never even seen a dragon. I've only read about them in books, and even then they were only parts of fairy tales. I...I wouldn't know how."

"You wouldn't need to know how," Ecson chimed.

"It's in your blood. It's instinct. You won't know until you see one," Maddux added excitedly.

"She's not our hero," declared a shout from behind the encouraging crowd that was forming around me.

The fairies turned. There stood a boy no more than one or two years older than me. His fiery red hair hung long in the front but was kept short in the back. I thought it amusing he resembled a fox dressed in a black gambeson and grey tights. A fox boy that carried a sword at his waist. Interesting.

"She's merely a child," he continued. "She knows nothing of the dangers of our reality. Fairies and dragons are mere storybook fantasy to her. What would she care if we all were destroyed? Once we're through, I'm sure she'll just mosey back to her England or whatever her world is called."

"Watch your mouth, Nevel," Maddux warned. "It doesn't matter that she's not from around here. She's a dragon watcher by blood. Now *that*, in my book, is more honorable than a shape shifting fox boy like *you*. And let's not forget, without this girl, you'll be the first one to run out of food, and you know it."

"You forget, my *friend*. I'm a moss eater by choice so I could live here away from Haggin's destruction. If I wanted to switch back to eating small helpless animals like *you* in order to survive..." A sly grin crossed Nevel's face, and he quickly added, "*I could*."

"That was an awful thing to say, Nevel," Myrilla flew forth, her arms akimbo.

"I'm sorry, Myrilla," he apologized half heartedly. "You and the others know I would never do such a thing, especially since you all took me in knowing I could if I wanted to. I'll always honor my promise to never eat another creature.

"However," Nevel glanced at Maddux, an untrustworthy look in his eyes, "I can't guarantee I won't make one exception."

Maddux thrust his wings and flew towards the red headed mischief-maker. He delivered blows all over, as Nevel blocked him and chuckled. He was athletic and robust for a fairy but compared to Nevel, his punches were little more than modest taps. Nevel began to swat Maddux with his hands, stinging the persistent fairy. It was more than I could bear to watch, a helpless eight inch fairy getting clobbered by a nuisance boy. I pulled my whip from behind me and cracked the popper on the ground to get a good feel. It was the first time I had used my whip since arriving in this strange, new world or reality or whatever it was. As I approached them, I drew back the whip one more time before sending it forward, the fall wrapping around Nevel's wrists before he could strike Maddux again.

"That's enough," I commanded. "Alderek is dying at the hands of King Haggin and the fenova. It wouldn't matter who eats who in the end. We'll all perish eventually if nothing is done."

I released the whip from Nevel's hands, as Queen Pavia glided towards me. Maddux and Nevel quickly bowed and offered their apologies.

I turned to the queen, "Tell me how to find the dragons."

"It's a few days journey," Queen Pavia responded. "Myrilla will be your guide. She's been there before to speak to the dragons with no luck."

"How do we get there?" I asked.

The queen opened her palm revealing a frosty glass gem. The ends of the gem extended until it was as long as a walking stick. She sprinkled dust on the forest ground before her, and a map of Alderek appeared. Using the glass stick, she traced the route we would venture to rescue my parents. "Make your way to the opposite end of this forest from which you entered. On the other side of the thorny wall, there will be another forest where you will find a stream. Follow the stream to the Valley of Mintz. You will find plenty to eat in this valley. Make certain you and the others stop to restock your supplies because there may not be too many chances after this point. From here make your way to the Foothills of the Greeves."

"What is this over here?" I pointed out what looked to be an entrance in the hillside. "It looks like it could be a shortcut."

"It's the Cave of the Smalls. Avoid it at any costs," she briefly warned.

"Yes, Queen Pavia," I nodded slightly. With a name like Cave of Smalls, it hardly seemed like a treacherous place to be. Still I knew it would be unwise to question the queen. I had to remind myself that what Nevel had said was right. I knew nothing yet of the potential perils of this supernatural world.

The queen continued with the map. "I can't tell you where to go between the Cave of Smalls and Sutters Valley where there will be a bridge. The maps is constantly changing. When a village is destroyed, its location disappears on the map. Just find your way to the bridge at the end of Sutters Valley. Take care not to venture too quickly here. There's a cliff on the other end where sudden fog will make it more difficult to see the cliff and the sudden drop below. There is no easy way down the cliff except to fall. You'll most likely want to climb down to the three doors. One of those will lead you to Kasus. Myrilla will know from here where you can find the dragons' lair. Once the dragons are with you, they can take you past the Living Forest to the highest peak. This will be Mount Iris where your parents and the others are locked away."

"We'll need backup," Myrilla said. Despite the obvious dangers we had ahead of us, she seemed ready for pumped and ready for the journey.

"I'll go with them," said Maddux.

"If Myrilla goes, I will, too," chimed in Ecson.

I glanced over to Willox, "We could use your magic as well."

Willox nodded in agreement.

"You call that backup? A bunch of little fairies and an old guy?" A chuckle escaped from Nevel, as he shook his head. "If the fenova don't clobber you first, the Beast will."

"He's right," Queen Pavia announced to everyone's surprise.

Nevel crossed his arms, a smug look on his face.

"Which is why," she continued, "they'll need someone fast and clever to outwit the Beast. Nevel, you will go with them."

"What? No!" Nevel exclaimed.

"You're not suggesting you would rather be left out of the team that saves Alderek, are you?" Queen Pavia said.

Outwitted by the queen and unable to find another way to save Alderek without joining the group, Nevel finally gave in.

"Fine," he huffed. "But if any of them go missing, don't immediately blame me. I've got better things to eat out there than puny, ol' fairies."

He sneered and made a point to shoulder bump me as he left the group, nearly knocking me over.

"Everyone get your rest tonight," Queen Pavia ordered. "Before the sun rises, Astrid and the rest of the group will begin their journey. I guarantee it won't be an easy one, but I have faith now that our dragon watcher is here. It is my hope she will bring Alderek back to all creatures before it is too late."

No pressure, I thought to myself. What have I gotten myself into? The fate of Alderek is in my hands. Me, a dragon watcher? And my parents, they're alive. I'm not sure if I'm living a dream, or if I'm slowly sinking into a nightmare.

CHAPTER 5

The sky loomed dark. I shifted in my bed of leaves at the base of a thick tree. Although I was exhausted by the previous day's marketplace mayhem, the chase to rescue Pike from the agents, and surreal transport to an unknown world where mystical creatures and magic collided, I couldn't sleep a wink. It felt as if I'd only gotten an hour of shut eye, at most.

The stars shone brightly overhead, even through the thick forest canopy. If I was in a different world, I couldn't tell. The evening sky on Alderek looked similar to the one I observed back in England. It was stunning. I wondered which way we would travel, the direction that led closer to my parents. Memories of being a part of a family were so few. I'd often questioned whether or not they were real. Over a decade had separated us. Would they be expecting the return of a child and surprised to see a teenager? Why did they have to leave me? What danger were they trying to protect me from? No doubt, I was full of questions. If only I could get to my parents and fast. There was no telling how long our journey would take, or if we would even survive it.

We had planned to leave the rest of the colony hours before the break of dawn. I figured I had another hour to try to rest before then. Gently shutting my eyes, I allowed myself to sink into slumber.

"Wake up, sleepyhead! No time to drool. We've got a long way out of this forest," his voice grated on me. Did he ever take a break from being boorish?

"Nevel, when are you ever going to learn?" Myrilla brushed past him, carrying a large bowl of steaming soup. She set it down in front of me. "Drink this as quickly as you can. It should wake you up and keep you energized for road ahead."

I picked up the hot soup, took a whiff, and coughed. It smelled like rotting mushrooms and burnt ginger. I glanced at Myrilla who hastily urged me again. Without further hesitation, I gulped the entire contents of the bowl down. The putrid flavor lingered on my tongue and burned down my throat.

"What was that disgusting concoction?" I gagged.

"You don't want to know," Ecson said as he made his way past us.

Myrilla placed a reassuring hand on my shoulder, "We've been waiting for this day to finally come. For the child of the dragon watcher to speak to the dragons and convince them to fight alongside with us for Alderek. I'm so happy that you're here."

I smiled to acknowledge her, and she flew off with a hopeful gleam in her eyes. When she left, the edges of my smile quivered. There was so much faith these fairies put in me to speak to the dragons. When I was younger, I remembered trying to speak to the birds that would find their way into the factory through the broken windows. There was one sparrow in particular that stayed with me in my room for a few days until it flew away and never returned. I liked to think they understood what I said to them. How I wished they would stay forever and keep me company. None of them ever did. If I couldn't speak to the birds, how could I ever convince a dragon to fight a war against a nefarious king bent on taking over the world?

We each received a satchel filled with water and food to carry. Upon leaving, Queen Pavia placed a curved machete into my hands.

"It was mine long ago, given to me from a very powerful and honorable warrior," Queen Pavia said. "Use it to protect yourself and the others. And when you meet *him*, use it to destroy him."

I pulled the weapon out of its leather sheath to examine it. The weight of the machete alone felt foreign. Although I'd been in numerous situations where I had to rely on my whip to protect myself, not once did I ever use it to seriously injure anyone, much less *destroy*.

"Who, Queen Pavia," I asked, "do you intend for me to destroy with this?"

She was standing in front of me, so close that I could see the delicate peach fuzz on her face. Her youthful look was astounding. It almost seemed as if she truly glowed, literally, as if some kind of bioluminescence oozed from her pores. Despite her radiance, a heavy melancholy fell from her eyes as she looked to the ground.

"Haggin," she said with grief in her voice. "Use it to destroy King Haggin."

Without another word, the queen turned and was gone. Before I could think more of it, Myrilla waved me over. "Come on, Astrid!"

The others were already yards ahead of me. It was vaguely bizarre to see the fairies fortified each with a different weapon. Ecson carried a double-headed battle ax, Myrilla was armed with a crossbow, and Maddux had a blow dart gun. How I ended up being an orphaned English girl protecting my fellow starving orphans from butchers to becoming a warrior girl with a family in a world I'd never dreamed could possibly exist with a powerful wizard, a conniving fox boy, and three very well-armed fairies was beyond me. I holstered the machete and rushed to the group I'd only met the day before, but would entrust to keep me safe in this world I barely knew.

For the most part, the trek out of the forest was a simple hike. It was extremely dark. The trees grew to such magnificent heights in this part of the forest that it made whatever moonlight there was unable to reach the forest grounds.

Although we relied on the near perfect night vision of Nevel and Willox to lead us out of the remainder of the forest, I must've tripped at least half a dozen times. My night vision wasn't as terrible as the fairies', though. Ecson tried his best to follow the shadows of our guides as best he could, but still collided into branches and leaves. At one point, he found himself in a sticky situation as he ended up tangled in a fairly massive spider web. Everyone couldn't help but laugh at the ordeal. We were on a perilous mission to either save this world or lose our lives. I think we were entitled to a good laugh. Of course, until Nevel noticed the foot-long spider that set his sights on having Ecson for an early breakfast. Making quick use of the machete, I carved Ecson out of his predicament, being extra careful not to slice him in the process. He fell to the ground. The spider, more interested in an easy meal and not a fight, retreated into the shadows.

"Well, that was a close one," Ecson sighed as he batted away at the thick web that draped him.

"That was a big one," said Maddux. "Hopefully, they don't get any bigger than that around here."

"The Argon is rising," Willox cautioned. "We have move faster out of the forest and as far away as possible before the fenova make their sweeps."

"Who's Argon?" I asked.

"It's the first sun," answered Maddux. "It rises about an hour before Vromen, our second sun."

"Which means Willox has a point. We don't have time to stand around chit chatting," Nevel said as he made his way past the group. "Remember what they say, 'With Argon looms an eerie calm, but with Vromen burns the fire.' If the fenova are going to find us, let's get as far from the forest as we can. If Haggin finds Queen Pavia and the rest of the fairies, his army will be pretty close to unbeatable."

"Well, then. Let's go," I said, helping Ecson to his feet.

The light from Argon was enough for those of us without near-perfect night vision to make out what was several feet before us. The forest beyond that was still as dark as night. We followed Nevel and Willox, but managed only a few short steps before they stopped in their tracks.

"What's going on?" I asked Nevel.

I withdrew my bullwhip. By the look in his eyes, I could tell he'd spotted something lurking in the darkness. What it was, I didn't know, until *they* came forward and down from above.

"Everyone stand close," Willox calmly instructed.

"Oh my goodness, mother of all beasts," Maddux gasped. "They do get bigger..."

There were at least a dozen of them, each with multiple green and black eyes staring back at us. We huddled as a group, our backs turned to each other and weapons drawn while ten-foot wide spiders surrounded us on all sides.

"We should've let them have their breakfast," Nevel said, nodding over at Ecson who still had remnants of the cobweb on his clothing.

"Why stop with Ecson when they could feast on larger fare like us?" I quipped.

He let out a nervous laugh, "That doesn't help, sweetheart."

"Well, maybe you can be the hero and offer them an arm while we all sneak on by," I winked.

"Sounds like a fabulous idea," Maddux smirked.

Ecson chimed in, "I second that."

Nevel raised an eyebrow. "Well, I'm glad we've got each other's backs here, don't we?"

Movement from above caught our attention and our eyes sprung up. A massive sheet of spiraled webbing dropped from over us. Just as it was about to drape our bodies, Willox raised his arms. The cobweb landed over the dome force field he created.

"Obviously, I can only hold this for as long as my arms can stay up," Willox said matter-of-factly.

The spiders drew closer. They had fangs the size of my torso, if not larger. Their hairy legs were covered in what I first thought was morning dew. As they inched closer, I noticed the true source of the moisture. They were salivating heavily. It dripped from their mouths as they eyed us, their prey.

"There's no way we're going to let a bunch of creepy crawlies get in our way," Myrilla said. "Okay, guys. Time to show these spiders some pest control."

"Pest control?" Nevel grimaced.

"I'm actually not feeling that either," Maddux added.

"Oh, forget it! There's no time for this," I gritted my teeth, "Let's fight!"

Nevel raised his sword, "Now that's what I'm talking about!"

As Willox lowered his arms, the force field dissipated. I spun my machete over our heads, slicing through the cobweb before it could envelop us. We all split up, taking on more than one arachnid at a time. A black spider with a red hairy collar around its head lunged at me, nearly missing my waist with its fangs. I snapped my bullwhip on the ground and it hissed at me. I hissed back. The duel was on.

The spider raised its two front legs like a horse rearing. I ran backwards just in time to avoid getting impaled by his javelin-like legs. I wrapped my bullwhip around the two legs and brought him down to what would be his knees, if spiders had any. His head struck the ground, and I took the opportunity to spear him with the machete. It hissed and wriggled, all the while still clamping its fangs at me until he lay motionless.

Once I pulled the machete out from the spider, I felt the force of something great hit my stomach and I was propelled backwards onto the ground. Pulling myself to my feet again, I noticed a sticky ball of white silky thread on my clothes. Looking up, I was face to face with the culprit. She hissed and drooled as she clamped her fangs near my face. Never in my life did I realize spiders could have such terrible breath. I'd only hoped the others were better off than I was. Her drool slipped onto my boots, and I could tell she was ready for her first taste of human blood. She flung herself forward and snapped her fangs where my neck would've been if I hadn't ducked quickly enough. I ran underneath her belly, caged by her eight hairy legs. She danced around, lifting her legs and trying to spear me as she thrust them down. I grabbed onto one of her legs and pulled myself up to her back, while she turned and snapped at me like a dog with a flea. Luckily, her head couldn't reach as far back as a dog. Once on her back, I drew my machete and drove it into her carapace.

Her legs rapidly curled under. Unable to hang onto her back as her body dropped, I toppled to the ground. I opened my eyes in time to see that Maddux had just riddled the eyes of one of his predators with poisonous darts.

"Oh, no," Maddux called out. "Astrid!"

The blinded, dying spider was about to fall in my direction. My back was still throbbing from hitting the ground so hard, it was taking me a while to get to my feet.

Just as I contemplated the irony of getting flattened by a massive spider like a regular old house spider, I saw a flash of red out of the corner of my eye. It was a red fox, as quick as lightning and as adorable as...

"Nevel?" I spurted out as I watched him transform into his human form again.

"No time for chit chat, sweetheart," he said. He grabbed my arm and pulled me away from the falling spider. The force of its fall caused a quick gust of air that lifted us both off of the ground before we fell back onto it again.

"No need to thank me," he said. "It just looked like you needed a hero."

The nerve of this boy to think I would need him of all people to save me. I wiped the dirt from my already filthy dress.

"I could've gotten up just as fast if you didn't get in the way," I said.

"You're welcome," he smiled. He gave a quick bow and then went on his way to help Willox and Ecson with their last predator.

I looked around and saw Maddux hanging onto a spider's palps with one arm. It swung him around, trying to get him closer to his mouth. With the other free arm, Maddux aimed his blowgun and shot a dart into the spider's jaws. The spider writhed and Myrilla pelted its eyes with her nunchucks. The poison of the single dart was not enough to bring the spider down, and Maddux had run out. The spider grew angrier. Although Maddux and Myrilla could fly, the spider was relentless and snapped at them, determined to have fairies for breakfast.

I cracked my whip on its abdomen, hoping to take the attention away from the others. It worked. The spider turned and clambered in my direction. Instead of running away, I stood my ground and waited for the right moment. When the spider got close enough, I wrapped my whip on its palp and pulled myself off the ground. The spider attempted to spray at me with its sticky webbing , but kept missing as I swung myself back and forth. I swung in front of the spider to the underside of its belly until I could finally reach the flesh of his abdomen. The machete pierced through and I hung in midair suspended between the machete and my whip. Thick glob-like jelly oozed from out of the wound and onto the handle of the machete onto my hand. Like the walls of a collapsing building, the legs of the spider crumpled inward. I pulled the machete out and swung underneath past his head before he hit the ground. The spider gave a final twitch before it was finally over. The rest of the group came rushing towards me.

Willox pointed at the sky. It only took a moment to notice the blood orange halo rising over the trees.

"Vromen has risen," he said.

We could hear more crackling overhead and feel the extra eyes carefully watching us.

"Well, let's go before there's more eight-legged chaos to deal with," I urged. "Come on. There's no time to lose."

Without looking back, we fled as swiftly as we could toward the edge of the forest. Vromen's rays were getting bright and hot. The extra daylight finally allowed us to move much faster. Within a few minutes, we spotted the thorny branches that signified the perimeter of the forest. Willox spread his wings and the first layer of thorns parted. Just as Nevel was about to walk through, Willox brought down his wings and the branches closed again.

"What was that all about? I almost walked right into those little *impaley* things" Nevel motioned towards the thorns.

Willox metamorphosed into his human form and raised his hand to silence Nevel. At first, we could hear nothing but the light crackling of leaves on the other side of the thorny branched wall. Then, like the sudden clasp of thunder from an approaching storm, we heard it. Dozens of footsteps over twigs and dried leaves. Low grumbling of voices could be heard but nothing comprehendible. It sounded as if the other side of the forest was being pillaged, if a forest could be pillaged. Pounding, yelling chaos. The sound of an army of monsters capable of nothing more than destruction.

I couldn't let this happen. How could we stand and listen to this? If this was a battle against the fenova, we needed to be there. If there were other helpless creatures living on the other side of the wall, why were we standing here doing nothing?

I pulled the machete from its sheath and prepared to break through the thorny wall on my own. Nevel held his arm out, stopping me in my tracks.

"We have to do something," I insisted.

He shook his head and hushed me.

Myrilla pulled me aside. She whispered, "The fenova are on the other side of the wall."

"Then shouldn't we go out there and fight them?" I protested. "Bring Alderek back to the fairies, right? We can't let them destroy any more or there'll be nothing left."

This was the first time I noticed her eyes were quite massive. Although they seemed to sulk as if to sympathize with me, they still seemed fairly large above her equally rounded cheeks. She pushed a stray strand of hair out of my eyes.

"Thank goodness for your passion, Astrid. I'm glad we have you on our side. But we have to remember not to act on impulse. The other fairies along with Queen Pavia are shielded in this forest behind these thorny walls. If we come out charging now," she hesitated, reflecting in the thought. "If we charge now, the fenova will know where our colony is hiding. They'll capture the queen and change the rest of us into fenova."

I felt helpless, but I understood that what Myrilla said was true. The destruction of whatever lay beyond the thorny walls was a sacrifice to keep possibly the last remaining fairy colony safe. It was a painful reality that we had to stand and listen to the destruction as it was happening. Every brief moment of silence gave us hope to breathe again, hoping it would be end of the devastation.

"I don't think there are any colonies of creatures living out there," said Myrilla, perhaps more to convince herself than to comfort me. "The fenova like to destroy anything they think may be a food source. King Haggin wants every living creature to depend on him to live. That's how he operates. Food and fear. The fear of no food."

"When will it be over?" I fell to my knees as I remembered the hungry orphans I left behind in England.

Then just like that, silence. The obliteration beyond the wall was over, but in my mind I knew something else. The battle had just begun.

CHAPTER 6

Everything around had burned quickly to a crisp. The trees left standing were like blackened matches, scorched bare to their core. The ground was still warm, although Willox sent a brief chill through the air to clear some of the smoke. Ashes continued to descend from the sky as scattered flames littered the area. All that was living that couldn't run had been engulfed by the fire. What was once a thriving forest of trees on the other side of the thorny wall was now reduced to lifeless sticks and soot.

"What do we do now?" Ecson said as he picked up the black dirt in his hand and let it run through his fingers.

"We get out of here like we planned," Maddux said, "and hope we don't run into any of the fenova."

I turned to Myrilla, "Is there another path we can take to the valley? The fenova will likely follow the stream. It's best if we can prevent crossing paths with those demon fairies. At least for a while."

"I agree," said Maddux. "I don't think any of us expected to be nearly trampled by monster spiders."

Myrilla nodded, "Give me a moment to think about it."

"Great," I continued. "The sooner we can get to the dragons the better. We'll need as much help as we can get to get to the mountain, especially if the fenova are this ruthless."

"I've got it," she said. "It'll take a little longer, but that'll put greater distance between us and the fenova. We can go through the Garden of the Hanging Vines. It runs parallel to the stream perhaps a few miles from here."

"That sounds lovely," I chimed.

Her very apple-like cheeks blushed as she grinned proudly. "Oh, it is! I've flown through once before."

"What are we waiting for?" said Nevel as he gestured to Myrilla. "Lead the way."

The twin suns were at their highest peak. Out of the burnt forest, there were no longer any towering trees to offer shade. We traveled through a meadow with blades of grass three fingers wide and as high my shoulders. Willox trekked with us on foot, while the fairies flew below the blades to keep from getting spotted by rogue fenova. Everything seemed larger in this meadow, the occasional flowers that we happened upon, the beetles that brushed up against us in the grass, and the ants that scurried below. It felt as if hours had passed, but the blades of grass were never-ending. I started off using the machete to clear a path for us as we passed through, but soon my arm tired and I had to stop. Nevel took up clearing the path with his sword, but he too promptly grew tired.

"Couldn't you carve a way for us, Willox?" Nevel suggested. "You know, like do that thing you do with your hands and then whoosh! Everything parts and we can walk through."

"If I could, my dear Nevel, I would. But as time would have it, I'm still an old man underneath this hat," Willox said. "Everything I do drains me just as much or more than you. It's best I conserve my energy for if we encounter the fenova or worse, King Haggin."

There was no end to the passage through the tall grassy prairie. Day turned into night and night back into day. The grass seemed to reach higher towards the sky the further we trudged. The fairies randomly peeked above the blades of grass to get an idea of which way to go. Direction proved difficult to find though. For miles, it seemed, the grass stretched on and on. There was nothing in the distance to give any inkling of hope that the terrain would alter or, better yet, end. We watched the twin suns rise and fall thrice with little hope for change. Our water supply was running low and, although I was accustomed to going on for days with little or no food, I could hear the bellies of the fairies rumble and growl. They grew more irritable. Frustration consumed them when no visible mountain or hill broke the smooth rhythm of the ever-expansive grassy fields. Their wings grew exhausted, and they took breaks riding on our shoulders during the day. On the fourth day, change didn't come from above as much as it did below. The dirt gave in under my feet and I fell down into a dirt hole. I slid and tumbled my way down until I finally reached the bottom at least fifteen feet below the surface. Just behind me, Nevel slid. He'd shifted into his fox form and was tucked neatly into a ball as he rolled down the dirt, eventually bumping into me. Above us, we could see the falcon and fairies hovering over the hole.

"Are you all right down there?" Myrilla called down to us.

Nevel stood on all fours and shook his head rapidly. The shaking passed through to his neck, then body, and out his hind legs and tail until he was no longer covered in dirt. He shifted back into his human form, clean as a whistle. I glanced at my dress, the same one that smelled of fish and dried ham hocks. It was now covered in red dirt and so were my hands and face.

He shrugged, "It could be worse, right?"

"We're coming down," Maddux said. The ground began to tremble fiercely, knocking us off our feet. Dirt from above fell through. I grabbed a hold of Nevel and crawled with him further from the opening as we covered our heads. The hole we had fallen into closed up and all around us was now in darkness. Willox and the fairies were above the ground we were buried. We'd been swallowed by the land.

"Nevel," I whispered into the darkness. "Nevel, where are you? I can't see a thing."

I held out my hands in front and around me, hoping not to run into the tunnel wall. Ours hands touched and he intertwined his warm hairy fingers around mine. I quickly pulled away, annoyed by his possible motives.

"Really," I scoffed, "This isn't the time nor the place to get all touchy feely. You could just say something to let me know you're here."

"Oh, sorry," Nevel said, his voice distant. "I'm over here."

My heart froze as I realized he was nowhere near me. Instead, he sounded as if he was at least twenty feet behind. If he was back there... I pulled my bullwhip from its holster. Who touched my hand in front of me?

"Nevel," I tried to sound as calm as I could, "if you're far behind me. Can you see me very well with your night vision?"

There was a teasing pause before he answered just as calmly, "Somewhat."

"Well then, who or what is in front of me?" I swallowed.

The sound of a match scratching against a surface filled the tunnel. A torch was lit and my question was answered.

"Hello," squeaked the six foot tall squirrel.

"Squirrel!" I gasped.

Although still in his human form, the squirrel must've realized at that moment what Nevel was. For when the light of her torch shone on his face, she gasped just as anxiously as I had, "Fox!"

Without warning, she retreated through the tunnel taking the torch and our only source of light with her.

"Wait!" I called out to her, hoping she could lead us to a way out.

She was swift. Had she been the size of a normal squirrel, my effort to follow after her would've ended abruptly. Despite my repeated plea for the squirrel to stop running, she raced on. Through turns and dips, I chased her in the tunnel. Once or twice I slipped but managed to keep on track, never losing sight of her tail for more than a few seconds after she'd round a corner. I could hear her breathing heavily, panicked.

"Please, stop!" I pleaded. "He doesn't even eat meat."

"It's true," Nevel exclaimed from behind. "Well, maybe the occasional beetle or cricket, but I haven't had a squirrel in years."

"I wouldn't suppose you disliked that experience very much, did you?" the squirrel called back as she continued to dash ahead.

Nevel was silent. Since there was never a good answer to follow in the wake of his silence, I said as I ran out of breath, "You have my word - he nor I will have you for any kind of meal. Just...please...stop..."

And just like that, she did. I was already beginning to slow down, drained from the previous days' walking. I managed to stop a few feet to the side of the rather giant squirrel. Nevel, on the other hand, didn't anticipate the chase to end so unexpectedly. He rammed into me but not before transforming into his fox self. I plummeted to the ground as I felt paws slap my shoulders and a tail whip in my face. The squirrel gazed over us in amusement.

"Thanks for the brief animal encounter," I said, helping myself up.

He briefly shook his head, gaining back his composure. "Glad you appreciated my quick thinking. Thought it would be less harsh for a soft, furry animal to slam into you, rather than a strapping young lad like myself." He shifted into his human self and ran his fingers through his disheveled red hair.

The squirrel giggled. "I like this one's self mockery," she gestured towards Nevel.

"There was no mockery intended," murmured Nevel.

"Why did you stop running?" I changed the topic.

The squirrel raised her eyebrows and answered simply, "You gave your word."

"That's it?" I asked.

She nodded.

"If only I knew it was that simple to catch a squirrel back in the day," Nevel mumbled to himself.

"It's squirrel's honor," the squirrel said. "If someone, anyone, pledges their word, we're inclined to give them the benefit of the doubt. No questions asked as long as the someone giving their word was not an obvious predator, of course. We have to draw the line somewhere."

I glanced over at Nevel who shrugged. "Understandable," he said. "She looks a lot less threatening than me. I get it."

"I'm Astrid," I offered, changing the topic. "The fox boy is Nevel. We were on our way to Kasus to find the dragons when we got separated from our group on the prairie before falling into your burrow."

"I'm Nellie," the squirrel responded. Her name struck me as so ordinary for such an extraordinary creature of her size and intelligence. Still, it was very fitting. The name was remarkably simple, and, although she was an oversized squirrel, Nellie projected a personality that was rather easygoing and simple herself. She continued cautiously, "Why, may I ask, are you looking for dragons? I do hope you're being silly with me."

"Why would I lie about finding the dragons?" I inquired, hoping to gain insight on what other creatures thought of them.

Nellie was cautious. Her eyes darted around making certain no one else had miraculously appeared. Then she said in a hushed tone so not even the walls could hear, "Come with me. We're not safe in these tunnels. Even the walls have ears."

We followed her through more tunnels, some more narrow than others. Although Nellie had to squeeze through a tapered passageway, she did it with great ease. Only then did I realize how much of her fuzzy exterior was actually just a thick coat of fur. At the end of the slender tunnel was a door. Nellie opened it and bid us to follow her in.

"Mama! Mama! Mama!" squealed three squirrels each the size of a fairly large dog. They looked just like Nellie, only on a smaller scale, with cheeks that protruded on either side, as if they were permanently stuffed with the largest acorns they could find but never intended to ever swallow or store away. The baby squirrels bounced around Nellie with arms outstretched. She scooped one up in each arm. The third squirrel sat on her foot as she held onto her leg, the next best alternative to her mommy's arms.

"Why aren't you taking your naps like I told you to?" Nellie scolded her children in a playful manner.

"Tasha and I couldn't fall asleep," yawned one girl in her arm.

"And why not, Annie?" she asked.

"Benny kept playing skunk but we wanted to sleep," said Tasha, whom I assumed was the other girl on Nellie's leg.

"I couldn't help it," pouted Benny, as he straightened the glasses on his face. "Eating dried leaf soup every day makes my tummy feel funny. I miss eating acorns."

Benny's stomach rumbled loudly and was quickly followed by several whistles that I assumed also came out of Benny. Annie groaned, and Tasha jumped off her mother's foot where she was directly under the arm that held her brother. Nellie placed her other children down.

"Children, these are Astrid and Nevel. They're going to be our guests for tonight," she said. The little squirrels looked over and gasped as if noticing us for the first time. Benny's jaw dropped when he saw Nevel by the doorway. "Don't worry. He doesn't eat meat. They gave their word."

Annie tucked Benny's jaw closed, but his eyes didn't hide his lingering disbelief.

Tasha came over to me and took my hand. Her eyes were soft and brown much like her mother's. "You're pretty, Astrid" she said.

"Why, thank you," I blushed. "I can't help but notice you have very lovely eyes."

"Mama says I got my eyes from my daddy," she fluttered her lashes. Her eyes grew larger and welled up with tears. "He was in a tree collecting acorns when the fenova burned the forest we used to live in."

"Oh, I'm so sorry to hear," I didn't know how else to respond. I remembered the forest the fenova burned only a few days ago. What other creatures had lost their lives or the life of a loved one? How many more broken families had King Haggin created?

"Would you read us a bedtime story before we go to sleep?" Tasha asked shyly.

I've never been asked to read anything to anyone else before, much less a bedtime story. I didn't know if I could or if I knew how. Tasha's large brown eyes gazed, beseeching me to say I would. "Of course," I finally gave in.

"Save it for another day!" Nellie interrupted the moment. "Okay, kiddies! Off you go."

She nudged her children towards their bedroom.

"But, Mama! They just got here. Can we play a little?" they whined in unison.

"If you took your nap, yes. But you didn't, so no," she answered firmly. "Now go to bed."

The girls ran off while Benny stood in place. His face contorted as his body shivered. "Dig your hole to lay your droppings in, Benny. Don't forget to cover it up when you're done and go to bed," Nellie advised him. He quickly obeyed and ran off, leaving behind scented reminders of his presence. Then Nellie turned to us and said casually, "Finally, we can talk. Anyone hungry for some warm leafy dumplings?"

She brought in a second helping of dried leafy dumplings. They were surprisingly tasty, and our stomachs were not fed enough to be picky. Nellie went out of her way to be hospitable towards us. Although we were unexpected guests and practically strangers, it felt as if we were on a routine visit to an old friend's home.

Opening up to us, she explained how she came upon raising her three squirrely children alone. It was a year ago when they'd begun to hear about neighboring villages above ground coming under attack by fenova. Communities were wiped out in a matter of minutes, disintegrated to the ground. Nothing left behind, not even a trace or memory of living history. Many of their friends and family disappeared eventually. She hoped the majority of them had enough time to flee. That was her wish. Nellie and her family were fortunate enough to make their lives underground. It wasn't something that was common anymore since it was decreed by King Haggin years ago that all creatures were forbidden to hide beneath the soil, except the dragons. It was his way of keeping everyone in check. Despite the possible consequences, Nellie and her husband, Hubert, secretly kept their burrow. It was easy for them to venture above ground in order to visit others or to gather supplies without getting noticed. The entrance leading to their burrow was well hidden by the tall grasses. The regular prairie quakes helped too by shaking the dirt over any exposed holes if they'd forgotten to close it up. One day, her husband decided it was time to venture out of the burrow to see for himself what had happened to some of the villages. He wanted to gain some closure for them, so they'd know for certain if they could remain hopeful or if they were truly alone. Nellie recalled that day was beautiful. The sky was blue and Argon had just risen. Hubert left with hope in his eyes when he looked back on their family as he exited the burrow. She knew he would be back, and she waited for him to bring them good news. That was a year ago almost. Occasionally, she'd take walks through her burrow when the children slept just as she did this day when she came upon us. She'd think perhaps she would find one of her friends, family, or any other creatures from one of those burned villages. Perhaps she'd find her husband with the same light in his eyes that was forever planted in her memory. She hoped survivors would come to her burrow. It would give her great strength because it would mean Hubert, too, could be a survivor.

"Hubert would never let anyone stop him from coming home to his babies," Nellie sniffled. "If he didn't come home, he will one day. Not one fenova or an army of them can stop him. That's just how he is."

"He sounds like a fighter," said Nevel.

"And a survivor," she quickly added. "My Hubert has been branded before by the fenova for a crime he didn't commit. He stood his ground and never admitted to any guilt, so they branded him again."

"Branded?" I asked.

She nodded and pointed to her shoulder, "The fenova hold a weekly gathering where they offer food rations in every village that still stands. Hubert took my two girls to pick up our weekly rations. You have to be present in order to claim your food, but Benny was terribly ill that day. That boy has the most sensitive stomach, I don't know if you've noticed. Anyway, Hubert collected two extra rations on behalf of Benny and me. It was the fenova that gave them to him. They've seen our family before and knew he had two more family members at home. You see, not all fenova are terrible. There are some that still..."

As she had done in the tunnel, Nellie's eyes darted around as if to make absolutely certain no one else was around. She leaned in to us and said in a hushed tone, "...remember."

She sat back in her chair and continued in her usual demeanor, "There are still a lot of fenova that are hard core, stand-by-our-king-til-the-end kind of fighters. Those are the ones that branded him for stealing. One brand, and you're warned. Two brands, and...well, nobody knows. I suppose you disappear. To where, I'm not sure."

"Could the fenova have him now?" inquired Nevel. "Perhaps they've taken him in for another crime they've conjured up."

"Perhaps," her voice trailed. "Or, perhaps, the dragons found him."

"The dragons," I uttered. "Why would the dragons pose any danger to him? Aren't they isolated underground?"

"Because the dragons were the ones who destroyed the first fairy village," she said. "It was an attack out of nowhere. Those dragons are stealthy and not to be trusted after what they've done. That's the reason the fairies rebelled against the dragon watchers and joined King Haggin before he banished them underground. The dragons are the reason all creatures of Alderek have to suffer. Would you care for some more tea?"

Nevel and I declined and thanked her. If what she said was true, that the dragons were the cause of the rebellion and King Haggin's rise to power, then our journey to seek out the dragons would result in more chaos. If the dragons agreed to help us against Haggin, what would they do to us once he was no longer in power?

"If I may ask," she began, "why are you interested in finding the dragons?"

"She's a dragon watcher by blood," Nevel spoke before I could. "We need their help to defeat Haggin and the fenova. Queen Pavia believes she can speak to them, convince them to join us."

"Interesting," she raised an eyebrow. "I didn't think there were more dragon watchers besides the ones locked in Mount Iris."

"No one knew of her existence until a few days ago," he said.

"Our first priority is to find the rest of our friends and together defeat Haggin," I said, deflecting the topic away from me.

"If we don't stop the fenova now, Alderek will burn until there's nothing left except what Haggin will want to give us. We'll be forever at his mercy, the children too. We can deal with the dragons and their crimes later."

Nellie pursed her lips in thought. Then she said, "If you really are a dragon watcher, they may listen to you. But they've been in isolation for many years now, so their tempers will be high and your chances of success will be as low. Legend has it that the first dragon watcher summoned the frost that cooled their throats when the dragons got temperamental. Now, how he did that is beyond me, but I thought you should know just in case you didn't already."

"Summoned the frost," I repeated, baffled. "I'm not sure what that means, but I'll remember. Thank you, Nellie. If there's anything we can do for you for your hospitality, please let us know."

"Bring back Alderek to the creatures," she said. "This wasn't the kind of world Hubert and I planned to raise our children."

I nodded. We slept on the floor of the living room where the occasional trembling of the ground lulled us to sleep. When I woke, Nevel was no longer in the spot where he had lain. I heard muffled noises coming from another room around the corner. I looked into the room and found him. On his back, Annie had her arms wrapped around his neck as she hung on. Tasha and Benny each clung onto his legs. He ran around the room in circles, dipping down and popping up. The squirrels giggled. Benny and Tasha begged for a chance on his back, which Annie shrieked for more. I had to admit, it was nice to see Nevel do something nice and not ask for anything else in return. Unexpectedly, I could feel the corners of my mouth creep upwards. Just then a hand touched my shoulder and I jumped, startled.

"Sorry, dear," Nellie apologized. She handed me our satchels. "I filled these up for you with more water and leafy dumplings. Just enough to get you to the Valley of Mintz where you can replenish again."

"Thank you, Nellie," I said. "If there's anything I could ever do for you..."

"Bring down Haggin," she nodded as she interrupted. "And bring back the peacekeepers."

"We will," Nevel said in a strained voice. All three squirrels were hanging on his back now as he did his best to gallop passed us.

"One more thing, Astrid," she said. "If you could. I mean, if you see him...He has a mole where his whiskers grow out on his left cheek, and he wears glasses. He'll never leave behind those glasses or he'll be blind as a bat."

"We'll bring Hubert back to you if we find him," I assured her. "I promise."

They led us through tunnels underground that took us beyond the grassy prairie. It was there that the tunnels ended, the soil was no longer hard but moist and swampy. It was like leaving our home, a mother and siblings, when we finally ventured out of the burrow. In almost the same way we got trapped in the hole, the ground shook and the hole we climbed out of closed and disappeared.

CHAPTER 7

The land beneath our feet was spongy. The longer we stood in one spot, the further our feet sank and we were forced to move forward. There was no shortage of woody vegetation around us. Vines dangled freely from the trees to the ground. Others wrapped tightly around the trunks of their hosts, leaving them strangled. A warning to all who pass through perhaps, and overstay their welcome.

Further into the swamp, the water level began to rise. In a matter of minutes, it went from barely covering our ankles to submerging us just below the hip. Our weapons were drawn as we trudged through the murky water. After all, water was the source of life, regardless of good or evil. Every disturbance in the water kept us on our toes. Strange beetle-like insects climbed down the vines and into the water. They swam towards us and nipped anywhere our skin was exposed. Nevel was ahead of me as he attempted to swipe at the pests with his sword. It seemed as if this only aggravated the beetle infestation even more. Beetles that were under the water came up and swam frantically to the surface. If they could find a vine to crawl onto, they quickly made their escape. Some mistook our arms for vines and sought refuge on our bodies. Nevel continued to swipe at them in the water.

"Wait, Nevel, stop splashing the water," I urged as I swatted beetles off my shoulders. "I think it's making things worse."

Without delay, he stopped splashing. We focused on keeping the beetles off our bodies with minimal movement. I observed the beetles swim to the surface of the water. They frantically looked elsewhere for some safe ground.

"What are they trying to run from?" Nevel said aloud what we both wondered.

Not too long after, our question was answered. A disturbance in the water behind me caused us both to turn. Although we'd missed whatever had caused the sound, the evidence it left behind was clear. It was a massive animal of some sort. The ripple it created spread smooth and evenly towards us.

"Maybe I was wrong to assume your splashing got these guys all worked up," I said.

He raised an eyebrow. "You think so, lass?"

"We have to get out of the water," I said nervously, "and fast."

Looking around, there was nowhere we could possibly go. The swamp water spread out as far as my eyes could see. I watched the beetles as they made their way onto vines and out of the water.

"Up," I blurted aloud.

"What? Is there something up there, too?" Nevel readied his sword and looked around frantically.

At that moment I felt something thick bodied and scaly slither against my leg. By the fear I could see in his eyes, I knew that Nevel felt it too. Out of nowhere, the terrifying head of a black serpent propelled six feet out of the water. It's mouth yawning wide to let in as many beetles as it could. It's multiple rows of teeth and yellow beady eyes were enough to send my heart jumping out of my chest. Before it retracted into the water, I yelped, " Up! Get up the tree. You're a fox. Climb!"

"What about you?"

"I'll think of something," I said, my mind raced for ideas. Finally, it came to me. The vines! They hung from the trees, thick and seemingly sturdy enough. For a moment, I feared this would be a stupid idea. One tug on a vine and it would come crashing down, unable to hold my weight. Time was running out, and I had to do something fast. Surveying what was going to be on the menu next, the serpent grazed my leg. That was my signal, do it or die trying. I flung my bullwhip and wrapped it as high around the nearest vine I could find. The serpent sank back in without a splash, leaving behind only ripples in the water. Nevel transformed into a fox and was able to swim to a tree and climb its trunk. He perched above on its highest branch before changing back into his human form. I barely pulled my feet out of the water as I climbed the vine. Years of climbing the wall to get in and out of the marketplace were helpful in building my upper body strength. Still, my clothes were drenched and my fingers were wrinkled from overexposure in the water. I made progress at a sloth's pace until I was finally a safe distance above the water.

"You're not planning on hanging there all day, are you?" he asked as he wrung the bottom of his shirt.

Unfortunately, he was right. Although I was high enough from the jaws of the serpent, I could only hold on for so long. I pulled my bullwhip back and flung it towards the branch where Nevel sat.

"Whoa! That was close," he flinched.

The bullwhip wrapped around the branch. I let go of my sanctuary vine and swung over to the tree. My toes skimmed the top layer of water forming a wake behind me.
"Air bubbles following your trail" he pointed out. "Looks like the serpent is lurking just below the surface."

I pulled myself up the whip. An anxious Nevel continued to urge me along.

"He's probably got his eye right on you," he said softly, motioning me to hurry. "Be ready, he could burst out at any moment and..."

"Thanks, Nevel. I get it," I said bluntly. "Now, please stop your chattering and give me a hand."

At the moment he reached out and our hands gripped, the open jaws of the serpent lurched out of the water. I could feel his warm breath surrounding my legs as I briefly dangled in his mouth. Nevel screamed and yanked me onto the branch the instant the serpent snapped his mouth closed. The creature once again retreated back into the water.

"Heavens to fairies! That was the close one," Nevel gasped.

Snapping its jaws feverishly, the serpent sprung out of the water under us. Shrieking, Nevel pulled his legs onto the branch.

"I hope this thing doesn't give way with all the weight we're putting on it," I mentioned.

He paled, and I had to stifle a giggle at the expense of appearing insensitive. It felt like ages since we'd last seen Willox and the fairies. With hopes to encounter them along way, we agreed to continue our journey to Kasus. The future of Alderek diminished every second King Haggin remained in power. We were determined to stay focused, to find the dragons and recruit them in our venture to free my parents and take down Haggin and the fenova. There was one dilemma, however, that stood in our way. The water below. Trees surrounded, some a good distance apart, but one slip off a branch and we'd be falling into a deadly bath. There was no telling how many surprises were lying in wait down there. In the end, it was the only way to go, and we found ourselves vaulting from tree to tree. Nevel, as a fox, glided with ease and great balance. I tried my best to stick my landings, but it wasn't always as easy. Eventually, the trees grew too great a distance apart that there would be no way I could make the jumps. Machete in hand, I'd hack a hanging vine and swing to another branch as far past Nevel as I could get. Every time I came out in front, Nevel's ears bent back and his nose pressed forward. It became an unspoken competition after a while, with both of us alternating in the lead.

"Nothing can beat this hot fox in pursuit," he warned as he attempted to gain speed behind me.

"Right," I shouted back and maintained my lead. "Nothing except this girl who's only a mere child and should mosey on back to my England or whatever world it may be."

"Are you still sore about what I said back there with the fairies?" he panted.

"Not anymore since I know I'm going to beat you," I laughed.

He ran beside me as I glided on the vine. "If I cared about whether or not you're going to like me, I won't do what I'm about to do."

"Oh, really? And what is it that you're about to do?"

"Beat you," he grinned broadly and shot ahead.

I'm never fiercely competitive. I'd rather avoid the limelight winning usually brings. Yet something inside me stirred, and I realized there was no way I was about to lose to him of all people. Someone had to bring him down and put him in his place. I slashed vines, clutched onto them tightly, dove off branches, and glided far and fast from tree to tree as I could go. I winked as I traveled past him and watched his jaw droop. There was no prouder moment, and I relished in it until...

SNAP!

It was much colder and deeper, I could tell because I kept sinking further to the bottom. There was nothing below to stop me. The broken vine floated out of my fingers. I was running out of air and needed desperately to kick to the surface. As much as I thought about moving my legs, I couldn't get my body to respond. The water kept pulling me down, down, down, like a vortex. I was numbed by the cold, so I didn't feel any pain when the hook pierced my shoulder and I was reeled out of the water just before the serpent could nip off my legs.

CHAPTER 8

"If you stare at her any longer than you should, your eyes will roll out," an old woman cautioned.

"I'm not staring. I'm admiring," informed a rich, deep voice.

My eyes fluttered. I could see nothing. Understood nothing.

"She's waking," screeched the old woman.

"Don't be so alarmed, Mirdeth. She's only a girl."

"She's more than just a girl, and you know it."

I stirred as the strange voices seemed to swirl around me. I couldn't discern if I was dreaming or they were real. Mirdeth, the anxious old woman and the man with the distinctive, silky baritone. There was not enough strength in me to care.

"She has a companion," warned Mirdeth.

"He's not here."

"He saw you pull her from the water. He'll find her."

"We'll wait until he gets here and then..."

I couldn't stay in this dream if I wanted to. My breath felt heavy. Back again into the pit of darkness.

When I finally woke, the aroma of something savory roasting wafted beneath my nose. A fire burnt in the middle of a pit several feet from where I laid on a bed of layered furs. Sunset was quickly approaching, and whatever daylight was left streamed through the limestone bedrock. Although I could hear water trickling all around me, I couldn't locate the source. Once I sat up, the fine red dirt immediately painted my boots. My head swirled and nausea danced in my belly. There was nothing and no one else in the cavern that I could see. My stomach churned, and I was once again drawn to the attention of the delicious smell of something roasting. I turned to where it originated over the fire, large chunks of meat cooking over a make-shift wooden grill. As I ventured closer, I saw what it was that made me salivate under the dim light. Then I saw it, the head.

"It's the serpent that nearly killed you," a deep male voice caught me off guard. I reached for my bullwhip and realized it wasn't on my holster. My holster!

"Don't worry, my Aunt Mirdeth has your weapons." I turned and there was the statuesque man inches from my face. "If you brought a stranger home after rescuing her from the deep water vortex and you discovered she was carrying a whip and machete, you would confiscate her weapons too," he informed me.

"I suppose I would," I said warily, as I spoke to the man's chest. He was like a tower. "But I don't think I would've brought her home in the first place."

He wore an elaborate pendant strung onto a thin, dried vine around his neck. I could make out the shape of a swan's head and neck with wings spread out, ready to take flight. The wings were not ordinary birds' wings. They were intricately designed and almost transparent. It was so lovely, and I immediately had my suspicions. This man was a thief. He may have saved me from sudden death, but something about his cool demeanor told me not to trust him. Anyone claiming to be a hero most certainly has some other ulterior motive, and I had to be vigilant. I'd bet this man would turn me in to the fenova if they put out a hefty reward on my head.

"You didn't look very dangerous," he said.

"Then perhaps taking my things was unnecessary," I remarked.

"You were about to draw your weapons on me just now. Maybe it was a good thing we took them," he said defensively.

"I wouldn't have hurt you," I responded with sarcasm.

"I don't believe you."

"Well, you didn't need to save me if you thought I would hurt you. I was with a friend anyway. I'm sure he could've gotten me out."

"You sound ungrateful." He shrugged, "I didn't see your friend anyway."

"I'm sure he's looking for me."

"You've been here for two days already. I don't think he's looking."

Two days?

"Nevel," I grew worrisome. "Maybe he's in trouble."

The last time I saw him, we were racing in the trees. What if he jumped into the vortex to save me but couldn't get out? What if a serpent got to him before the stranger could see him? Troubling scenarios raced through my mind.

As I turned away, lightheadedness overcame me. I felt myself fall but someone caught me before I could hit the floor. The stranger breathed down on me in his arms, and I was forced to raise my chin to look him in the eyes, a move I deeply regretted. Our eyes locked and for once my attention was drawn away from instinctive suspicions. He was handsome. No, he was more than handsome. He was strikingly gorgeous. If someone told me the color of the crisp blue sky the day after it rained was inspired by his eyes, I wouldn't argue. Although my strength seemed to escape every pore of my body before I could make use of it, the tips of my fingers ached to touch his wavy, light brown hair.

"You haven't eaten in days, nor have you had any water," he said soothingly. "We can eat now and build your strength. When you're ready, we'll go find your Nevel."

"He's definitely not *my* Nevel," I corrected him. Then faintly added, "I was foolish. I didn't mean to sound so ungrateful for your hospitality and the fact that you saved me from being swallowed by some swamp vortex."

"I understand."

"No," I insisted as I truly felt awful. "I'm not used to being helped or cared for. It almost makes me feel uncomfortable."

"I can make you comfortable," he said, every word delivered so beguiling.

This was ridiculous. Absolutely absurd. Here I was malnourished and dehydrated, while in the arms of some guy I just met. I'm sure my eyes were especially sunken and my hair nappy. There was a great chance I reeked of swamp water and squirrel. Still, I didn't want to move a muscle for fear of losing the moment. If that sounded pathetic, then perhaps I didn't mind being pathetic for a few more seconds of my life.

"Xander!" the penetrating shriek of Mirdeth killed the moment. She was still a good distance away from us in the shadows of the cavern. "Maybe you should take her to the Collectors now while she's knocked out. I have a feeling that girl could be a fighter when she wakes."

The old woman approached out of the darkness. Her hooked nose was thick and had large pores, while her cheeks laid flat and hollow on her face. Her grey hair was wavy and untamed. Was this reflective of the woman I was about to encounter? She was short with a hunched back and used what looked to be a stalagmite for a cane. I was able to stand with help from Xander and watched as her black eyes broadened when they caught sight of me.

"Well, perhaps I was wrong" she said softly, abruptly changing her tone as she looked me over. "Make sure she eats and regains her energy. The Collectors will pay more if they can see she's capable."

"Collectors?" I asked.

Xander handed me a sizable chunk of skewered serpent. Although it smelled fabulous, something told me it may be better to starve if I was going to keep in the presence of these people.

"You've never heard of the Collectors?" Mirdeth was suspicious.

I shook my head. Xander nudged me, urging me to eat. Reluctantly, I took a bite.

"In exchange for a wanderer like yourself," she continued as she picked at the serpent meat directly over the fire, "the Collectors offer us protection from the fenova. Without them, Haggin will take all of our water. And without water, there will be no more serpents to eat and our swampy paradise will essentially turn into a desert."

"You can't possibly sell me," I said astonished.

She turned and placed her leathery finger over my lips, "Ah ha! But, you see, I can. You wandered onto my land, little girl, and now you have to pay for your stay."

"It wasn't my intention to stay," I explained. "I was just passing through."

"Stay or passing through," the old woman shrugged. "You're still a wanderer, and the law says we must deliver any trespassing wanderer at once to the Collectors. In turn for our loyalty, we gain protection. And if we let you be on your way, our land is destroyed. But, don't worry. The Collectors will do you no harm. In fact, they'll feed and clothe you. All you have to do is work long hours on the food fields for the remainder of your life."

"Life? Who's law is this?" I said. "It sounds more like a threat to turn in innocent people so they could use them as slave labor."

Mirdeth grinned. She grabbed the seared head of the serpent off the rack as if it hadn't been cooking above flames for hours. With her bare hands, she split the lower jaw off the head and bit into it with teeth, burnt scales, and all. After swallowing much of the meat and bones, she spit the teeth onto the cavern floor. Her black eyes burned into me, reflecting the fire light. "Your innocence is not my concern. Neither is your life." She turned to Xander who stood closely by me and said, "After she's done replenishing herself, take her to the boat. I'll be waiting there. Collection is in an hour, and we mustn't be late."

"Yes, Aunt Mirdeth," he willingly complied.

I took one last bite of the meat in my hands then flung it at the old woman's face. It hit her on the forehead and plopped onto the ground. It may have been my imagination but I thought I heard Xander chuckle before quickly suppressing it. With no time to waste, I bolted for the cavern exit, wherever it was. There were three archways that led into tunnels. The one to the far right seemed more brightly lit than the other two. Perhaps it led out to the open.

"Get her!" Mirdeth howled.

Before I could even get under the archway, I hit the floor and hard. My legs were bound together by a bolas, and Xander was quickly approaching. I had to break free. Hastily, I removed the bolas and threw the weapon at Xander. He dove and it flew over his head, smacking Mirdeth, who followed behind him, on the forehead.

"Don't make me use my magic on that girl," she growled. "Get her and bring her to me now!"

Magic? Who was this woman? Although I raced through the cavern tunnel as swiftly as I could, I felt my body slowing down. Part of me wished I'd taken more time to fill up on more serpent meat. Xander was not too far behind me. I could hear him panting, trying to keep up.

"Don't go," he pleaded. "She doesn't threaten to use her magic lightly. You'll be much safer with me. There's nowhere but into the water at the end of the tunnel, and you don't know how to handle the serpents around here like I do."

"I've been through much worse," I said. "I think I can handle myself, thank you very-"

ZAP!

A bolt of energy hit the cavern ceiling above me. I backed up as stalactites came crashing down like knives spearing the ground. They created a barred fence in front of me. Hands grabbed me and picked me up from behind just in time before a final stalactite pierced the spot I once stood.

"Listen to me next time, and you'll be safe," his baritone voice whispered into my ear. "Just play along."

Xander used the bolas to tie my hands behind my back. Mirdeth drew near until her nose touched mine. I could smell the serpent on her breath, but it smelled foul as if she'd eaten some raw. Observing her so closely now, I could finally see. She was a witch.

"Try a stunt like that again, pretty girl, and I'll make sure those stalactites don't miss. You're lucky my boy seems fond of you, but I have a feeling his infatuation won't last," she threatened. Then she turned to Xander, "Wrap her up some more, then meet me in my quarters."

Mummified is pretty much how he wrapped me from my shoulders down. He fed me until I couldn't eat, not another bite. "What's the point?" I asked when I saw that Xander stocked my satchel with the leftover chunks of meat and filled my canteen with water. "I'll be property of the Collectors within an hour."

"Trust me, you'll need it," he shoved the satchel into my arms.

"Really? But Mirdeth made it sound like a great life. They'll feed and clothe me, while offering me a chance to earn my place. It's a great deal, right? Now I'll know what I'll be doing in my old age, and I'll have you both to thank for it."

"Don't be crazy," he said avoiding my eyes.

"Xander!" the witch bellowed.

"I'm coming," he answered.

"What does she want? What's she going to do to you?" I blurted, unaware of my growing concern. Although I didn't trust fully him, I couldn't help but worry about what Mirdeth would do to him after he saved me from impalement. Could she really control someone's feelings so they couldn't feel compassion anymore? What would she do? How would she do it? Magic?

"Don't worry, just trust me," he quietly reassured, his gentle eyes rested on my shoulder. He rubbed a lock of my hair between his fingers. His eyes glided to mine as a smile crept onto his face. Before I knew it, he turned and was gone.

The wooden boat was simple and uncomfortable. I sat as best I could in my man-made cocoon at the bow. Thankfully, Mirdeth sat as far from me as possible at the stern. I faced Xander who was rowing not too far from me. When he came back from the witch's quarters, it was as if a wall was suddenly resurrected between us. Not once did he attempt to speak to me or look at me. Anger filled those eyes and visible creases developed between his brows.

She saw me studying his face and snarled, "You're nothing to him. Never will be. So save it." Mirdeth pulled her legs onto her seat, curling into a ball. She closed her drowsy eyes and draped a sheet over herself from head to toe.

The minutes passed and the old woman's breathing became heavy and more steady. This would be my chance to work on Xander, convince him to let me steal away.

"You once said you would keep me safe," I kept my voice low as to not wake the witch. "Should I still trust you?"

"No," he said flatly.

I shifted in my seat. "I thought maybe we had a special connection. At least it was something I felt. I can't explain it. Maybe

I'm just not used to people being so attentive or caring, but I was hoping you felt it, too."

Silence was all he could afford me. This would be harder than I thought.

"What are you doing here?" I dared to ask. "She's obviously not your aunt but a witch. Who is she to you?"

His eyes lifted, brows furrowed. "As far as I'm concerned, *you're* the witch. Whatever spell you cast on me in the cavern has worn off. That woman raised me since I was a baby, abandoned by my mother. She saved me, and I'm grateful," he said. Then he added under his breath, "Probably more than you can say."

I let out a breath I hadn't known I was holding. It was no use. It was obvious the witch had more power over him than I expected. His strong exterior was no indication of his broken self. What did it matter anyway? His loyalty was never to me, a girl he'd met only hours ago after waking. The witch was... Who was she really? I needed to get my head out of the clouds and back to reality. I never asked him to care for me. Still, I couldn't suppress this feeling of sorrow for him. Could it be possible I cared? No... Why was I wasting my time trying to figure out Xander and this crazy witch lady? Nothing good ever came out of developing attachments or feelings for anyone. Look at what happened to my parents whom I thought I lost at a very young age. I loved them deeply, and, without warning, they staged their deaths to get away. Sure they had a reason to do so in order to protect me and keep me from looking for them in the future, but it still sucked. Then Pike was used as a decoy by some guy masquerading as an Agent and almost died because of me. Now Xander... I needed to focus, distance myself, and get back on track. Alderek. Suddenly, my mission was clear once again. I had to rescue my parents so they could save Alderek with the help of the dragons. Then, I could get back to Pike and the other orphans. A plume of black smoke rose in the distance. Another home, another village lost to the fenova.

"I'm not a witch," I said gently. Once again, I was met with only more silence.

We'd finally reached the rugged shoreline and what seemed to be a village was immediately before us. Beyond the docks were cobbled streets lined with small shops. Banners crossed over from rooftop to rooftop advertising the arrival of the Collectors today. It was a gathering of hundreds of people and creatures leading their captured trespassers to huge open wagons. The Collectors were long slender creatures, similar to fairies except larger and sea foam green in tone. Their tattered wings were too weathered to lift their elongated bodies more than half a foot off the ground. *Fenovas.*

"Bring your trespassers to the carts," they instructed the new arrivals. "Find a line and get ready for inspection. Only healthy individuals accepted. Untie them but keep them under control. Collectors will not be responsible for any captive that runs away. If this happens, your land will be at risk of destruction unless they are recaptured in a timely manner."

Mirdeth continued to slumber in the boat. Xander took out a machete, and I recognized it immediately. It was mine. He used it to break me loose from my wrappings, but my hands remained tied behind my back. The gathering was bustling with commotion all around us. Captives broke free, pushing and shoving through the crowds. Captors ran after them or utilized weapons and nets to bring them back, some more successfully than others. He led me to the middle of the swarm, then did the unexpected. I felt the rope slice apart, and I was free.

    He spun me around, facing him. His tender eyes looked upon me as he cupped his hands around my face. He spoke quietly. Although the ruckus of the gathering polluted all around us, it seemed as if only his words could reach my ears. He said, "The witch has ears like a hawk. Even in her sleep, she could hear a pin drop. We're safe here. She can't come out of the boat without being recognized by a fenova as a witch. If they catch her, they'll destroy her for sure."

    "Why would they destroy her? How would that help them?" I was curious.

    "I don't know, but I'm guessing King Haggin has some insecurity issues. Only one known entity is allowed to use magic, and even he has a bounty on his head."

    Willox! He rescued the girl in the prophecy King Haggin is so fearful will strip him of his power. The only surviving being with magical powers in Alderek is now a fugitive. But who is Mirdeth? How did this witch manage to escape Haggin's initial sweep of witches and wizards? There was barely any time to prod for more information, and Xander had already moved on before I could ask any more.

"When I was a child," he continued, his voice silencing whatever questions that arrived in my head, "the Omaan came to our cavern and told us about a girl who I would save and love instantly. He said in turn, she would rescue me from a life of solitude and an early grave. I know that sounds crazy, but it really did happen. I didn't believe him at first until I saw you lying on my boat. Mirdeth couldn't handle that."

Xander kissed my forehead. Uncertain of what to do next, I grabbed his face and brought it down to mine. There on his forehead, I planted a kiss. He let out a laugh, probably not something everyone around us expected to hear at a gathering like this. Creatures eyed us suspiciously. They wandered further away from us, perhaps not wanting to be accidently associated with us in any way. As the crowd parted, a yipping sound moved closer towards us.

"Stop that fox boy!" hollered a portly man, fury oozing from his pores. "He's getting away!"

I turned towards the yipping noise when suddenly I saw him. Weaving through the obstacle of legs with a net over him, he finally arrived and leapt into my arms.

"Nevel," I exclaimed, grateful to see him again.

I placed him on the ground and pulled off the net.

Gasps echoed through the crowd. "She released someone's trespasser!" a woman said with disbelief.

"Traitor!" another yelled. Soon, there was a mayhem coming in from all directions.

Nevel transformed into his human form and grabbed the machete and my bullwhip from Xander's holster. "You won't be needing these, but she will," he said. Then he held his arm back and delivered a blow across Xander's face. As he turned to hand me my weapons, I slapped him.

"What was that all about?" he winced, then motioned to Xander. "Isn't this guy your captor?"

Nevel looked over at Xander. He shrugged, "It's complicated."

"Complicated? How complicated can it get? We've only been separated for two days."

"Who are you again?" Xander asked, a hint of annoyance in his voice.

Nevel closed the gap between them and the two were nearly nose to nose. "I remember you. You're the one who shot me out of the tree with the tranquilizer dart. I woke up and the next thing I knew I was tied up and held prisoner by some troll."

"Sorry. It's nothing personal."

"Well, it got personal when you took Astrid and tried to sell her to the Collectors."

"Are you for real? Can't you see, I released her? I'm trying to *help* her," Xander said through gritted teeth.

"How is releasing her in the middle of the *fenova central* helping her?" said Nevel facetiously.

Before he could release another net over Nevel, I heel kicked his portly captor, sending him back into the crowd.

"Nevel! Xander! Enough already. Things are going to get a lot more complicated if you guys keep it up," I quipped. "Less talking, more action."

Xander raised his eyebrows at Nevel, "They don't get any better than her." He slammed a fist into his open hand, ready for a showdown.

Inspired by my freedom, as well as Nevel's, captives everywhere began to break loose from the grasps of their holders. Chaos unleashed almost immediately. Those whose detainees became impossible to subdue immediately sought their revenge on us. The three of us fought back as much as we could, but there seemed to be no end to the stream of livid captors.

"Please, tell me we're not taking this guy with us to Kasus," Nevel said as he held a troll in a choke hold. He released him, sending him headfirst into the belly of another.

"As much as I would really love to get to know you better too, my fiery friend," Xander answered as he side kicked a minotaur, "I have a home to protect with my aunt. I don't think the Collectors are going to let us off easily after this."

"Good. I'm sure you'd get bored after a while anyway, you know, being the third wheel." Nevel quipped. He sent an uppercut into the jaws of a captor twice his size.

"I don't think I'd have to worry about any problems like that," Xander said as jabbed an elbow into the nose of a troll. The troll fell to the ground but not before Xander pulled the sword from his sheath and claimed it for his own. He then proceeded to indulge further in his raillery with Nevel. "I think it's you who may need a reality check. Is she your girlfriend?"

I rolled my eyes. I continued to listen to their silly banter, as I dodged getting hit by an airborne baton.

"No," Nevel answered, seemingly offended. "She's not even my type. But I don't think you're hers either."

"Interesting," Xander responded, taking a hit in the gut. "You could've fooled me."

"Maybe it's you who needs a reality check," Nevel shot back but not before suffering a blow to the face.

Two armored fenova grabbed each of my arms as a third rushed towards me with a net. I sprung up, using the fenova as mounts, and back flipped behind them. Before they could realize where I was, I thrust them forward into the third fenova and they tangled in his net.

By now, I was further from Xander and Nevel than I wanted to be. I could hear the continuous back and forth banter between them but could no longer make out their exact words. Eventually, the stream of captors slowly abated and the two faced each other once again. I raced towards them when suddenly, my path was blocked by a hefty minotaur. He wore an iron helmet and armor draped over his chest and back. When he grunted, a dusty spray came out of his nostrils. I took my whip and attempted to snap it back. Before I could, he grabbed my wrist.

"Dragon watcher," he said in a low, guttural tone. Then he lifted me up so I was hanging by my wrist at least three feet off the ground. He proclaimed victoriously, "Dragon watcher!"

The minotaur squeezed my wrist some more. I could feel my bones crush between his fingers. I gritted my teeth and winced in pain. The crowd ceased in their tracks and immediately grew quiet. Xander and Nevel came charging, each jumping onto the minotaur's arms. He struggled as he attempted to shake them off. Taking advantage of the distraction, I pulled my machete out of its sheath with my free hand. Nevel bit down onto the exposed neck of the beast. The minotaur threw back his arms and shoulders, sending both sailing into the air. I jabbed the machete with full force through into his fleshy side until he released my crushed wrist. I fell to the ground.

Xander darted to my side and held me like he once did in the cavern when I nearly fainted. "Astrid, are you all right?" his voice full of concern. He held my limp hand in his.

"I've been through much worse," I managed to smile and sit up. Without warning, he pulled his shirt off exposing an incredible work of muscular art. He effortlessly tore his shirt into strips and began to bandage my wrist.

Nevel approached and gestured towards Xander, "Oh, come on. Even if I was interested, how do you expect me to compete with *that*? What do you do all day, wrestle water serpents and then eat them?"

"I think he does," I said, thinking of the serpent we ate.

Xander glanced at me and winked. When he was done, he helped me to my feet. For the first time, we turned our attention to the crowd and noticed that they were already focused solely on us. With me centered between them, the three of us stood in a protective stance together, ready for the next battle to ensue.

"Look what you've done now, big boy," Nevel patted him on the back. "You've attracted an audience."

"I don't think they're staring at me," he answered, then looked over at me.

The crowd stood silent, captors beside their captives. Armored fenova and minotaur marched through the crowd. A few of the fenova were as tall as the people around them, their wings blackened and terribly frayed. One of these fenova led the army directly towards us. He stopped with only a few feet left between us. He was different from the other fenova in that his forehead bulged and his ears were longer and curved backwards like horns. His nostrils flared and his exposed teeth were small yet jagged and undeniably sharp.

"I am Colonel Bojra," he said in a strangulated voice. "Welcome. We've been waiting for you. King Haggin has sent me here to kill you."

"That was quite a welcome," Nevel said under his breath.

"Please, send King Haggin a message for me," I said firmly to the Colonel.

"Yes," Colonel Bojra stretched the word out ever so slowly.

"Tell him," I began. "Tell him if he wants Astrid Noble dead, he'd better come find me himself before his army is destroyed."

Without warning, I linked arms with Xander and Nevel. They lifted me up, as I struck Colonel Bojra in the face with alternating legs. He crashed back into the minotaur behind him, and when they finally got him up again he lashed, "Kill her! Kill them all!"

The infuriated warriors flooded towards us at the same time those in the crowd came forward, too. We were outnumbered for sure. Then something miraculous happened. The captors and captives for once were not fighting each other nor did they attempt to ambush us. Instead, they fought alongside each other bringing down minotaur and fenova.

"The prophecy is real! We're saved," someone shouted.

"Down with King Haggin!" another cried out.

"Free Alderek," many chanted.

I grabbed hold of fenova wings with my bullwhip and flung them hard onto the ground. I looked around to see how the boys were holding up. Nevel was quick with his sword, slicing through as many armored minotaur that came his way. Xander. Where was he? I searched for him frantically, striking with my bullwhip in one hand and slashing with my machete with the other. There was no time for pain in my broken wrist. Any fenova or minotaur that got in my way stood no chance.

"Retreat!" one of the minotaur bellowed. With the crowd rebelling against their army, they finally realized they were outnumbered.

As the crowd chased after the withdrawing army, damage of the battle became more apparent. Bodies of people, trolls, minotaur, fenova and other creatures of Alderek littered the cobblestone street. Then I saw him, lying on the ground with blood pouring from his chest.

"Xander!" I rushed to him and applied pressure on his wound with the shirt he'd wrapped around my broken wrist. I laid my other hand on his cheek. It was cold. "Xander. Stay with me. Don't you go," the tears welled in my eyes.

Movement. His eyes fluttered, and soon I was looking at blue sky again. "Hey, Astrid," he said with much effort. "You never told me you were the girl in the prophecy."

"Which one?" I snorted, as hot tears rolled down my face.

"Well," he swallowed. "If you can somehow save me from dying right now, I guess both."

"Shut up," I scolded. "You're not dying."

His eyes rolled back and then closed.

"No, no, no," I choked and patted his face frantically. Was this it? Were those the last words I would ever say to him? Did I really just tell a dying man to shut up?

"What's wrong?" he said weakly, barely opening his eyes. He smiled, "Did I scare you?"

"Don't you dare do that again!" I scolded him once more. I just couldn't seem to learn. A figure was drawing near us, and I squinted to make out who it was. He had untamed red hair and walked with a swagger. "Nevel!" Seeing that Xander was grievously wounded, he rushed over.

There was no time to think, no time to search for other options. There was only one person who could save Xander, and I knew what I had to do.

"Quick. See those boats in the dock?" I asked. "There's an old woman in there. A witch. Tell her it's Xander, and he needs her help."

"A witch?" Nevel seemed perplexed.

"Nevel, please, just go!" I urged.

CHAPTER 9

We were back in the cavern, the same place where hours earlier she'd tried to kill me. I remained cautious on the boat, aware she could throw me overboard at any moment. Once we docked safely in the cavern, she summoned me to follow near the fire. She placed an empty cauldron over it began fill it with items that littered shelves behind her. The liquids boiled, while the solids steamed as they dissolved in the bubbling broth.

She grabbed my broken wrist, and I flinched to get away. Instead of using force, she calmly held up a finger with her other hand. Then she pointed to the cauldron and nodded. Something told me to trust her. She had her chance to use her magic on me once we were out of sight on the boat. If she wanted me dead right, why go through the trouble of brewing up a potion in a cauldron? I let her dip my arm into the smoky concoction. It neither hurt nor burned. Muscles tightened, nerves tingled, and bones shifted. When all was done, my hand felt renewed and a bit stronger. She ladled the same broth into a bowl and brought it to Xander's bedside. She poured it onto the wound on his chest while he lay unconscious. We watched as the blood bubbled and washed away to reveal renewed skin underneath.

"I can only patch up the bones and the flesh. If he's lost too much blood, there is nothing I can do. It may take days for him to recover," Mirdeth said.

"Thank you," I said.

"No," she shook her head. "He is like my son. I would save him with my own life."

"Mirdeth," I began. "how..."

"No questions," she sounded tired. "I'm a witch. You've already figured that out. How Xander came to live with me is not something I'd like to discuss with you or anyone else, even if you are a dragon watcher. If you know anything, I shouldn't even exist in Alderek. The fenova will come looking for anyone who helped you rebel against King Haggin at the gathering today. If they find Xander, then they'll find me. I won't be able to help him anymore after that. It'll be all over for my boy then."

"He can come with us," I uttered. "We can wait until he's regained his strength, and he can help us get to Kasus. If he's on the move, the fenova will have less of a chance to find him. You can come, too. If we all work together we'll have a better chance of defeating Haggin. There's another. He's a wizard. His name is Willox."

"No! Never," she hissed in my face. "Be on your way and let us be! I will never join forces will that evil wizard, Willox."

Xander stirred in the bed that was once was used by me. "Astrid," he gasped, his throat coarse and dry.

I moved passed Mirdeth, but she immediately clasped my arm. Nevel drew his sword. She opened her hand and, as if a ball of energy was released from it, pushed him to the ground. She held up one finger. The nail grew long and sharp. Without warning, she slashed my palm until droplets of blood dripped freely onto the ground. She dragged me close to Xander's bedside and pressed her nail into his upper arm until blood flowed from the wound created. She held my hand over his wound and droplets of my blood fell onto his. It sizzled on his skin, and I watched as his brows furrowed in pain.

I withdrew my hand from hers, and shouted, "What are you doing?"

A twisted grin washed over her face. She seethed, "You can never be together, see? You aren't the girl in the prophecy the Omaan gave him. You can *never* be the girl. Your blood is toxic."

I won't pretend that what she said didn't sting. It did. It stung greatly. It took all that I had within me to not bark back at her. Every part of me wanted to strike at full force and in every way. Instead, managed only to say, "I never asked to be the girl in any prophecy."

"Astrid," Xander breathed through dry lips. His eyes opened weakly as he reached an arm out to me. I couldn't take it. I saw our blood mix and boil. What did that mean anyway? What if I was toxic for everyone? I would have to keep my distance. *Focus, Astrid, focus,* I reminded myself. *Save Alderek and go home.* It was better to not get attached. No good ever came out of getting close to anyone.

"Find your strength, Xander," I said. "The fenova will find this place eventually and stop at nothing to burn it down."

I motioned for Nevel to follow me, and made my way to the tunnel that would lead us to an exit.

"Wait! I'm coming with you," Xander called out.

I turned to see Mirdeth grab onto his arm. "Not a good idea," she said. "You're too weak to do them any good."

He shook her off, as I continued through the tunnel. Mirdeth shrieked after him, "I raised you. I was the one to save you, not her! How dare you leave me. Come back." Her tone changed quickly from anger to desperation, "When the fenova come, it'll be all over for me. Won't you stay, Xander? Stay and help me protect our home."

"Mirdeth," I heard him stop in his tracks, "I'll never forget who took care of me growing up when there was no one else. I'll forever be grateful to you. But, please, you have to understand, this is bigger than our cavern and the swamp. If I don't join Astrid to free Alderek, this place will never have a chance to survive. Nothing will."

The further I traveled through the tunnel, the less I could make out the conversation between them. I had an inkling Mirdeth would use her manipulative ways to convince him to stay. Xander would never leave her if he knew she'd be at risk of danger from the fenova. It wasn't too long after, though, that I discovered I'd misjudged the witch. Someone seized my shoulders and spun me around. In an instant, I was facing him. He tried his best to quell any signs of his aching muscles and tired breathing, but I could tell it wasn't easy. He said, "Give me some time to gather a few things. I want to come with you. Just wait for me. You can't do this alone."

"She won't be doing it alone," Nevel stepped in closer.

He gave Nevel a quick glance, "No offense, Nevel, but she's just a girl and you're just a-."

Nevel drew his sword. "She's a born dragon watcher. If you knew her longer than you do, you'll know she's completely capable of dismantling trolls like you in seconds."

Xander stepped around me and advanced towards him. "Sounds like you know this from experience."

I drew my bullwhip and quickly pulled the sword from Nevel's grasp onto the floor. "Homes are burning and people are dying," I scolded. "This is no time to fight. If either one of you wants to join me, I'd suggest you leave behind your egos and grow up!"

My words flittered into thin air. Dragon watcher or no dragon watcher, there was no way to get them to listen. Hopefully my inability to get through to these stubborn two doesn't reflect what will happen when we encounter the dragons. They would have to battle it out like children fighting over a toy. With both of them unarmed, they decided to charge at each other with fists flying.

"You've got to be kidding me," I said under my breath. "Okay, boys. You've left me with no other choice."

The end of the tunnel was near, and the last rays of Vromen burnt just above the horizon. I stopped just before the boat to take me to the end of the swampland when I heard a twig snap behind me. I drew my bullwhip. Then I noticed the water leaking into the boat. Holes had been drilled into the wood, and it was recent. I crouched down and twirled around, as I lashed out my bullwhip. It caught onto someone's legs in the shadows. I pulled him near. A fenova!

He was tall and lanky with a bulbous forehead. "Seize her," he said in a strangulated voice. Colonel Bojra.

Nets dropped down over me, and I quickly pulled the machete from its sheath. I sliced through the netting as Colonel Bojra freed himself from the coils of my bullwhip. Once freed from the nets, two husky minotaur narrowed in. One grabbed me around my arms from behind, while the other took hold of my thrashing legs.

Colonel Bojra crept up towards me. He put his face close to mine. His breath smelled of rotting flesh. His tongue resembled one of a snake's. It seemed to have a mind of its own slithering in between the cavity-ridden gaps of his teeth.

"This must be my lucky night," he rasped. "I came here looking for the witch who stole from the king, and I found the dragon watcher girl instead. Haggin will be pleased when I bring both of your dead bodies to the palace."

His arm reached out as he wrapped his fingers around my neck. This was not the way I imagined how I would die. It was too easy, too quick. The last image that would burn onto my cornea would be that of a maniacal, mutant fairy. This wasn't the way it was supposed to be. I could feel my breath slipping away as his grip got tighter and my neck squeezed thinner. My eyes began to roll, and he cackled while he concentrated on my killing.

"Did you really think you'd be able to save everyone by coming to Alderek?" he spat. "Almost half the planet is in ashes and more creatures are brought to the king to do his bidding every day. Once his work is done, the fenova will rise and take back everything. Someone so fragile as you can't place a dent in our plans."

This would be it, if I let it be, but I wouldn't. With all the strength I had left in me, I pulled my legs in and kicked out with all I had. The minotaur by my feet fell hard onto the ground. The other minotaur behind me lost his footing from this force and backed into a tree. The impact caused him to release me as he slid to the ground. I grabbed onto Colonel Bojra's hands and pried them from my neck. His fingers were bony and clammy. He leaned in, fangs exposed. I skirted left, avoiding his sudden tactic to maul me. Without warning, he came at me like a vampire thrust forward by wind. Machete drawn, I swiped. In one clean swoop, Colonel Bojra's head was airborne. It finally landed with a splash and drifted atop the swampy water. I could make out a slow ripple in the distance. There was a short screeching noise that echoed as the serpent's head broke the water. In one swift swallow, the head of the colonel was gone.

"I think that was more than a dent, Colonel," I proclaimed. The minotaur grumbled as they picked themselves up and rapidly disappeared back into the shadows from which they came.

Onto my hands and knees I dropped. Back in England, death from starvation and sickness were never almost inevitable realities. But this was different. I was a warrior, and with warring came casualties at every corner. This was my life in this strange world. I wasn't sure I could ever get accustomed to the careless disregard for life and the planet.

I coughed and gasped for breath but only for a moment. I stood, regaining my strength with every new breath I drew. It wasn't over. It was only the beginning. There was no way I would let King Haggin take anymore.

I'm coming, I closed my eyes as I told them without breathing a word aloud. *Be ready.*

The ground beneath me trembled and a soft groan could be heard in the distance. I didn't doubt it for one bit. They had answered. King Haggin had his army of fenova and minotaur. I was confident I would have the dragons.

"Did you feel that?" Nevel's eyes widened.

"Feel it? Did you hear it?" Xander replied.

They raced out of the cavern, no visible injuries on either of them. In fact, Xander wore a new shirt and was now armed with a double-bladed sword. I decided not to question how their boxing match went down, as I figured all was well now between them.

"Quick," I said. "We have to get to Kasus before it's too late."

Nevel glanced at the slowly sinking boat. "But how? We'll never be able to swim safely out of here."

"The minotaur," I murmured to myself. And then I was off in the direction of Colonel Bojra's men.

Fortunately, their burly frames and hefty armor slowed them down. They hadn't gotten far and were about to get into their boat. Xander threw a bolas and brought one down. The second was already in the boat. He cut the dock line and began to steer the boat from the shoreline. I snapped my bullwhip, and it coiled around one of the boat's cleats. With the help of Nevel, we were able to reel it in like a fish on the line. Xander jumped on board and, in one swift blow, sent him overboard.

We took turns rowing, keeping low as we traversed the village where the Collectors held their gathering. Hidden once again amongst the thick woody vegetation of the swamp, we allowed ourselves to drift along the current. The moonlight reflected on the water ahead of us, the only witness to journey through the swamp river. Xander fell asleep behind me. I was surprised he had the strength to keep up with us this far.

Nevel drew a cape he'd found in the boat left behind by one of the minotaur, ready to turn in for the night. "Are you sure you don't want me to take first watch? You look like you need the rest more than I do," he said.

I shook my head, "I'll be fine."

"If you change your mind," he began.

"I'll let you know," I answered. "Thank you, Nevel."

He nodded and rested his head. The night was still, yet the water remained very much alive. I listened to the occasional gentle breaks in the water, the dips and dives of creatures oblivious to the intentions of Haggin. Reaching into my pocket, I felt around for the amber amulet Willox had given me when I first arrived. It lay in my palm, as I wondered how to make it call the images of my parents. I gently rubbed it with my fingers with no luck, blew on it already knowing it would produce nothing, and finally stared at the stone until I grew weary. Unable to make it work, I folded my fingers over amulet. I'd longed to have a moment to myself to see their faces once again, but I'd have to wait some more.

"You have to speak to it," Nevel's voice startled me.

"What?"

He got up and sat beside me. He pointed to the amulet hidden in my tightened fist. "You have to ask it to show you, and it will. It doesn't have to be out loud." He held out his hand, "Here. Let me show you."

Sensing my hesitance to give up my valuable stone, he said tenderly, "I promise I can make it work. Let me show you."

My fingers opened to reveal the amulet. He took it into his hand, and, with no effort at all, it began to glow. The projection of my parents lingered before us, standing at the altar as they gazed lovingly at each other.

"These are your parents?" he asked.

I nodded. "I barely remember what they looked like. It's hard to believe they were once a big part of my life. A distant memory, yet I somehow I miss them so much."

I took the amulet from his palm and the image faded away. "Thank you," I whispered.

"I lost my parents, too," he said softly, "but there's no chance I'll ever be reunited with them."

"I'm sorry."

"Don't worry. Every creature and person you'll meet in Alderek has a story about how King Haggin has done them wrong. Whether it be their homes were raided or their entire village was burned down. Maybe a friend or family member disappeared because of Haggin's laws. We all have our tragedies. Mine is no different from everyone else's. That night, like so many others, the fenova were ordered to destroy our homes. I managed to escape and so did my father. He was so grateful I made it out alive. He kissed me, held me, and told me he loved me. It wasn't long before he realized my mother was still in our home. We could hear her screaming. It took only a few seconds for my father to make it into the house. And it took only a few seconds after that the roof collapsed and my mother's screaming was finally silenced. I was about ten at the time. I remembered everything. I watched the fenova cheer and hail Haggin while my parents and neighbors perished. I fled knowing one day Haggin would die at my sword."

I squeezed his hand reassuringly, "Your parents didn't die in vain. We'll do it. We'll end Haggin's reign and put a stop to the fenova once we get to the dragons."

The boat entered a clearing where the moonlight danced more freely on the ripples, uninhibited by invasive vegetation. Nevel looked at my hand on his, and I coyly pulled away. Grateful for the shadows of the night, masking what I could feel were my burning red cheeks.

"When I first met you, I didn't think you'd survive a day here," he grinned in reflection.

"I wasn't too sure of myself either," I sighed. I fidgeted in my seat. Having a cordial conversation with Nevel wasn't something I've ever imagined happening. Needless to say, it was awkward.

"If that's true, you hid it well," he said.

"So, what happened between the two of you?" I changed the subject as I gestured to Xander in the back. As much as I enjoyed our bickering-free and noncompetitive time together, I could feel it was time to put up a wall. Walls I should've built a long time ago before I let Pike or Xander in. "First you guys were at each other's throats, and now you're sleeping on the same boat. No one's afraid of the other throwing them overboard?"

He shrugged. "I'm tempted, trust me. But I think we've realized we're on the same team against Haggin. It doesn't make any sense to knock out someone on your side, especially when there aren't too many of us in the first place."

"You don't like him," I said.

"I don't trust him," he corrected.

"Why not?"

Nevel rubbed the back of his neck and raised his eyebrow. Before he could answer, Xander stirred behind us.

"Is there something I missed?" Xander yawned.

"No, no. Not at all," Nevel said, sounding somewhat flustered. Was he relieved at the chance to evade my question? Why didn't he trust Xander?

"Good. I can take the next shift now if you both want to catch some shut eye before the suns rise," Xander said.

I swapped places with him, while Nevel moved to the front of the boat. My eyes closed, unaware of how exhausted I'd been. As I drifted to sleep, I felt the warmth of a blanket placed over my arms.

"Good night, Astrid," I heard someone whisper. My eyes drowsily fluttered open, expecting to find Xander by my side. Instead, I was alone, draped in a cape once owned by a minotaur.

CHAPTER 10

I awoke to the enticing smell of charred fish. My stomach growled, eager to get me up and moving. The boat was docked, and I could see Xander several feet inland with large fish over a hot bed of rocks.

"Hungry?" he grinned as he offered a chunk of meat.

"Famished," I replied. The fish was light and flaky and tasted sweet and fresh. I wolfed down my piece before Xander handed me more. As my belly filled, my concentration wandered further from my stomach and more to our surroundings. The land was flat and lightly dampened by the thin humidity in the air. Boulders and trees with wide trunks were scattered everywhere, covered in a mossy sheet of green.

"Where's Nevel?" I asked as I finished the last bit of fish. "Didn't he find the fish appetizing?"

Xander shook his head, "Said he didn't want to eat anything that could possibly remind him of the small creatures he used to eat. He went off in search of berries or flowers. Not sure how much he's going to find around here, though."

Just then, a chilling lament cut through the air. I glanced over to Xander, wondering if what I'd heard was real. Then it happened again. It was a deeply mournful cry, all the more terrifying because when we realized we knew the source. With no time to lose, we abandoned our campsite to follow the sounds that would lead to Nevel. His cries echoed north of our boat, directly along the water's edge. Adjacent to the shoreline stood the dark and barren hill with a carved entrance leading deep into the darkness within. A cave. The river forked and ran through and around the cave.

We darted into the mouth of the cave, dimly lit by the meager sunlight that was able to make its way through the jagged rocks that guarded it. The scent of mildew and something decomposing filled my nostrils. I felt my stomach turn as I saw the remains of an animal that I couldn't identify rising and falling with the tide. Phosphorescent algae bloomed above us, casting an eerie blue glow. As we journeyed deeper, the pulsing waves of light tapered off and the darkness consumed everything. Xander found what seemed to be a leg bone on the ground. He scraped some of the algae off the wall. It came off as a thick goo that he placed on one end of the bone leg. When he was done, he gave the make-shift torch to me and made a second for himself.

"Are you sure the sound was coming from inside this cave?" Xander began to doubt. It had been quiet since we left the campsite, and there were no other clues that would lead us to Nevel.

"I'm sure," I said, although I felt a meager amount of self doubt lingering. We thrust forward into the cave, keeping careful not to walk into the river that ran alongside us.

"Do you have any idea where we are?" I asked Xander.

"You are in the Cave of Smalls," dozens of ubiquitous tiny voices echoed at once.

"Where are you?" Xander demanded. "Show yourselves."

"We are nowhere," they answered from one direction.

"But we are everywhere," they giggled from another.

"What have you done with our friend?" I implored.

For a long time, we stood in silence. Every second that passed without us hearing from Nevel made me anxious. Did I lead us in the wrong direction? If he was not in this cave, then where was he? Would he die because I delayed our finding him? My heart sank. It took everything within in me to keep from collapsing, from giving up. We had to find him. Finally, the voices spoke up again.

"You mean, the one you let wander alone in this unfamiliar territory while you two stayed together?" they teased. "Was *that* your friend?"

"They're right. I should've gone with him," Xander's voice cracked. "I never cared for him really, but I shouldn't have let him go off on his own."

Although it was dark in the cave, our only source of light were the ends of our glowing bones, I sensed Xander was overwhelmed with guilt. This wasn't like him, nor was it like me to give into my emotions so easily to the point of contemplating giving up. A sense of foreboding clutched my stomach. Something wasn't quite right.

Visibly distressed, Xander ran his hand through his hair continuously. With sunken eyes, he turned to me, "We have to get out of here. I'm feeling overwhelmed. I'm sorry. I can't do this anymore. We need to get out."

"But what about Nevel? We can't stop looking for him."

"We haven't heard anything from him since we came into this cave. I don't think he's in here. You led us in the wrong direction," he said accusingly. Then, his face fell into his hands, and he shook, "I'm sorry, Astrid. I don't know what got into me. If Nevel is here, it's probably too late. We have to leave before it's too late for us."

"No," I gasped, astonished those words came out of Xander's mouth. It wasn't normal. It wasn't like him to abandon ship. I held his arms and looked him in the eyes, "Xander, look at me. We'll find him, and we'll do it together. Whatever it is they're doing to us, fight back. Find yourself and fight back. It'll be okay." *I think.*

Flustered, I turned to the voice, "Where are we?" I inquired again.

"The Cave of Smalls," they repeated. "Your memory is brief. Or perhaps, you had doubts about your knowledge? We have that affect on those that visit us."

"I think so. I'm not sure," I said, frustrated. It was difficult to concentrate when my focus kept narrowing in on how helpless I felt. I had to stay strong, redirect my focus. *Pull yourself together, Astrid.* I continued, "I meant to ask, what is this place? And what are you doing to us?"

"Do you want to know about your friend?"

"Yes, of course."

"Then heed our warning carefully because you haven't much time. Even if you do reach him, it'll probably be too late for all of you. For at this moment, we're feeding on your energy, the strength of your emotions, your egos and your character," one of the voices cautioned. "Your friend is succumbing to his weaknesses as we speak, drained of anything that once held his chin up high. By the time you reach him, you too will be on your knees begging for second chances you know you'll never be granted. So do what you must if you can. Just know you have to make a choice and make one fast. Use the last of your energy to get to your friend, or use it to rescue yourself from out of this cave before it's too late."

The voices broke into a convulsion of taunting giggles. Xander dropped to his knees and began to sob. I felt my cheeks grow hot with frustration. I didn't come so far into Alderek to have whatever these voices were deplete me of my strength and existence.

"How do I know you're not wasting my time, telling me he's in there when in reality he's probably nowhere near this cave?" I challenged. "For all we know, you want to feed on the energy of two people of strength. You'll stop at nothing to keep us here, even lie to us."

The laughter abruptly stopped. "Lie? How dare you accuse us of using such a strategy. Are you insinuating we lack character?" they shot back, obviously offended.

Xander's shoulders that had slumped over since we entered the cave rolled back. His head lifted once again as he realized my approach. He dried the wet streaks from his face as he stood. Was he back? I tried hard to avoid any eye contact with him to save him from any embarrassment and regression. When he stood tall once again, he declared, "Anyone who steals from others is certainly questionable. In this case, you're acting as thieves of the very things people work their whole lives to guard and achieve, character, pride, and their self-esteem."

Yes! He's back.

The voices didn't hide their annoyance, "We don't *steal*, we *feed*."

"What would happen if years went by without creatures entering this cave? Would you starve and cease to exist?"

"Nothing will happen. We'll simply sink into hibernation until someone ventures into our cave."

"So you take from others what you don't necessarily need to survive," I chimed. "Not that you should take from others in the first place, but we do what we must within limits to endure."

"That wasn't our intention," the voices sounded aggravated.

"Ah, but it is," I insisted. "Unless you find it within yourself to change. Instead of taking from others what they've worked so hard to build, why not develop your own character with what you already have. I'm sure you're an energy source within yourself. If courage, pride, and self-worth are what you really are made of, do what many other honorable creatures and people do. Build on it. Live it. Don't wait for someone to come along so you could take theirs. That's not having character."

It was difficult to make out for certain, but at that moment I swore I could hear a faint weeping. Suddenly, the noise grew louder until all of the voices were sniveling simultaneously.

"We never meant to take from others," one could be heard sobbing.

"We've always thought it was our duty to drain the strength of others," another lamented.

"It made us feel almost stronger, more superior than anybody that's ever set foot in our cave," yet another whimpered. "We never realized…"

"Never realized…" the voices repeated all together. Whatever they meant to say drowned in their sudden excruciating moans. We shielded our ears.

"Pull yourselves together," I hollered over the commotion. "There is a way to make things better."

Their painful sobbing quickly subsided. "What do you mean?" inquired one voice. "Our strength and character have never been our own. How could we possibly make things better when we're reduced to an absolute nothing?"

"You don't have to use anyone else's ability to do what's right," I said, trying to sound hopeful. "You know what's right, and that's where you can start."

"You mean a second chance?" another voice piped up.

"Yes. That's exactly what it is, a second chance."

Pulsing blue lights lit up below them. It lit up a path that led deep into the cave. At the end of their trail, I saw him. He lay on the cold ground, motionless.

I ran to him, scooped him into my arms. "Nevel," I gasped. "Nevel, wake up. It's me, Astrid."

Xander knelt down beside me, "We have to get him out of here."

I shook my head. He was barely breathing, and his fingers were like icicles. If the voices drained him of his strengths, he needed something to refuel. I leaned over so my lips were close to his ear. Then I whispered two simple sentences. When nothing happened, I glanced at Xander.

"Let's take him outside," he said.

Just then, I felt the warmth radiate from Nevel. His fingers started to twitch and his eyes slowly opened. "Hey," he said when he saw me.

"Hey," I smiled back.

"I was scared of the dark," he responded drowsily.

"You don't have to be anymore. We're here."

"Astrid, what did you say to get him back?" Xander cocked his head with curiosity.

"I'm not sure what it was," I said, a bit flustered. "Some words of encouragement."

"What words of encouragement?" This time he directed the question to Nevel.

"I don't remember," he said as he rubbed his head.

Xander helped him to his feet. "Well, whatever she said pretty much saved your life."

"I guess it did," Nevel said. "I won't forget it."

"Good," Xander patted his back. "Now, let's get a move on out of this place before something else goes wrong."

"The colonel's boat is in the vicinity. Start searching in here and all around the perimeter," a hoarse voice echoed into the cave.

"Fenovas," Nevel gasped.

Their rhythmic footsteps gained momentum and grew louder as they drew nearer. The intensity of their burning torches brightened the cave walls in the direction we came.

"We have to get out of here," I said looking for a way out.

The blue pulsing light of the cave voices glowed in the direction of a dark passageway. I motioned for my friends to follow. "Quick!"

Without a moment to lose, we pursued the direction the blue lights led us but not before being spotted by the first line of fenova.

"Captain!" one alerted. "We've found them. They're over here!"

The passageway seemed endless. The walls were extremely closed in on either side of me, it was difficult to sprint through without an occasional bump on the shoulder. I took a quick glance back. Xander followed behind us, doing his best to side step through to keep up.

"Are you doing all right back there, Xander?" I called out.

"Never been better," he replied as the fenova got closer. They were slender and swift, unhindered by the obstacle of the constricted passageway.

"Duck!" Xander ordered.

I swooped low, keeping my pace. I watched as a flaming boomerang flew overhead and disappeared into the pitch black tunnel. I continued to race through. My heart pounded in my chest as I saw the flaming boomerang fly full force towards us once again. This time it was my turn to holler, "Duck!"

As I crouched low, Nevel followed suit. I watched in horror as Xander faced the boomerang head. With barely seconds to spare, he dodged it leaving no time for the fenova behind him to see what was coming. It was like a domino effect after that. The first fenova was knocked back by the boomerang into the fenova behind him and so on until five were on the ground. The rest of the fenova army struggled for a while to pass their fallen comrades, widening the gap between us.

"Either you have a death wish, or you're really crazy, Xander," Nevel exclaimed as we continued to dash through the passageway.

"Well, I sure don't have a death wish, I can tell you that much," Xander casually replied.

"I knew it!"

We neared the end of the tunnel and daylight was up ahead. I raced outside, grateful for some open space, but stopped suddenly. We were atop a rugged hillside which plunged abruptly to the valley below. The water that flowed into the cave continued its way out a separate passageway from which we came. It flowed over the edge of the cliff, creating a massive waterfall that flowed into a lake below. The water roared as we watched it cascade over the mountainside.

"Now what do we do?" Nevel said. "That's a two hundred feet freefall. There's no telling how deep the water is below."

"We jump," I blurted.

"We what?" he gasped.

Xander threw his arm over my shoulder, "See? I'm not the only crazy one here."

"If we're going to do it," I said, "we'd better do it fast."

Someone grabbed me by the hair and pulled me from Xander's arm. The next thing I knew, I was in a chokehold under the arm of a fenova.

"You're not going to do anything," she said. She pulled my hair back again, and her sharp nails dug into my scalp.

I seized her arm around my neck. I managed to lift her elbow enough to squeeze out of the chokehold and pin her arm behind her. One direct kick in the back of her knee, and she collapsed to the ground. Before she could lift herself back up, I dropped my elbow and struck her in the neck. She groaned as she hugged the dirt floor.

"Nobody tells me what to do," I said, wiping my chin. I turned to the other half dozen fenova that had gathered and motioned to them, "Who's next?"

Nevel shook his head. "You made her *mad*," he chastised.

"She's *crazy*," Xander nodded with a grin.

A female, almost identical to the one I'd just taken down, snarled. She bared her yellow teeth, and I could tell it was personal. She advanced towards me, her shoulder heavy with revenge. Behind her trailed a massive fenova, wielding a mace club embedded with steel spikes. She raised one arm and let out a guttural roar. Before long, all the fenova charged. Xander and Nevel moved forward. They intervened just in time as clubs and axes swung at me. They each took on two fenova and left me to deal with the demented female and her club-brandishing male counterpart.

I removed the machete from its sheath in one hand and held my bullwhip in another. Something told me I wouldn't be in combat with them separately. My instincts were right. As she attempted to slash at my face with her massive claws, the club came swinging towards my head. I ducked down just in time. I snapped my bullwhip against the male's leg and pulled him off his feet. Then I spun around and stood up in time to kick the female in the torso. Finally back on his feet, the male twirled his club erratically as he approached. When he got closer, he swung with full force, determined to annihilate and destroy. Every swing he took at me, I managed to block with the machete. Thankfully, I was strong, but it was obvious he was stronger. With each blow I blocked, I was pushed back closer and closer to the female fenova as she picked herself back onto her feet. He swung. I blocked. I could feel her heat raging behind me as he forced me with his blows closer to her. When she was directly behind, ready to sink her claws into my neck, I bolted to the side. His mace club raised high, too late to stop the downward swing already in motion, thrust down and onto the female. It was over for her, but not over for me as the male came rushing towards me. He threw his mace club at me. The force was so strong, it knocked the machete out of my hand. His clenched fists sprung open, and he held them in front of his face. One by one they came out. His claws were as sharp and long as my machete.

"Haggin requested we kill you immediately," he said gruffly and lowered his hands to reveal the smug grin on his face. "But I'd prefer to take my time and have a little fun first."

While I knew it would slice in an instant, I held my bullwhip in front of me. I was ready for battle although it might have looked like I was ill equipped.

"I don't have time for fun, buddy," I scoffed, as I snapped my whip around his wrists. His claws intertwined against each other. Humiliated and angered, he charged towards me. He lost his balance and fell to the ground, impaled by his own claws. I winced as I retracted my bullwhip.

Looking around, I saw Xander and Nevel retrieving their weapons. We could hear the shouting of more fenova from within the cave.

"Time to jump," I said indifferently, as I headed to the edge of the cliff.

Xander stood next to me. "I'm not sure that I ever want to remember what life was like before I met you, Astrid," he said.

"A little safer, I'm sure," Nevel chimed in.

Fenovas poured out from the cave opening.

"Jump!" I urged.

Without further hesitation, we were in the air, feet first, plunging straight down into the pool below us. I hit the water, and it stung momentarily. When we broke the surface, I glanced up to see the fenova watching us from over the cliff. They seemed afraid of even looking, as if fearful of heights.

"Will they follow us?" I asked.

"Sure, they'll follow us," Nevel replied, "but not by throwing themselves off a cliff like we did."

"Why not? It'd be a lot faster. Makes their job easier."

"Not for fenova. Something strange happens to a fairy during transformation. I mean, besides the obvious physical changes. They suddenly develop a fear of flying and of heights."

"Well, I can see why. To go from flying everywhere to barely being able to lift yourself off the ground must be traumatizing," Xander added.

"It's no wonder those guys have severe insecurity issues," I said. "Colonel Bojra said the fenova were planning on overthrowing King Haggin. Why would he say that? I mean, why not just do it? He's clearly outnumbered."

"I don't know," Nevel shrugged. "But I do know the fenova are a bit shifty. They'd like to make you believe they're a pretty tough army when in reality they run at the first sight of a mountain."

"He did mention something about waiting for Haggin to be done with something before making their move," I pondered. "What could Haggin achieve that they couldn't do no their own?"

"Not much, probably. Come on, Astrid," he coaxed. "Let's get swimming before it gets too dark and the serpents get hungry."

Just then, we felt a tug at our ankles. Nevel screamed, and I kicked whatever it was in the water.

"Hey, take it easy," Xander laughed, as he broke the surface.

"Why did you do that, you idiot!" Nevel said, shaken.

"It was funny," Xander chortled, as Nevel splashed him. "Loosen up, fox boy."

"Don't call me 'fox boy' unless you want your throat ripped out."

"Oh, come on! Does it have to get ugly?"

"Ugly? You haven't heard ugly!"

"I don't have to hear it, when I can just *see* it," Xander barked, as he stared directly at Nevel.

"I'm sorry," Nevel said sarcastically. "No one forces you to look into the mirror every day."

"Nevel, you are one big a-"

I couldn't help it. I knew it would be inappropriate, but it was too difficult to contain it any longer. I burst into a fit of laughter. They turned and stared at me in curiosity.

"I think she finds us amusing," Xander remarked.

"You guys are so funny," I slowly managed to get out, each word a challenge between breaths. "Here we are in the middle of who-knows-where after we nearly killed ourselves by jumping off a cliff, and you're acting like little kids."

"She's right," Nevel sighed. "I'm sorry. I don't know what got into me."

"That's all right. No harm done. I think I'm rather getting used to our random spats," Xander smirked.

"I think it's Nevel's way of saying he likes you," I winked at Xander.

"Huh? What?" Nevel was flabbergasted.

"Yup," Xander chimed. "I know deep down he really does like me. Maybe even looks up to me like a big brother."

"Oh. No, no," Nevel insisted.

It was uplifting to have this moment after all we'd been through so far. It was hard not to laugh. The water was warmer than we expected, enough for us to continue swimming downstream as much as we could before it got too shallow. By the time we climbed back onto shore, we were at least a few miles away from where we'd dropped into the water.

We were soaked to the bone and the air began to cool down rapidly. A chill ran up my spine, and I got the feeling there would be no sanctuary on this shore. After taking some time to wring out our clothing, I glanced over to find Nevel staring off into the distance. He was pale as day although night had already begun to cloak the sky in darkness.

"Nevel?" I approached him cautiously. "Is everything okay?"

I watched as he swallowed hard the lump that had formed in his throat.

"We're here," he said under his breath.

"What do you mean *here*?"

"This is it," he continued, as if everything around him was frozen in space and time. "This is where they died."

"Who? Who died, Nevel?"

"My parents."

Then he did something I didn't expect him to do. He walked straight into the darkness beyond the trees until I could see him no more.

CHAPTER 11

"Stay close," Xander spoke softly as he grabbed my hand.

Nevel must have seen something familiar with his night vision eyes, but, for us, there was nothing much to see except blackness. We ambled warily, hand in hand, feeling for trees or anything else that may be in our way. Finally, after what felt like an eternity, we could make out what appeared to be a log cabin. Smoke bellowed from the chimney, and a warm orange glow pulsated through the window. Someone was home, but where was Nevel?

Remnants of a community that melted away were still apparent. Burned wooden foundations where lives were possibly lost were overtaken by vines and moss. The lone log cabin was clearly a new resurrection after the destruction. But who would choose to live amongst the memories of this tragedy? Perhaps Nevel would know, but where was he?

Xander led me to the doorstep of the log cabin. I could hear the crackling of the fire inside, someone was feeding the flames. Xander lifted his fist, ready to knock on the door.

"Wait," I whispered, squeezing his hand. "I think I heard something."

He cocked his head to the side, then shook his head. "No, nothing." Then he raised his fist again.

"No, wait," I insisted. "There it goes again."

This time it was more obvious, repeated soft tapping against a wall.

"It's coming from that building over there." I tugged on Xander's hand and urged him to follow.

We made our way to the building where the noises were coming. It was a charred structure no larger than the log cabin next to it. Part of the roof was caved in and the windows were shattered all around. This was possibly a home, somebody's home a long time ago. Then it hit me, and I realized why we were here. This was where Nevel's parents died. The sounds of a struggle mounted as we drew nearer.

"He's inside," I declared as I shot through the door. The light from the bright lanterns that hung around the cabin next door streamed through the cracked and broken windows. Then I saw them, two foxes, one red and the other a pale, sandy blonde. They wrestled on the floor, nipping at each other's ears and noses. When Nevel finally escaped the grip of blonde foxes teeth over his ear, he darted away. He ran along the walls as she chased him closely behind.

I helped myself to Xander's bolas and waited for the right moment when the blonde fox lagged a little more behind Nevel. Then I tossed it. The bolas wrapped around her front legs. As she tripped and rolled on the ground, she transformed into a human girl. Her longer legs helped her slow down until she was finally in an upright sitting position. Her hands were tied with the bolas. She desperately attempted to break herself free.

Nevel transformed back into his human form and ventured over to us. "Thanks, Astrid. I don't know where she came from, or why I felt so compelled to just leave you guys in the dark when I wandered over here. I'm truly sorry."

"That's twice in one day she had to bail you out," Xander chastised.

"I know."

I wandered over to the girl that sat on the ground, still struggling to free herself from the bolas. She was about my age, perhaps even a year or two older. Her sandy, blonde hair resembled the curvy tail she wore as a fox. It was tied back and laid perfectly curled over one shoulder, displaying no evidence she was ever in a struggle. She briefly glanced at me with her cold hazel eyes warning me it would be wiser to keep my distance.

"Who are you?" I wondered aloud.

She continued to wrangle with her bolas.

"Do you live in the log cabin next door? Is there anyone else that lives with you?"

Annoyance seemed to strike her, as she shot me a look of pure abhorrence. "Do you really believe I want to talk to you right now? You're in my territory, so you should be telling me who you are not the other way around."

I tried not to let her affect me, although the heat within my chest rose and flushed my cheeks. "I'm Astrid. I've come to Alderek from England to kill King Haggin," I said bluntly. "Now it's your turn. Who are you? And why did you try to kill my friend?"

She raised her eyebrows, "I didn't try to *kill* him. He's on my property, and so are you. I live in the house with my aunt and uncle. Years ago, when the fenova burned our village, everyone fled or died, but not us. There was nowhere else for us to go, so we stayed. This was the home of a family I once knew. A boy lived here with his parents." She lowered her head and continued. I could barely hear the words she spoke next, "He was my dearest friend, but they all perished."

Nevel stepped forward. "Eden?" he gasped.

She looked up at him, her eyes filled with tears.

"Eden," he said as he kneeled by her side. "It's me. Nevel. I'm alive."

She gazed at his face as if to study him. Then the flood gates opened and the tears streamed down her perfect cheekbones. He untangled the bolas around her wrists. The second she broke free, Eden embraced him, and I knew right away I didn't trust this girl.

#

Eden and Nevel sat shoulder to shoulder on the rug in front of the fireplace, their legs sprawled out before them as they each sipped on warm cups of broth. I stayed with Xander at the table after we'd filled our bellies with the meal prepared by Eden's aunt, Eolande. She was a gentle, older woman with a hunchback and the uncanny talent of transforming the most bizarre ingredients into a delicacy. Slug slime never felt nor tasted so pleasant. With her hunched back, she had lost her ability to shape shift into a fox. Her younger brother, Eden's Uncle Kian, was more eccentric and physically sturdy. He had more red facial hair than anyone I'd ever met before, and seemed uninterested in greeting his unexpected visitors. Once Kian was done with his meal, he promptly excused himself for bed. He never spoke much, but I think he preferred it that way.

I tried not to be obvious that I was hard at work eavesdropping on the conversation by the fireplace. I sipped my broth and warmed my hands on the mug as I did so.

"Your hair is still the color of flames, just as I remembered it," Eden said, as she playfully spiked up Nevel's hair.

"My hair may be the only thing about me that hasn't changed much," he patted his hair down.

"How about me? Have I changed much?"

He took a moment to observe her face. *Pretty sneaky*, I thought. *I bet that was exactly her plan.*

"Nope," he replied and shook his head. "You're still the same Eden I remember from years ago. Only, of course, you're older."

"Older?" she was disappointed.

"And prettier," he quickly added.

She smiled approvingly of his answer.

"What happened to you after the fire? Why didn't I see you or Uncle Kian and Aunt Eolande?"

Then she spoke so softly, I could barely hear, "The entire village was burned to the ground in a matter of minutes. Our friends and family were gone so fast and without warning. Sometimes I feel cursed I wasn't there when the fires started. Uncle Kian took my aunt and me hunting that night. He taught me how to set up traps to catch rabbits and ground squirrels. I guess it was beginner's luck because I caught two rabbits that night almost immediately after I placed my traps. We weren't aware that while we were having a successful time hunting, our people were dying. My mother and father died tragically along with so many others. We found them in someone else's home, collapsed at the foot of the door. They were carrying an older couple out, but the smoke got to them too soon. There was just so much smoke in the house and all around the village. I think that's how most of them died, trying to save each other. It's hard for me to even think back to that day, much less talk about it. I looked for you when the fenova left, but I gave up hope so quickly. Now I wish I hadn't stopped looking. Did you ever think to look for me, too?"

Nevel drew in a deep breath. It was obvious the subject was difficult on him, too. "I heard and saw terror that night. I heard the moment my parents died. It's not something anyone should ever have to witness. Perhaps I was too angry to feel any glimmer of hope. Maybe there was none in the first place to be had. All I wanted to do was to put an end to the fenova and King Haggin. To stop them from doing this to other people. That's why I'm here with her."

Her? I thought. *Is he thinking of me?* Eden must have been thinking the same thing because that was her next question as well.

"By *her*, you mean Astrid?"

"Yes," he said. "She has just as much reason to bring an end to the fenova and remove King Haggin from power."

"Oh. Is that why she's here?" Eden remarked candidly. "Maybe we should change the subject to something a little lighter, shall we?"

For a while, they chatted amongst themselves. As much as I tried to listen in, it proved to be difficult with Aunt Eolande sweeping the floor beneath our feet and all around us.

"More broth?" Xander offered.

I shook my head and thanked him. He was keeping to himself a lot. I wondered if he, too, was interested in what Eden and Nevel were talking about. Either that or he knew about my eavesdropping and was being careful not to interrupt. That would be embarrassing. I needed to stop. Why should I care about what Nevel was talking about with his stunning, long-lost, childhood friend? I had a feeling she didn't care for me either. That was fine with me because I was finding it difficult to be in her presence as well. Prior to dinner, Eden gave me a set of her clothes to change into, announcing to everyone that mine were too worn and hideous. She was more slender than I was, leaving the shirt to be extra form fitting but still comfortable enough to battle in if I had to. I had to roll the sleeves since she was slightly taller also. The black leggings she paired with it had to be adjusted at the bottoms. Otherwise, they were snug and a welcomed change to my tattered dress. Also during dinner, she seemed to go out of her way to keep Nevel from speaking to me. She spoke nonstop about anything and everything. It was difficult to get a word in edgewise. Perhaps, I was just being a bit paranoid. I reminded myself she hadn't seen Nevel in years. She thought he didn't survive the fires and to find him again must be a great gift. Of course she would be possessive of Nevel. Why should this even bother me? It shouldn't, and I was determined that it wouldn't.

    Just then, Aunt Eolande rested her broom against the wall and left the room. The volume of the conversation on the rug unexpectedly became audible once again. Eden threw her head back and giggled. Suddenly my interest peaked for a second round of eavesdropping. *Darn it! What did it matter?* My conscience shook me from inside.

    "Do you remember how inseparable we were," she cooed. "No one could ever find us when we were planning out our naughty little pranks. They never knew about gargantuan tree with the cavity we used to hide in. Do you remember that, Nevel? Do you remember that tree?"

Nevel sighed, "How could I forget? Some of our greatest pranks were thought up inside that tree."

"You eat," someone shoved a bread roll in my face. It was Aunt Eolande. She wore a grin and nodded for me to take the roll.

"No, thank you," I patted my belly. "I'm so full. Dinner was wonderful." Little did she know I wanted to listen in on her niece's conversation.

"You eat," she insisted again. She picked up my hand and placed the roll into my palm. "It's good for you. You feel better."

You feel better? Was it that obvious I wasn't feeling quite myself this evening?

I broke off a piece of the roll and put it into my mouth to show her how much I appreciated her offering. It was warm and chewy on the inside. She was right, it did make me feel slightly better. I offered half the roll to Xander, but Aunt Eolande insisted I finish the one she gave me. She would return with another for him. When she finally bid us good night, I'd just swallowed the last chunk of bread and Nevel and Eden were still talking.

"Remember the time we convinced Perama's older brother into eating the black mushrooms?" she giggled.

"The ones that made him transform every time he coughed or sneezed?" he asked.

"Yes! And you'd stand next to him with your pockets filled with dried lotus flowers, knowing he was allergic."

He shook his head, "I regret we did anything so childish."

"But we *were* children. There was nothing we could do to know what would happen to everyone else. Fenova was not even a word we knew existed until they took everything from us." She took his hand into hers and rested her head on his shoulder, "I thought you were dead for so long."

I shifted in my chair. Suddenly, the fireplace had warmed the house too much for my comfort, and I broke out in a light sweat. Feeling faintly lightheaded, I excused myself from the table before heading outside.

I stood outside in the chill air, making certain I didn't wander too far beyond the lantern lights. The door of the cabin swung open, and I immediately knew Xander had followed me.

"It'll be a nice change tonight from sleeping on the floor of a cave or in a row boat," he said, as he stretched.

The night seemed brighter now that the clouds began to roll away, exposing a few bright stars behind them. The sky was littered with all their sparkling and twinkling. A part of me wished I could reach up and take one down to keep in my pocket for another dark day. The chill ran up my spine, and I shivered.

"Cold?" Xander asked.

"I'm all right," I lied. I wanted to do what she'd done. I wanted to rest my head on someone's shoulder, shut my eyes, and just breathe. But, alas, I didn't have a clue about how to do that. Why was it so difficult to freely express my emotions? Did I ever nuzzle against my parents before they left me? Did I feel their warmth before they abruptly decided to take it away? Was I afraid it would happen again? Better not chance it.

"Is everything really all right, Astrid?" he frowned.

I shrugged and shook my head. "How could it ever be? Willox, Myrilla, Maddux, and Ecson are out there, somewhere. I don't even know if they're safe or terrified. I mean, here we are, well fed and getting ready to sleep in beds tonight. My parents, on the other hand, are at the top of some mountain locked up in a cell. And the orphans, I can never forget the orphans. Pike. If only there was a way get home, a portal. We can't stay here for very long, Xander. There's too much at risk to lose."

"Like Nevel?" he asked casually.

"No," I answered, flustered. "I mean...What do you mean?"

"Astrid, it's okay. It's obvious, at least to me, that you're bothered by the whole Eden and Nevel thing."

"I'm not bothered," I said, offended. "They're childhood friends. There's nothing I can possibly do to change that. They've got a bond and years to catch up on. I mean, it's...it's nice."

"Nice?" he snickered, amused.

"Yes," I insisted. Then asked curiously, "What's wrong with *nice*?"

"Nothing's wrong with *nice*. *Nice* isn't so bad. After all, it's always nice to have someone you've known for a while and can trust, especially when it seems like the world is falling apart all around you."

I took in a deep breath, as I wiped the buildup of sweat beads on my nose. There was a blackened tree stump where I decided to sit down until the lightheadedness passed.

"Are you feeling all right?" he asked, concerned.

I nodded and scooted over to make room for him to settle next to me. "Tell me about Alderek, Xander. Since I've been here, I've seen more callousness and destruction than anything else. Tell me this world is worth saving, that there's more beyond this pointless savagery and hatred."

His lips pursed in thought. "Well, do you have some time to listen?"

"I have all the time in the world for you, Xander," I beamed.

"That's the best thing I've heard all day," he beamed back. Then he began, "This place of ruin, this mess...None of this is what Alderek was before Haggin's forces grew strong enough to take it all away. The people of Alderek could roam freely, explore endlessly. We didn't have to worry about trespassing or the Collectors."

"You mean, you haven't been wrestling serpents every day of your life and rescuing damsels in distress from watery vortexes?" I teased.

"Ah, yes. The good life," he sighed. "You know, I wasn't always confined to living in the swamplands with my aunt. Although, I have to admit, she was more overbearing than most caretakers. I wasn't allowed to travel much of the world like so many others. So it was a good thing it wasn't really a desire for me to do anyway."

"Why do you think she sheltered you as much as she did? Especially as you got older. I mean, you aren't exactly built like you can't handle yourself."

"I never knew why she was so protective," he shrugged. "But, then again, I never asked. What I did get, however, was she was a loving person who taught me well."

"I'd love to hear what you thought was your most valuable lesson," I said curiously.

"Well, I remember she took me once to a carnival in a town we'd never visited before. I mean, it was rare for Mirdeth to take me anywhere beyond wherever we lived at the time, so I knew there was a special reason why she did it. She warned me not to focus on the games, the food, or the events. We were there for a lesson, a very important one indeed, and she made that clear. We had fun, or, at least, I did. But, she really forced me to observe those around me. So I did. Astrid, it was incredible, a real eye opener. This was the first time and the only time I've experienced anything like this. Every type of life form you can think of on Alderek attended this carnival. It was a diverse array of creatures and people, all mingling together with the same purpose, to have fun. And it all happened because it was possible for everyone to set aside their differences and to share the common bond of the joys in life."

"That sounds beautiful. So peaceful. Exactly what life should be," I said.

"This is what Alderek was all about, unity in the face of differences," he said before he hesitated. "Of course, all is gone now since Haggin got a taste for greed. Unfortunately, the greed and indifference to each other spread. Trust is a difficult thing to come by in this world. People are betraying each other everywhere to keep their homes safe from the fenova. You experienced it firsthand when Mirdeth tried to make me turn you in to the Collectors in return for temporary immunity."

"How could I forget," I cringed.

"She isn't what I remembered her to be growing up. But I can't blame her. With our world turning upside down right before our eyes, pillaging and annihilation in a matter of seconds a definite reality, desperation has made it more difficult for people to think clearly."

"Xander?" I said faintly. "Do you ever wonder where your parents are or whatever happened to them?"

He reached under his shirt and pulled out the pendant I'd admired when I first met him. The swan taking flight with transparent wings. It was as lovely as it was when I saw it first.

"This belonged to my mother. I've always thought the wings were the most beautiful part of this piece."

"They remind me of Queen Pavia's wings. So lovely," I said.

He smiled and tucked the pendant back behind his shirt. "I don't remember either of my parents. I was told my father died when I was only an infant. It wasn't long after that my mother fell ill and never recovered. Maybe that's the reason Mirdeth has always been so protective. I have no one else but her," he said.

"That's not true," I said softly, as I turned to him. "You have me."

"It's *nice* to have you around, Astrid."

"*Nice* isn't so bad," I smiled tenderly.

"Ahem," someone cleared his throat. We turned to find Nevel with his arms crossed and a look of consternation on his face. "Am I interrupting something?"

"Just a good heartfelt conversation between close friends, buddy," Xander said, as he patted Nevel on the back and headed towards the cabin. He yawned, "Time for some shut eye, guys. Don't stay up too late. We've got more villains to fight and an entire world to save. I'll see you in the morning. Good night, Astrid. I hope you're feeling better."

"Night, Xander," I waved.

Nevel took a seat beside me once we were alone. The space he left between us let in the chill until it was fully embracing me.

"You're not feeling well?" he inquired.

"No, I'm feeling fine. A little lightheaded a while ago, but I think was just tired," I replied.

He looked up to the sky. "Do you see those two really bright stars there? They're shining right beside one another?"

"Yes."

"Now, look closely. Do you see it? It's very faint."

The sky was ominously dark with few scattered stars across it. I stared into the darkness between the two vivid stars. The longer I concentrated on the dim spot between them, the more I could see something pierce through the darkness. There it was, the third star. Small and barely noticeable. "I see it," I said.

"Great. Now don't take your eyes off it. Focus. You're about to witness something even more amazing." It seemed like forever that I watched this tiny star appear out of nowhere, brightening with every second that passed. Finally, he gave me the cue, "Now, look at the sky."

I let my eyes roll away from the sparkling gem. What I saw was breathtaking. Faint, yet glittery silver stars speckled across the black emptiness in the sky.

"It's beautiful," I breathed. "Who taught you how to do this?"

"No one. I used to watch the sky a lot after my parents died. The stars kept me company, it's pretty sad. Anyway, one night I was just staring into the heavens wondering if there was more to...well, everything. Nothing seemed to have any meaning anymore, you know. Then, I spotted those two radiant stars over there. It almost seemed like they were competing for attention. Which one can outshine the other? Or something like that. So I grew tired of giving either one the attention they were receiving and instead decided to find more in the space in between. When I found what I was looking for, the entire sky lit up. It was like-"

"Magic."

"Exactly," he rubbed the back of his neck. "It's been a long day."

"It could've been worse," I said, as I stared at my hands.

"I got myself into some dangerous predicaments twice today."

"But you survived."

He nodded, "You're right, but I did because of you."

I glanced up to find him staring at his own hands. "The second incident wasn't so bad. She would never have hurt you."

"She didn't know who I was at the time. I think she could've done a lot of damage if she wanted to. You don't know Eden."

"But you do," I said, my voice trailed.

He shook his head, "We were friends as kids. Most of the time we spent together was nonsense. We were too young to know any better. I'm pretty ashamed, actually."

"It must be nice to at least be reunited with someone you knew before the fenova attacked the village."

"I can't lie," he mused. "It's much better than *nice*. It's a relief, quite a relief to see her again. It means there could be more of us that survived that night. Seeing Eden again was like...the best thing that's happened to me in a long time."

I wasn't sure how to respond. My head wanted me to be happy for him. Eden shared a special time in his life that no one could ever get back for him. Her memories of their childhood were his. Some they shared alone together, and some they shared of each other's families. It was also difficult to deny the fact that Eden was drop dead gorgeous. She was dainty yet tough. Perfection from head to toe.

"But, Astrid," I was grateful he broke the silence before I could. "I didn't come out here to discuss Eden."

"You didn't?" I inquired. Why did I suddenly perk up? What was I expecting? If only I had the ability to stop my cheeks from turning crimson.

"No, I didn't," he smiled. "I've been wanting to speak to you all day since the cave."

"You did?"

He nodded and leaned towards me. "I wanted to tell you-"

"That tomorrow I'll be teaching each of you how to battle against the fenova using combat weapons I made with my uncle," Eden chimed in. She sat between us on the stump and nearly pushed me off the edge. "Nevel and I have been talking. He told me about you being a dragon watcher."

"Did he?" I asked, amused. I rose from the stump and opted to stand.

She waved her hand in the air, "It was really quick. He didn't go into details or anything like that."

"Oh."

"I guess there wasn't much time for that, or he just didn't have that much info about it. So we got into talking about how we keep the cabin out of harm's way from the fenova."

"How do you keep them from destroying the place?" I was suddenly curious. "It looks to me like building a new home on top of a village they destroyed was like an act of defiance."

"You're quick. I like that," Eden said facetiously. "In a way we were making a statement, yes. The fenova could never drive us away from our homes no matter how much fear they thought they instilled in us. Anyway, that's beside the point. I digress. I'll get to the bottom of it. My uncle and I supply weapons to the enemy."

My jaw dropped or, at least, it felt like it should have hit the ground. Here she was, the elephant in the room, confessing to being the enemy's accomplice. I knew there was something about her I didn't trust. Now I knew what it was.

"Don't be so quick to judge. I know what you're thinking, and we're not traitors. If anything, we're helping the rebellion," she added matter-of-factly.

"Please, help me to understand. How are you helping the rebellion by supplying the enemy with weapons to kill and maim the good guys?"

"Look around you, Astrid," she said. "Where do you think you are? Our home is a safe house. We're in an uncovered and unprotected area. Do you have any idea how many people and creatures pass our way that are trying to keep away from the fenova?"

"A safe house?" I wasn't convinced.

Nevel spoke up next, "The only reason Eden and her family can stay put is to turn something in to the fenova that would be of value to them like weapons. Of course, they can turn in trespassers like us to the Collectors, but they choose to help us get closer to where we need to be in order to defeat Haggin."

"Your friends," Eden continued, "the falcon and the fairies. They lost their way from you but found my home."

"Willox and the fairies," I gasped. "Are they all right?"

"The wizard seemed weak, but we did as much as we could to nurse him back to health. They were headed to Mt. Iris," she informed, "but that was days ago. They should be there, if not very close to it by now. Do you trust me now?"

"How many kinds of weapons do you manufacture?"

"Three."

"When do we start?"

"At the break of dawn."

I hesitated, wondering if I was being fair by not giving Eden the benefit of the doubt. Still, I couldn't place my finger on what it was about her that made me feel leery, and I was left to prolong my uncertainties. I declared, "I'll trust you once the three of us leave from here safely, and I find my friends alive and well."

"Why don't you like me, Astrid?" Eden frowned, as she scooted closer to Nevel on the stump.

"I never said I didn't like you, Eden," I said bluntly.

"Astrid, Eden's only trying to help. Maybe you should cut her some slack," Nevel retorted.

I felt the aggravation mount within but decided it wasn't worth arguing. I had no solid evidence against Eden, but, at the same time, something was telling me not to let my guard down completely. "Let's hope you're right that she's truly trying to help us," I forced myself to say calmly.

Nevel then turned to her and said, "I think Astrid's got a lot going on right now, Eden. You have to understand, it can't be easy to trust someone you've just met, especially when that person's just confessed to supplying fenova with weapons."

"When I explained it to you, you understood. But I guess you're right," she pouted. Then she added, "She doesn't know me the way you do."

Was that supposed to be a jab at me? If I hadn't already seen her transform, it wouldn't have been too difficult to guess she was a sly, manipulative fox. I feigned a yawn.

"Good night," I said. "If we're getting up to do some early morning combat, I'd want to be fresh and ready."

"Good night, Astrid," Nevel said. I expected them to follow me inside. We all needed some extra rest after all we've been through that day. Instead, they stayed back on the stump. The space between them absent.

CHAPTER 12

Xander raised the curved horn hilt to his ear. He activated the spring-loaded triple blades as he aimed for one of six wooden fenova cutouts one hundred meters out. With precision, he flicked his wrist and sent the blades spinning forward. They sliced the mock target's throat then came whirling back to reattach onto the hilt.

"Darn it," he cursed. "I was aiming for the forehead."

"Oh, Xander," I chuckled. "Sometimes I worry about you."

We had ventured out into the clearing just as Argon peaked over the horizon. The air nipped at our noses, and not one of us was left without red noses and rosy cheeks. I felt a hard tap on my shoulder and turned around. It was Eden, and Aunt Eolande was hovering behind her. She held out a steaming roll of bread.

"Take it," she said indifferently.

The night before proved difficult for me as I lay in bed to sleep. Since the discovery of who Eden was, I wasn't exactly proud of my behavior towards her or my feelings. How callous I'd been to someone I didn't know. Why didn't I just trust that Nevel trusted her? I vowed to give Eden "some slack," as he'd put it. If not for me becoming a better person, then for the sake of my friendship with Nevel.

"Thank you," I offered her an appreciative smile.

She pulled out what looked to be my bullwhip from her belt. "Here," she said, her face expressionless.

"My bullwhip. Where did you get this?" I asked, rattled.

"I snuck into your room while you were sleeping. Don't worry. I fixed it for you."

"I wasn't aware it was broken," I said, wishing she didn't have to make it so difficult to like her.

"It wasn't," she said and shrugged. "I made some improvements. I hope you like it."

Did she, too, feel guilty for our subtle actions against each other the night before? I felt hopeful we could start over again. "Thank you," I said again, as I accepted the peace offering. "What did you do to it?"

Nevel approached us, eyeing my bread. He held his hand out. "Yum. Breakfast."

"Snap the whip," she ordered.

"At Nevel?" I said, my eyebrows raised.

"Just a super, light tap on his hand will do."

I did as I was told, making certain to strike him on the tip of his finger only. It made a crackling sound as it moved through the air. When it made contact, blue electrical discharges jolted him and he jumped back in shock.

"Ow!" he cried. "What was that?"

I pointed to Eden who wore a huge grin on her face. "It's the new lightning whip," she said proudly. "The more contact with the tip of the whip, the more of a stun your opponent will suffer. Activated only by cracking the whip first." She held the tip of the whip in her hand to demonstrate it was safe to touch.

"Sweet," Nevel was impressed but quickly moved on. "Bread, please?"

Aunt Eolande waved her hand and said, "No, no, no. Please. I have more for all of you. I'll bring you all food. Just wait."

While she ventured back to the cabin to get more food, Eden was more than happy to steal Nevel away to show him the weapon she'd made for him. I made myself comfortable on a nearby rock and ate my roll. It was sweet this time but tasted delicious. With all the delectable dishes this woman could possibly make, I was surprised Eden was as trim as she was.

Nevel gripped the grooved handle of the weapon she gave him. When he squeezed the handle, massive tri-blade stars slid out on either end. He twirled the baton between his fingers, than manipulated it around his body before flinging it hard at one of the targets. One end of the double-sided baton sunk deep into a wooden fenova.

Eden clapped graciously. I shook my head as I stuffed my mouth with the last bit of the bread roll. "Show off," I teased.

"You're just jealous I have a better weapon than you do," he scoffed.

"I highly doubt it."

"Can you do better?" he said, as he came towards me.

I took his weapon and gave him a wink. "I think I can."

"Let's see what you've got," he winked.

It was heavier than I expected it to be. I had to give Eden and her uncle some credit. They really knew how to design and build these things. As I approached the targets, a wave of dizziness came over me. I must have been dehydrated or in need of a larger breakfast this morning. Luckily, the wave passed, and I was able to get to where I wanted to be to strike. I focused on the wooden targets. Although I'd never seen him, the face of King Haggin took place of the blank cutouts before me. His eyes were dark and his skin was grey. The hatred in his grin made me feel sick, literally. I threw my arm back and then forward as I released the baton. It landed hard, deep into the wood. Each star struck one of two side by side targets in the head.

Eden gasped. Nevel cheered. I heard the muffled call from Xander as he shouted out my name in a panic. For a moment, I viewed the world through quickly narrowing tunnel vision. Xander ran towards me, his arms stretched out. Blackness engulfed me, and it was too late.

The crisp crackling of a fire, the sweet scent of freshly baked bread wafting through the air, and a warm woolen blanket over my skin. These were the luxuries I sensed around me as my mind awoke. My whole life was spent living in an abandoned factory with cold cement floors, beginning and ending the days with hunger filling my belly, and fighting for the survival of a world I never knew existed. *Let the past be a dream*, I tried to convince myself. *Don't open your eyes. Fight it. Fight it.*

"Wake up," Eden's unsympathetic voice ordered, as she shook me. Reluctantly, I opened my eyes. She held a roll of bread out to my face. "Eat it," she ordered.

Then I understood. The bread. Why did they insist I eat their bread and never share my rolls with the others? Immediately after consuming it, I'd find myself lightheaded and dizzy. I looked around. The only ones other than myself in the cabin were Eden and Aunt Eolande. Where was everybody else?

I sat up and slowly shoved the roll further from my view. "The bread. Every time I eat it, I get dizzy. What have you been putting in there?"

"Leak leaf oil. It's a poison," she answered flatly. Then she pushed the bread she held into my hands. "This one is clean. You won't have to worry."

"Poison?" I repeated, repulsed.

"Calm down. We didn't put enough in there to kill you, only enough to make it seem like you were dead."

Aunt Eolande came over with a cup of broth. She placed it in my hand and pointed to the bread. With a gentle smile on her face, she urged, "Eat." Then she returned to the kitchen where she continued her endless sweeping.

"I don't understand," I shook my head. "Did you want me dead? What's going on? And where are the others?"

"Listen," she drew in a breath. "Eat and drink. You'll need your energy for the trip we'll be taking."

"*We?*" I set the broth and roll on a wooden end table and promptly got to my feet. "We're not going anywhere until I have you give me some answers, Eden. You better start talking fast."

"I know you're upset," she began.

"You bet I am," I muttered.

"But if you want to be of any help to your friends, you're going to have to sit down and listen to me."

I figured it was the quickest and possibly the only way I could get answers. I sat back down.

"Good," she breathed out, relieved. "Now, eat your food."

I raised my eyebrow at her curiously.

"Don't worry. I promise there'll be no more poison," she insisted, and I reluctantly believed her. If she truly wanted me dead, she could have finished the job while I slept. She sat herself beside me and wrung her hands. "My uncle found out you were a dragon watcher and sent for the fenova to come and take you. He negotiated your life for a lifetime of immunity. The fenova wouldn't be able to touch us or our land for as long as we live, and we wouldn't have to make any more weapons for them."

"Is that why you poisoned me? To fake my death so the fenova wouldn't take me when they got here?" I asked.

"At first they wanted to take your body with them. Aunt Eolande had to convince them the poison she gave you was seeping out of your pores. They were all warned not to touch you, unless they wanted to share the same fate."

I glanced over at Aunt Eolande. She waved and nodded as she carried on with her sweeping. "Why? Why did you go through all that trouble to save me? I thought you hated me," I confronted Eden.

"I don't hate you," she frowned. "Okay, so I do. Maybe a just little. Or a tiny bit more than a little."

"Is it because of Nevel? You know, Eden, he and I..."

"You're all he ever wants to talk about. I've loved him all my life even when I thought I lost him. Then when he finally returned, he was in love with a dragon watcher."

"He's not *in love* with me," I assured. "I don't know how you could possibly ever believe he feels that way about me. I mean, we constantly bicker. If anything, he sees me as a threat to his masculinity. You know how he is. He's very competitive."

"He confessed to me after you left last night. He definitely loves you," she said bluntly.

"Oh," was all I could think of to reply.

"It's unimportant now. It'll never work out between the two of you anyway."

"It' won't?" I said, a bit offended.

"Of course not. Haven't you heard?" a conniving grin came over her face. Then she continued, "Why did the rabbit cross the road?"

I shook my head, "Why?"

"To get to the other side."

"I don't get it," I said, frankly. "Why are we telling jokes?"

Then she added, "Why did the fox cross the road?"

"To get to the other side?" I sighed, uninterested.

"No," she beamed. "To eat the rabbit."

"Are you saying Nevel will eventually eat me?"

"No, I'm saying you two are completely incompatible. You're from two different worlds, literally *and* figuratively. It's not that way with me, though. He and I grew up together. We've suffered the same losses and share a history. That sort of stuff runs deep. I think he'll get over you sooner or later when he realizes he only wants what he can't have," she said quite brashly.

"What do you mean, 'what he can't have?'" I asked, curiously.

"Oh, come on," she beamed at me, as if waiting for a confession. When she didn't get one, she abruptly replied, "Really?"

"I have no idea," I shook my head, unaware of what she insinuated.

"You're in love with Xander."

I was astonished. "I am?"

"See? You are!," she clapped her hands.

"No," I stuttered. "I didn't mean it that way."

"Don't worry," she leaned in. "Your secret is safe with me. It's obvious he how he feels about you, too. It doesn't take a genius to see it."

"I guess I'm as dumb as they get when it comes to..."

"Love?" she smiled. "Listen, you know the way I feel about Nevel, and now you know the way you feel about Xander."

"I'm not sure. I've never really thought about it, but you sure have," I said facetiously as my voice trailed. Never in my life had I been more confused than during this conversation with Eden. Was this some kind of mind game and she was trying to plant ideas into my head? Or was I just extremely out of touch?

"It's obvious. Don't deny it," she pressed. "Anyway, I like you Astrid. I really see us being close friends one day. Maybe even as close as sisters."

"I've never had a sister or a brother, actually."

"Well, neither have I." She hesitated, then added, "So, you know how I feel about Nevel, right? But things can never really progress between us if he believes there's even a sliver of a chance with you."

Mystery solved. "Do you ever stop doing that?"

"Doing what?"

"Manipulating," I said plainly.

She cocked her head to the side, ever so innocently. "I don't know what you mean?"

"I know what you're doing, Eden."

"What am I doing?" she challenged.

"You're trying to get me to drive a wedge between Nevel and me because you've never gotten over him."

"That's right," she shrugged. "But why shouldn't I? You don't even know how you feel about it him, but *I do*. He needs someone to support him, not to compete. Someone who isn't afraid of warmly expressing herself, not to bicker. It's only fair to him, Astrid."

But what if I did know? What if I knew exactly how I felt about him? Would it matter? How would I respond? Then I remembered the orphans that came and went over the years in the castle. How many of those children I chose not to get close to because learning about those that didn't make it back at the end of the day would be like taking a bullet through the heart. Maybe Eden had a point. I would be an emotional wreck for anyone. I needed to create some distance.

"I'm not sure what you think I feel for anyone besides friendship. Besides, I don't think these are the ideal circumstances to pursue any romantic relationships right now," I finally answered. "I'm staying focused on finding my parents and my friends. That is and always will be my priority. I can't lose sight on that."

"I agree," Eden nodded, optimistically.

"Fine then. We need to get out of here as soon as we can before the fenova realize Haggin will want definite proof that I'm dead. They'll be back here any time." I bit into the bread and chased it down with broth. It was crucial to build up some energy while I could. The closer we got to Mt. Iris, the deeper into fenova territory we'd be heading. "Where are the boys, anyway?"

"The fenova left you behind but took Nevel and Xander as payment for the month. But don't worry. The guys didn't leave without much of a fight." She pulled her shirt down from her shoulder and uncovered a dry bloodied cloth over her skin. "They both believed you were dead. Even though I tried to explain it was only temporary, Xander got me pretty good with the triple bladed dagger I made for him. Thank goodness the fenova came when they did. I don't think I've ever been so pleased to see them in my life."

"Why didn't you poison all of us? Why only me?" I was curious.

"Not enough leak weed to go around. It's difficult to grow them this time of year, and the oil we could squeeze out of them was only enough to feed to one. Naturally, we chose you." I must have looked as confused as ever because she went on to explain, "You're the girl King Haggin is scared to death of. You're the hope they spoke of in the prophecy."

Eden took my hand and looked deep into my eyes. Her eyes welled up as she spoke. It was possibly the first time I've witnessed her express herself so genuinely. "We can't live in fear anymore. We need your help, Astrid. Wake the dragons. Bring back Alderek."

I squeezed her hand, then told her, "I'll do my best."

"We need to go soon," she said. Then she stood and took two sacks of food and supplies from Aunt Eolande.

"By 'we', I hope you don't mean you and me," I asked, perplexed.

"Of course, I do. Do you really think you're going to save them all by yourself?" she said in disbelief and handed me a supply sack.

A quizzical look washed over my face. Then I muttered, "That was my plan, yes." I found my newly improved bullwhip and machete in a corner and attached them onto my belt. Nevel's baton and Xander's dagger were also there, and I carefully folded and packed them into my sack.

"Is this what you do all day? Squabble over everything?"

I shrugged. Then replied, "Hey, this is as expressive as I get. Most people back home get nothing but a few grunts and an evil eye. Consider yourself lucky."

"I'm not sure how that works but okay..."

I narrowed my eyes and grunted, and she gave a little laugh. We said our goodbyes to Aunt Eolande who stopped momentarily from sweeping to give us each hugs and kisses on either cheeks.

"I'd hate to run into your Uncle Kien right now. What do you think he'll do if he saw you walking out the door with a ghost? Do you think he'd turn me in to the Collectors?" I said as I followed Eden outside.

"No. I'd much rather shoot you and deliver your body personally to King Haggin," a thick, accented man answered.

"Uncle Kien," Eden gasped.

"Move aside, Eden," he said, as he tried to shove his way past her. "I don't expect you to know everything, but I didn't expect you to put us all in danger to save this troublemaking revisionist."

With arms outstretched, she guarded me from her uncle. "She's the one the Omaan spoke of. She can change everything. Gone will be the days of making weapons that destroy other villages like our own. Don't you understand? We can't live like this forever, Uncle Kien. It's destroying us. It's destroying the entire world!"

"I thought I'd already secured our immunity when I called in the fenova. Then you had to go ahead and jeopardize everything," he growled.

He grabbed her by the ponytail, as she transformed into a fox. His grip was now over her sandy, blonde tail. He dangled her in front of his face and growled. In a bold move, she bore her teeth at her uncle. He tossed her several feet away, and I could hear her yelp and whimper as she hit the ground. Eden returned to her human form. She clutched her leg in pain.

"Alderek can't and won't change overnight," he rebuked. "This is bigger than one little dragon girl can handle. I hope you can understand that. I've lost my home once before, and I'm not letting you or anyone do anything that will make us vulnerable to losing it again."

He began to pull something from his inside his coat pocket when I saw it, the gun with the ivory and wooden handgrip. It was the same gun the tall agent directed at me before Willox pulled me into the portal. My eyes raised until they locked with his. His eyes were as brown as the mud on my boots. It wasn't the same man. Uncle Kien aimed the gun towards my heart.

"Why don't you make guns for all the fenova?" I asked. "Wouldn't it make their war against everyone else a lot quicker?"

"Besides myself, I'm only commissioned to make guns for one other person. He doesn't trust those two-faced have-been-fairies to carry weapons as powerful as a gun," he replied dryly.

"What is he afraid of?"

"Rebellion," he answered without hesitation. Then he added, "And you."

"Haggin," I gasped. It was him, the man with the stormy grey eyes. He was there in London, the taller agent that took Pike and almost sent a bullet through my heart.

"That's right, girl," he licked his upper teeth. It was the first time I noticed his discolored, yellow fangs. Drool dripped from his mouth as he stared voraciously at me. "I believe His Majesty also commissioned to have you killed. What if I kept a leg to nibble on for later and give the rest of you up to the king? What do you think?"

"Are you sure you wouldn't much rather have a taste of my foot?" With quick precision, I high kicked his wrist and sent the gun soaring into the air. As he bent forward, ready to tackle me, I swung my other leg up. My foot kicked him just below the chin, and he fell onto his back. Aunt Eolande darted towards us from the cabin with various pieces of rope.

She knelt by her brother and checked his pulse. "He's okay. I'll take care of my brother. You go with Eden," she said as she coiled a piece of rope around his wrists.

I found Eden in the same location she'd landed. "How's your leg?"

"A minor sprain," she winced, as I helped her onto her feet. She limped on her right foot, then dejectedly dropped back to the ground. "It's hopeless. I won't be able to travel with you like this."

"If you transform into a fox, I can carry you in my sack," I offered.

Shaking her head somberly. "I'll only slow you down. I should stay back anyway. She's going to need some help getting him back into the cabin and knocking some sense into him," she gestured towards her aunt and uncle. "I'm sorry he almost killed you."

"No worries," I brushed it off. "I've gotten used to it by now."

"The fenova probably took Nevel and Xander to the collection compound. Keep heading north, about a half day's walk from here. It's where they cage all their collections at the end of the day. In the mornings, they transport them to the fields to work. So if you plan to free them before heading to Kasus, make your move at night."

"Thanks, Eden," I said. She transformed into a fox and carefully limped into my arms. After bringing her back into the cabin, I returned to assist Aunt Eolande carry in Kien as he moaned.

Then I was off, alone in this strange and foreign world for the first time.

CHAPTER 13

Rolling hills sparsely decorated with cypress trees and a clear dirt pathway wound through the valleys and hilltops. I'd been traveling for a few hours by now. Although the trees offered plenty of shaded protection from the two suns and a gentle breeze played along my hair, the clothes on my back stuck, wet and sticky.

The poison from the leak leaf reminded me it still lingered in my system. Twice, I had to stop unexpectedly, my stomach convulsing until I purged. Left weak and dehydrated, I rested against the wide trunk of a bald cypress tree and opened up the supply sack Aunt Eolande had put together. I dug inside and pulled out a large bread roll, perhaps triple the size of any of the other rolls she'd given previously. Unable to even handle the sight or smell of bread, I promptly returned it to the sack. I shuffled the contents of the sack with my hand, hoping to feel anything else that didn't resemble a bread roll. Thankfully, I found a leather canteen filled with water and a smoked leg of some small animal. When my body was replenished, I stored the leftovers back into my sack. I needed to make my food rations last long enough to get me to the collection compound.

Just beyond the dirt path, I told myself. If I can get to the top of the last hill, I'll be able to spot the collection compound from there.

The deeper into the valleys I traveled, the colder and more damp it got. Shadows blocked most of the light from the suns, and what should have been the middle of the day felt like dusk. A river seemed to appear out of nowhere and ran along the path. The further I followed the path, the wider the river spread. The current flowed stronger, the more I trudged on until finally I found its source. A magnificent waterfall spilled from the top of the highest hilltop. The river was glorious, vast and frothy, as the rushing water raged over rocks like white horses leaping over hurdles. I knelt down by the river to fill my canteen. For a brief moment, I swore I could hear trotting horses slosh through the water. I drank greedily. Dehydration and all the hallucinations it had to offer was not something I needed to add to my growing list of worries. When I was done and couldn't force myself to drink another drop, I froze. There it was again, the sloshing and trotting of horses. Either my body had suffered too much after being poisoned and my mental state was permanently altered, or this was real.

Over the thundering rush of the waterfall, the horses could still be heard. Then I saw them. From behind the crashing water, they ploughed through. Riders draped in all black from head to toe, with hooded capes that obediently flowed behind them. Five of them on black horses. Each horseman was armed with a sword tucked neatly away in black sheaths.

I drew my bullwhip, uncertain if they even noticed me. Their horses pounced through the water rather quickly, with no sign of stopping. Once they approached nearer, it was apparent. The men steered their horses onto the embankment, eventually surrounding me on the pathway. Everything from their noses downward was covered. Their eyes I could barely see under their dark hoods.

"Identify yourself or be killed on the spot," spoke a male rider I assumed was the leader.

I tightened my grip on the bullwhip, prepared to fight if these riders turned out to be loyal to the king. "Astrid Noble. Dragon watcher," I replied and carefully watched their reaction.

They remained silent and still. I shifted from one foot to the other. It was difficult to gauge what they were thinking when I couldn't see their eyes. Then, finally, the silence was broken by an unexpected noise. Laughter.

My attention shifted to the female rider that couldn't seem to contain herself. Soon, all the riders seemed to be besides themselves with the exception of the male I assumed was the leader. He pulled the cover from his face and drew back his hood. Underneath, a wide-brimmed smile was revealed along with stunning green eyes. His hair was short, silver, and wild. The others followed suit, revealing three males and two females all with different shades of either silver or platinum blonde hair. Their ears donned pointed tips. Fairies? But how could this be? They were as tall as Queen Pavia.

"My name is Jaxon. Forgive my siblings, Astrid," the leader replied. "It's not often we get visitors trespassing into our valley, let alone ones that claim to be powerful peacekeepers like the dragon watchers."

"But I am," I said without faltering. "What proof do you need to believe I'm telling the truth?"

"Perhaps you can summon the dragons," one of the females mocked. The rest of the siblings let out another wave of laughter, except Jaxon. He remained stoic.

"I can't do that. Not now. The fenova think I'm dead. If I call on the dragons now, they'll begin to look for me at the old fox village." A vibration that traveled from east to west shook the ground beneath us. "I can't put my friends at risk there."

"How *noble* of you," the girl teased again before the other siblings joined her in another eruption of laughter.

"That's enough, Hyra," Jaxon held his hand up calmly to silence them. Then he turned to me, "Is there something, anything, that you can show us to make us believe your claim, Astrid? If not, I'll have to wipe any memory you have of seeing us and leave you outside our protected boundaries. There will be no guarantee you'll be safe from the fenova or any beasts that still hunt within this area."

Then I remembered the amulet in my pocket and pulled it out for them all to see. The image of my parents appeared, diffused in a soft, white light. They gasped. The horses grew agitated and began to back into the water. Their riders struggled momentarily to calm them, and I put the amulet back into my pocket.

"I take it, your horses knew what that was?" I said, plainly.

"Where did you get that?" the other sister spoke up.

"It was given to me by Willox, the wizard. My parents, the man and woman in the amulet, gave it to him to give to me."

"Impossible," was all she could manage to respond. "Amoldine and Tyrus didn't have a daughter."

"But they did, Sye," Jaxon interrupted. "You were too young to remember when they escaped to have the child, only to come back alone."

"You knew my parents?"

"We and the rest of our colony owe our lives to them," Sye answered.

"Before they were captured and locked away on Mt. Iris, we were free," Hyra added solemnly. "Now we live in secret beyond the waterfall. No one knows where we are, not even the Queen."

"It was important to our mother that we go into hiding. She wanted to keep the colony safe," another brother chimed in. He bowed his head slightly and added, "The name is Servil, my lady."

I returned the gesture with a nod as well. Then I asked, "Your mother. Who is she?"

The last brother I didn't know the name of chuckled. "Why, Queen Pavia, of course!" He climbed off his horse and approached me. He seemed taller off his horse than on it. His smile exposed dimples on his cheeks that weren't there before. Then he took my hand and bowed to kiss it. "Ryder is my name, Miss Astrid Noble."

"Just Astrid will be fine," I blushed.

"Something is coming," Jaxon said abruptly. "Back on your horse. Ryder, take Astrid with you. I hear them coming."

"Who?" I asked as I mounted the horse behind Ryder.

"It's the beasts. They're headed this way."

In a matter of seconds, the ground beneath us trembled. Water jolted from the river and sloshed onto the pathway. The first one appeared, completely grey and threatening. Its head was that of an oversized panther's. It stood on its hind legs like a human, with shoulders hunched forward, rounded and fairly large. The beast held its arms outstretched in front, as if it was the walking dead. It let out a low growl as it bore its teeth, a cue for the others to show their presence. Another one appeared from behind a tree and another until there were a dozen pair of hungry eyes on all of us.

"Take as many as you can," Jaxon ordered. "Don't let them anywhere near the waterfall."

Before he could say anything more, the beasts charged. Swords were pulled from the sheaths behind the fairies' cloaks and the bloodbath began.

I held onto Ryder as tightly as I could as we tried to outrun one close on our tails.

"Hurry, take the reins," Ryder said. Once I took hold of them, he stood up. His black cloak lifted from his body as if an upward draft peeled it off him. He shot into the sky and turned so I could see his face. Head bent down and wings outspread with the rays of Argon piercing through them from behind, he was stunning. The beast clawed his way closer up the rump of the horse. The white flesh tore open, and red blood spilled like hot tears. With claws on his other paw exposed and aimed to pierce me next, the beast thrust forward. I felt a light scratch upon my shoulder before Ryder slammed his leg down into the chest of the beast. When I glanced behind, they were rolling on the pathway together. I yanked on the reigns and directed the horse back to Ryder.

Once close enough, I dismounted with my bullwhip in my hand. The beast was clawing ruthlessly through Ryder and his wings. Without a moment to lose, I cracked the whip to activate. It wrapped around the neck of the beast. Smoke rose from its flesh, and I quickly thrust him off of Ryder and onto the ground.

"Ryder," I turned him over. He was covered in scratches and his wings were tattered and torn.

"I'm going to be okay," he announced with a sly grin.

"The waterfall!" Hyra hollered.

My attention quickly turned from Ryder to the unattended entrance to the colony. The fairies were outnumbered. At least a dozen beasts were headed to the waterfall.

"I'll be right back," I promised Ryder.

"I'll be right here."

I raced back onto the injured horse, hoping he wouldn't mind one last ride to save the day. When we got close enough to the pack of beasts, I rushed towards them cracking my bullwhip from left to right warning them as I approached. All of them ignored my warning, turned their heads slightly and let out low growls. Once I reached the front of the pack, I flung my bullwhip. It wrapped around the wrist of one. Electricity surged through the beast, and I could easily fling him to the ground and get to the next one. After about two-thirds of the way through, I think the beasts were finally on to my technique. The remaining four decided to charge at me. I swung my bullwhip, and it brushed their bellies that left them with stinging burn marks. This only seemed to make them even more irate, and they lunged at once towards me. I drew Xander's spring-loaded triple blades in one hand and Nevel's baton with the tri-blade stars in the other. With a flick of the wrist, each of the triple blades cut through three beasts in mid air. It was too late to stop the last one from getting too close. The beast pounced on top of me and sent me to the ground. I shoved the baton vertically into its jaws. It was the only thing that prevented the beast from swallowing my head whole. The tri-blade stars on either end of the baton cut through its mouth. Bloody drool dripped over my face, as I continued to push the beast off me. Finding some strength in my legs, I kicked up with as much force as I could and sent the beast flying to the ground. I had just enough time to get to my feet before it came charging once more. This time I was ready for it. I swung the baton and released it. It hit the beast in the head, as it finally fell to the ground. I turned to look to where Ryder laid, but instead found Servil, Hyra, and Jaxon gently touching the ground as they landed before me.

"Good to know she's on our side," Servil said in wonderment.

"Ryder," I began. "Is he going to be okay?"

They parted to reveal my obstructed view of Ryder. He was sitting up with Sye beside him. Most of the scratches on his body were healed completely and only one wing was damaged. Sye placed her hand on a tear and a blue glow ensued. It didn't take long for me to realize, she was repairing his injuries.

"How does she do that?"

"We each have a gift," Jaxon explained. "Only fairies that carry our bloodline can have one bestowed upon them, usually by an elder once they are born. Our mother can see only a short distance into the future. Sye is gifted with the ability to heal, obviously. Hyra can move water. She's the one who placed the waterfall here to hide our colony. Ryder can make anyone fall sleep instantly, and Servil can freeze almost anything. Our half-sister, Zahra," he hesitated. "Before she died, she bestowed her gift upon her son now passed, too. It was the strongest and perhaps the weakest power of us all. She possessed two powers, one of empathy and the other the ability to turn anything into stone."

"Why wasn't the child born with a gift?"

"His father was human. Half-blooded fairies in our family don't possess gifts unless they are given. To give up your powers for another is often risky and essentially suicide."

"Your sister gave up her life to bestow her gifts onto her son?"

"Yes," he said. I could tell it wasn't easy for Servil to speak of his sister and what had happened to her. It must have been equally difficult for his siblings who no longer seemed to hold their chins up. I decided to steer the topic in a different direction.

"And you, Jaxon? What power do you possess?"

"Telepathy," I heard him say in my head. "I knew I could trust you long before you told us who you were. I never doubted you were a dragon watcher."

"On anyone else, I can freely read their thoughts," he continued to explain aloud. "On one of my siblings or someone with a higher level of thought like yourself or King Haggin, I could only do it if you are unaware, or if your mind is open to me."

Sneaky, Jaxon, I thought. He beamed back.

Evening was approaching. The purple and orange hues of the sunsets were already painting the sky.

"It's getting dark, and I have to be going."

"Thank you, Astrid. We are forever in your debt. I'm assuming your journey is taking you to Mt. Iris to see your parents."

"To free them, yes. But first I need to find my friends at the collection compound. I'll never be able to make it without them. Will you join us? Help us remove Haggin and restore peace in Alderek once and for all?"

"I wish it was that simple. Sye can take you as far as the collection compound, but from there she'll have to leave you. The beasts are the only creatures that know about our colony behind the waterfall. We'll need as much manpower as we can get to keep them out. I hope you understand."

Sye and a very much healed Ryder glided to where we were.

"Take my horse," Ryder insisted. "Sye can bring her back."

Sye placed her hand on the bleeding rump of the horse. Within seconds, the glow from her fingertips penetrated the horse's torn flesh and healed.

After we said our goodbyes, we mounted our horses. The day was coming to an end, but the war was far from over.

It didn't take long to near the top of the hill that overlooked the collection compound. We left the horses several yards down on the path and remained low behind the scattered cypress trees to avoid being spotted. Once at the top, I realized we weren't on a hilltop after all. Instead, we lay low at the rim of the mouth of a magnificent crater. A mountain range spanned in the distance. My spirits rose as I hoped to catch a glimpse of Haggin's castle atop Mount Iris. Nevertheless the dense clouds hid the mountaintops, guarding the secrets of the castle from my view. My thoughts turned to Willox and the fairies, hoping they were safe. I thought of my parents and wondered if they knew I was coming. From here, the mountain appeared so far away, almost untouchable. I couldn't lose hope, not now, especially when my friends needed me.

Turquoise water filled the basin below. An isolated island was situated in the center of this crater lake, and my mind raced as I scanned for a way to reach it.

"The fenova typically don't care for heights, but they have no choice but to reach the collection compound by air," Sye said, as if she read my mind. "They use jackal birds to take them to and from the compound."

"Jackal birds?" I repeated, curiously.

"They don't fly long distances and are easy for the fenova to train. Obviously, you don't have one right now to get you to the compound at the center of the island."

"So, how do I get down there?"

"I'd fly you there myself, but the fenova may detect me. We can't risk the chance of them following me and discovering where our colony is. I'd say, wait for dark. Then find a way to slide down the inside of this crater. There's a strip of land on the far side of the island that connects it to the crater's shoreline. You should be able to locate the compound from there."

"Any other options?"

Sye hesitated, as she thought. Then she replied, "Jump. And hope you land in the water."

"Okay, so not really," I said, cringing.

"Nope," she shook her head.

Sye embraced me, catching me off guard. She reached into a side pocket, pulled out a small pouch, and placed it into my hand.

"It's sleeping powder. A gift from Ryder," she explained. Use it carefully, there's not much of it left in there. Use it as you see fit. Just be careful to watch which way the wind is blowing. No one, not even Ryder, is immune to its effects. Good luck."

By the time Sye left with the horses, Argon was halfway in its decent. Vromen would soon follow, and the vibrant tints of golden left behind by the setting suns would fade into night. Facing away from the crater's basin, I nestled behind the trunks of two cypress trees that grew side by side. I took out the amulet Willox had given me. The image of my parents appeared, and for the first time in years I felt the loneliness I'd experienced long ago when I realized they were gone. I put the amulet away, and turned my gaze to watch the suns as they gradually set. My eyelids grew heavy. The golden tints in the sky were no longer streaks of light painted in the sky. They danced and glowed, red and orange. I felt the heat as it burned my cheeks. Smoke billowed and rose. Then I saw it. I saw what was burning so dangerously hot, engulfed in wild flames that flared from its rooftop, windows and doors. The abandoned factory back home. The castle. Screams of children rose above the relentless crackling of the fire. It was the orphans, they were inside, every one of them. I couldn't move. I tried to lunge myself forward but to no avail. If I had to run into the castle a thousand times to save just one, I'd be on my way. The heaviness in my feet prevented me from progressing even an inch. I felt as if I was trapped in a vat of dried cement. There was nothing I could do but stand and watch. The silhouette of a girl appeared at the one of the windows. She seemed to be waving her arms at me, the blaze quickly approached her from behind.

The haunting shrill of the girl echoed in my ear as she called out, "Astrid! Astrid, please help us!"

The girl, I knew her. It was Pike! I tried to call out to her, tried to assure her I was coming to save her. As much as I tore my throat shouting back, no sounds came out. The flames filled the window where Pike stood, and she was gone.

An ominous man's laughter filled the sky. He proceeded in a sinister disembodied voice, "Fulfill the prophecy and take my world away, Astrid. Just remember this, I can do the same."

I gasped for air as I shot up, awake from the nightmare that felt so real. My throat was sore, and I was drenched in sweat.

I heard him once again, this time in my ear as if the wind carried him there. "Remember," he whispered the warning. "Remember."

"Haggin," I said under my breath.

Without a moment to lose, I skidded down the slope towards the basin of the crater. Halfway down, I lost my footing. I log rolled and inadvertently tumbled to the bottom. I stopped just short of the frigid water and made my way to the strip of land that led to the island. The full moon only added to the mystifying ambiance of the island. It was hauntingly beautiful, although its ever-present history of forced slavery and captivity perhaps would forever taint its reputation.

I made my way through the island's mesic forest, towards the center where the compound was said to be. Out of breath and slightly disoriented after travelling through a continuous sea of trees, I took a moment to reassess my whereabouts. As my eyes adjusted to the dark, it became clear. I'd lost my direction and wasn't sure which way led to the center of the island or to the water's edge. I slumped down onto the ground and pulled out my canteen. It would be a dangerous prospect to continue the rescue mission in broad daylight, but wouldn't get us anywhere if we couldn't navigate ourselves off the island in the dark. Parched, I guzzled my water and settled against a tree for the night. When I woke, I cringed as I saw what I hadn't seen before. Beyond the trees was an expansive alpine grassland. I inched closer to the clearing, cautious not to be seen. I'd been only feet away from it all night. In the distance, a stone wall marked the vast perimeter of the compound. Carefully constructed and medieval in appearance, the wall was at least six feet in height. It would be a cinch for me to climb. Unfortunately, that wouldn't be the issue. The question was, however, how could I climb the wall without being seen?

    I lifted myself enough so I could inspect and take a quick peek. The compound was made up of several beehive stone huts lined up in rows. The fenova most likely used these huts for their personal living quarters. In between the rows, a long stone-walled building spanned from one end of the perimeter to the other. Every few feet was a new cell fitted with an iron-barred door. There were at least one hundred cell doors on either side of the building. Amazingly, there were no guards to be seen. This rescue mission, I hoped, would be a lot easier than I thought.

    I was about to hitch myself over the wall when I stopped short, hearing the clomping of boots. Two lines of uniformed fenova marched parallel to each other towards the prisoners' compound.

Each guard held a spear in his hand. Like clockwork, the lines split as each proceeded down the aisles in front of the cells. As they passed each cell, one guard would stop at an assigned door until there were no more doors and no more guards left over. Someone blew a horn in short bursts from the rooftop of one of the huts, signaling with each blast when to make their next move in flawless synchronization. First blast, keys out. Second blast, keys in cell keyhole. Third blast, turnkey. Fourth blast, open cell door.

Once the doors swung open, the prisoners slowly flooded out, each chained and shackled to the one before. Creatures and humans bound together. Five or six would emerge from each cell. Some of them were emaciated from laboring too many hours and from the lack of food they were provided. It was obvious controlling the food supply was not working for Haggin's empire. They were unable to supply enough to those living and working under their control.

"Nevel," I gasped, relieved to see him with a fighting look on his face. Although he had a minor gash on his temple and his hair was more than usually disheveled, he appeared strong and undeterred. But where was Xander? The fenova lined up the prisoners as they escorted them from the cell blocks.

A fenova with an swollen chest stood next to the lanky one who blew the horn. He wore a brown robe with golden trim. Just like Colonel Bojra, his ears were curved and longer than the others. Unlike the colonel, he had six inch horns that sprouted from his head and a black goatee under his chin.

The lanky fenova blew his horn. Then he announced, "General Skall with the daily address commands your attention."

Without uncertainty, all the fenova guards ceased marching with their prisoners and turned in the direction of General Skall.

"Today we add to our collection four more to our crew," his voice boomed throughout the compound. A fenova guard led through the front of the crowd two chained and shackled faun, a troll, and an elderly man. "Yesterday they were trespassers with no purpose in our kingdom. Today, they will be servants of Alderek, helping to provide food and the necessary supplies to make our world more powerful and efficient. Your hardships today will not be left unnoticed. Work hard and the future generations of our world will reap the great benefits of your toils. Those who choose to question or disobey act against our children. You will be traitors of the worst kind, punishable to only the harshest degree."

"You are the traitor! You've turned your back on our world to be a mere pawn for King Haggin. If we follow the king, we act against our children!" called out one of the prisoners from the crowd. He continued to chant, "Traitor! Villain! Murderer!"

General Skall squinted his eyes, as he honed in on finding the interrupting perpetrator. His searching gaze halted when he spotted the culprit, a feisty, stout troll. Without a second thought, he grabbed the spear from the horn blower's belt and sent it flying through the crowd with eerie precision. It struck the troll in the chest, quieting him indefinitely.

"Did you see that one coming from a pawn?" General Skall mocked haughtily. Then he added, "I didn't think so."

He wiped his hands together as if dusting a dirty deed off his conscience. "As I was saying," he continued addressing the prisoners. "We abide by the laws of the fenova on this island, no one else's. Any acts against *fenova* laws will be considered treason and punishable to the harshest degree." Without another word, he turned and disappeared into the stone huts.

The prisoners marched past me along the perimeter and were then taken around the huts to work in the fields. I picked up a rounded pebble from off the ground, then carefully returned to spy from over the wall. When he was only a few feet away, I tossed the pebble. It bounced off his thick tousled hair. No response. Quickly, I searched the ground beneath me for another pebble. This time, I found one with a sharp corner.

"Sorry, Nevel. It'll only feel like a prick, I promise," I uttered to myself.

Before he could get any further from my striking range, I tossed the pebble again. This time, it struck his neck. He looked back as he rubbed his scratched skin. The annoyance in his eyes dissipated once he caught sight of me. I offered a small wave. Immediately, he turned his gaze forward and collapsed onto the ground. He doubled over and groaned in pain.

"Get up," the fenova guard prodded him lightly with his spear.

"I can't," Nevel lamented. "It hurts so much. It must've been something I ate."

"Get up," the guard repeated, unsure of what to do next without orders from his superiors.

"It hurts. It really hurts."

The guard unchained Nevel's feet and led him into the nearest cell. He shut the door. "Stay here. No work, no food." He turned to another guard, "Stay here and watch him. I'll take your workers to the field."

In a short while, all the prisoners and guards were out of sight, except for the one that guarded Nevel's cell. I propped myself over the wall with little difficulty. I ran over to the prisoner compound and hoisted myself onto the roof. The guard was just below in front of the cell door. I gave a little whistle, and he looked up.

"Hello," I waved. Then sprinkled some sleep powder over him. It worked like a miracle, and he was out like a light in an instant.

I landed on the ground and removed the keys from the guard's belt. As I fumbled with the key to the keyhole, Nevel reached through the bars and grabbed my arms.

"I saw you die," he said.

"You can thank your girlfriend for temporarily killing me," I remarked sarcastically.

He let my arms go. "Well, if one of us had to die, I'm glad it was you. Wait, that didn't come out right. I meant it was better the fenova took us and left you behind."

"Don't worry. Apparently, Eden thought the same thing. I'm not sure how far you would've gotten on a rescue mission if the fenova caught me instead."

"I could rescue you if given the chance."

"Okay," I shrugged.

"No, I could. Really, I know I could."

"I don't doubt it."

"But you did."

"Listen, we can stand here and argue about this all day, or you can let me rescue you and be done with it.

"I see your point. Hurry up then, will you?" He nodded towards the keys. Then, he added, "She's not my girlfriend, by the way."

"Where's Xander?" I asked, changing the subject.

"They've got Xander in solitary confinement," he uttered. "He wasn't looking very good before they took him away. Not that he's ever really looked all that great in the first place, but that's beside the point. Astrid, he was practically near death when I saw him last. That was more than a day ago. I'm not sure if we'll get him back. I just want you to know."

"We'll get him back," I said, swallowing the lump that formed in my throat. I unlocked the door. "Let's get out of here. Where is solitary confinement?"

He pointed to the ground. "Somewhere under your feet."

My jaw dropped. "They buried him?"

"No." Nevel got on his hands and knees and began to frantically brush away at the dirt. "It's here somewhere."

"You mean, you don't know where it is exactly?" I fell to my knees and brushed the dirt away beside him.

"I don't know. I mean, I do know. But not exactly," he was flustered. "It's here in front of this cell, I know that. Somewhere. Just trust me."

"What exactly are we looking for anyway?"

At once, he ceased working and pointed to where I just brushed. "That!" He uncovered the dirt around it some more. It was a handle that connected to what appeared to be a circular door. He pulled the on it, revealing a dark hole.

"Ladies first," he gestured for me to enter.

I dangled my legs into the hole. Before I jumped in, I winked, "Only because I know you're scared of the dark."

He helped himself to my bullwhip, then said, "I probably should stay out here, or we'll have a zero chance of getting out. I'm not sure how deep it is in there."

I nodded, then lowered myself into the hole before falling a good ten feet. It wasn't as terrible as I thought the drop would be as I landed on a soft clump. I felt around, attempting to decipher what it was that broke my fall.

"That's not my face, by the way," the familiar voice said casually.

I held my hands up and immediately backed away, as I profusely apologized.

"Relax. It was just my knee," he responded. Then he did a double take, "Astrid? Is that you? I thought you were dead."

"Xander," I breathed, relieved he was alive and sounded relatively well. I searched for his hands and wrapped them around my waist in a hugging position.

"I didn't know you felt this way about me, darling. I've always thought you had an eye on somebody else less desirable."

"Just hold on to me as tightly as you can. Don't let go."

"Not a problem," he said, sounding almost intoxicated.

Nevel dangled the bullwhip over our heads. I grabbed hold of it and wrapped it around my arm. He hoisted us up. Once out of the hole, I got a good look at Xander. His left eye was swollen shut, the other squinted from the sudden exposure to the light. His lower jaw looked misaligned and his was bloodied on his back, as if he'd been flogged. Unable to keep his balance, he wobbled backwards toward the hole. Nevel caught him just in time.

"You're stronger than you look," Xander muttered through a crooked smile.

"Why did they do this to you?" I asked.

"I don't know. The big guy saw my pendant and kept asking if I was with *them*."

"By *them*, do you mean the fenova?"

"No, the fairies. Thought I was some kind of spy or something and trying to start a revolution."

"You kind of are," Nevel added matter-of-factly.

He shook his head, then realized it hurt to do so. "No. Not a revolution against the king. More like a revolution against the fenova, as if someone else knows about their planned uprising."

"Well, we're getting there," I said. "What did they do to you?"

Xander shrugged, "Whipped me, beat me, kicked me, gave me some strong elixir to make me stop screaming. I think they called it Vova or something like that. It really worked, too..."

The clomping boots of guards could be heard around the corner.

"We have to get out of here," I said hastily. Then I turned to Xander, "Can you run?"

"I can try."

"Can you jump?"

He demonstrated a pathetically low hop off the ground.

"We'll have to make do. Nevel, get him to the rooftop. We need to get him over the perimeter wall if we'll have any chance of getting out of here alive. I'll take care of the guards down here."

The guards made it around the corner, and at once spotted us. Nevel and Xander immediately hoisted themselves onto the rooftop using the iron cell doors as a ladder. Before the guards could get close to them, I cracked my whip and gave one an electric shock that sent him to the ground. The other grabbed at my belt and got a hold of the pouch with the sleeping powder inside.

"I wouldn't play with that if I were you," I warned him.

I darted towards him, but before I could get there he'd opened it up. The dust settled into his nostrils, and he unexpectedly sneezed into the pouch. Powder bloomed over his face and he collapsed onto the ground. In an instant, I stopped in my tracks, but it was too late. I'd breathed in enough to feel the sudden effects of the sleeping powder, but not enough that I couldn't fight back the drowsiness.

More guards were approaching. I raced to a cell door and began to climb. Almost to the top of the roof, and a guard firmly gripped onto my ankle. Yawning, I shook him off my leg. I stepped on a pipe as I stumbled onto the roof. The pipe came loose and knocked the guard out. The guard's six chained and shackled prisoners watched in awe. I threw them the key I'd used on Nevel's cell door. Then, I watched as an oversized squirrel with a mole on his left cheek and glasses as thick as a wedge of cheese catch it. His jaw dropped, and he mouthed the words "Thank you, dragon watcher."

I felt the close encounters of the spears that rushed past me as I staggered to the end of the rooftop. Then, I mustered as much energy as I could before I ran and jumped over the wall of the perimeter.

Nevel and Xander were on the other side already waiting for me. We could hear the commotion of the guards in the compound running alongside the wall. They were too afraid to climb it, so they decided to run towards the gate at the far end.

I yawned and scratched my head. I fidgeted and shifted. Every movement I made helped me to stay alert and awake. "They'll be here any moment. We have to find a way to get off this island," I said, trying my best to keep engaged.

Unaware of my sleeping powder mishap, Nevel tilted his head. I could tell he decided quickly not to ask what he was thinking. Time was too precious. Instead, he said, "I know where they keep their jackal birds."

"Great. Lead the way."

If it wasn't Xander stumbling over himself as we headed through the forest, it was me tripping over him. All I could see was through tunnel vision and that, too, was becoming moderately hazy. It was a miracle we made it to where the fenova had tied up their jackal birds, yellow and black birds that resembled gigantic goldfinches. There were at least ten of them, and we decided we would only need two. Nevel began to loosen their ropes of the others, and they flew off into the distance. He helped Xander onto one of the two remaining birds.

"Will you be okay riding on your own?" he asked, as he approached me. I could hear the growing concern in his voice.

I nodded profusely and waved him off, as I mounted my bird. "Don't worry. I'll be okay. Just follow my jackal bird. I know someone who can help Xander."

The guards drew nearer. Nevel patted my bird on the side and sent us off. We flew over the mesic forest of the isolated island, and as I looked below, I saw Nevel and Xander on their jackal bird ascending behind me. The spears of the fenova were thrown into the air but never took flight like our birds. Below us, we could see the prisoners in their chains and shackles cheering as they watched our escape. I was confident that they, too, would be free soon. The key was in their hands now. Rebellion would no longer be an option. It would be a reality.

CHAPTER 14

With heavy eyelids, I spotted the waterfall, relieved I was able to find it again. It was enough to give me the second wind I needed to get the jackal bird to land safely on the other side. The moment I dismounted the bird, Hyra took me by the arm and sheltered me behind her. Her other siblings stood in wait for Nevel's bird as they broke through the water. The bird fumbled as it landed, and they were catapulted from its back and onto the ground face down.

Nevel lifted his head and spat clovers out of his mouth. He froze, as Jaxon's cold, sharp sword blade slid under his chin.

"Rise," Servil firmly commanded him.

Nevel obeyed and cautiously rose his hands.

"He doesn't mean any harm, Servil. They're my friends. The ones I sought to rescue from the compound," I explained and rushed to Nevel.

Servil raised his arm, preventing me from standing by my friends. Then he said flatly, "He's a shape shifter. A fox boy."

"Who doesn't eat meat," I uttered.

He glared at Nevel. "Jaxon. Read him."

"She's telling the truth," Jaxon said and lowered his defenses.

Servil turned his attention then to me. "I'm sorry, Astrid. I hope I didn't offend you or your friend. I have a colony to protect. I hope you understand."

I nodded. Then he continued, "It was risk coming back here. The Collectors could have followed you through the waterfall."

"They're stranded for the time being," Nevel spoke up.

Servil quizzically looked at me for an answer.

"It's a long story," I offered. I kneeled down beside Xander and wrapped his arm over my shoulder. Ryder did the same on his other side. "My friend needs Sye's help. He's been badly injured."

Sye approached. She placed her hand on his chest. Then, she examined his face and his neck.

"Sye, is there something wrong?" Servil remained cautious. She uncovered his pendant and held it up for him to see.

"Servil, I need to heal him now," Sye said. Servil nodded. She placed her hand over Xander's forehead. A glow radiated from her fingertips in all directions and then extended from her palm until it was too bright to keep my eyes open. It felt like forever, bathed in her amazing white light. Then I felt Xander's arm from around my shoulders slip off.

"You can look now, unless you'd like me to kiss you," his silky baritone voice caressed my ear.

Although I'd witnessed Sye's healing powers on Ryder not long ago, it still amazed me when I laid my eyes on a perfectly put together Xander. I buried my head in his chest and held him tightly as he squeezed back. Embarrassed, I pulled away. What to do next, I didn't know.

"It's okay," Xander whispered, as if he understood.

Finally, it was Servil who helped break the awkward moment. "Take them to the chrysalis room immediately."

The tree was glorious. Its girth was as wide as a several dozens of the largest trees I've seen put together. Millions of fairies drifted in and out of its branches, blithely going about their business as if unaware of the turmoil beyond their shielding waterfall. We entered a door within the tree into a room bountifully filled with silky, white chrysalises hanging at every level.

"Amazing," gasped Nevel.

"I've never seen anything so beautiful in my life before," I added, as I turned and gazed at the magnificence all around us.

"This," Servil began, "is where fairies of hundreds of years go to begin their process of transitioning to the next world."

"You mean, where they go to die," Nevel said bluntly.

"If you must, yes. When their lives reach the end, their memories are stored in these chrysalises. They last for as long as the fairy lived."

"I don't understand," I said quietly. "Why did you bring us here?"

"Where did you get that pendant you wear?" he directed to Xander.

"My mother gave it to me," he answered. "I was young and don't remember, but Mirdeth told me it was from her."

"Mirdeth. The witch." It was as if something had clicked as Servil had found the answer he'd been searching for. He picked up a chrysalis like plucking a rose from a garden. He approached Xander and held it out for him to take. "This belongs to you," he insisted. "It was my sister's memories. Zahra would want her only child to have it, her son."

"*Of course*. He's part royalty," Nevel gasped, sounding slightly defeated.

"My mother was a human. This couldn't be hers. I'm sorry. You have the wrong person." Xander stepped away from the chrysalis.

"There are too many clues that point to you being part of our bloodline," Servil explained.

"I can't get into your thoughts to hear what you're thinking," Jaxon said.

"And you bear the wings of our family," Hyra added.

"I don't have wings," Xander laughed nervously.

The fairy siblings each pulled up a pendant that hid behind their clothing. The same shape of a swan's head and neck with wings spread out, ready to take flight hung from their necks.

"I've had this pendant since as long as I can remember. I've never seen it as anything more than a swan in flight. How is this possible?" he asked, by now truly flustered.

"Look closer. It is a fairy lifting up his head and his wings in the moment of victory. Only those in our family have these pendants. Your mother is the daughter of Queen Pavia, our mother as well," Servil said, as he offered the chrysalis to him again. This time Xander took it.

"But I have no wings and my ears aren't-"

"Your father was human," Sye consoled. "Those are just physical traits. They have nothing to do with the ability to possess powers or to have the spirit of the fairies forever in your heart."

He held the chrysalis in his arms and looked at it with both longing and trepidation. "What happens if I open this?"

"You'll discover the truth," Servil offered.

"What if I don't want to know the truth? What if I'm not ready for it?"

"Xander," I spoke gently, as I stepped forward. He was afraid. I'd never seen him so afraid before. "Do you know how many orphans out there dream about being able to find out an inkling about a parent. This is your chance. Her life is in *there*. Her memories of *you* are in there. No matter what you see in there, just remember nothing has changed. Nothing about you will ever change. You'll still be who you are. Nothing else can define you unless you allow it. Now, go. Go meet your mother. Don't be afraid."

He delicately peeled back the folds of the chrysalis until he could easily place his hand inside. Light and wind surrounded him, and he seemed at peace as he saw the personal memories of his mother. Although I couldn't see what Xander saw, it was almost cathartic to witness this gorgeous display of pulsating halos and swirls of wind.

Then it all ended so fast. Without a warning, Xander threw the chrysalis to the floor. Covered in sweat, he turned to Servil and seethed, "You knew I would see it. She died for *me* because of *him*. What were you hoping to accomplish by me knowing all this? What do you expect me to do?"

Servil stood motionless, his face stoic. For whatever emotions he tried to hide in his facial expression, he failed to hide in his broken voice, "She was our sister. You are the child we thought was dead. I'm not sure what I wanted to you to do. Perhaps in your own time, you will know."

Xander turned to leave the room. I grabbed his arm, but he brushed me off.

"Not now, Astrid," was all he said. Then he was gone.

"This didn't go down very well," Nevel stated the obvious.

Whatever Xander saw in that chrysalis, Servil knew what it was. They had just discovered he was their long lost nephew, someone they thought for almost two decades was dead. What was this memory they felt Xander needed to know and why?

I turned to follow Xander out the door, but before I could, Ryder called out, "Astrid, wait. Let him go."

"Let him go? How could I? He's obviously seen something very disturbing in there," I said, pointing to the chrysalis. "Is this what you intended to happen? He's hurting and you know why."

"Ryder's right," Sye spoke gently. "He needs time to process what he just saw. All those memories from his mother, a whole lifetime in a matter of moments. He needed to know the truth, Astrid. If not now, then when? Alderek and all the creatures that inhabit it don't have a great deal of time left. It's a lot of information, some of it disturbing, yes. But he needs to figure this out on his own."

"He reminds me of Zahra. She was charming but incredibly gullible some times. Because of her power of empathy, she tended to be more compassionate and understanding than anyone else. My sister always saw the good in people. She felt the good no one else knew existed. Some may say that was her weakness, but I've always thought it was her strength. If Xander is anything like his mother, he'll come through," Servil said, perhaps more to convince himself than me.

"You're right," I said, my shoulders sank. It may have been a shock to Xander to see everything his mother remembered in such a short amount of time. He never sought out to learn more about his mother. He'd been content with Mirdeth and all that she'd offered him. This was forced upon him, and I didn't exactly help to slow the process down either.

"I still don't understand," Nevel voiced curiously. "He said, 'she died for me because of *him*'? Who was Xander talking about?"

Servil drew in a deep breath. He slowly let it out before he surrendered his words, "His father."

"Isn't his father dead?"

Hyra stepped forward, her head hung low. "No," she said, almost sounding disgusted. "He's very much alive. The beast lives."

"Who is he?" I prodded.

Servil had turned to leave the room, as if ready to escape. He stood still at the door as he contemplated answering the question. For a moment I believed I would never know the answer. Then, to my surprise, he spoke as clearly and as carefully as he could possibly speak so there was no mistaking his words. "His father is Haggin. My sister married a beast."

He shut the door behind him. Suddenly, the chrysalis room had lost all its beauty.

CHAPTER 15

It had been a long night, but an even longer journey lay ahead. I could tell Xander was ready to move on when he allowed Hyra to embrace him. "Until we meet again, Xander."

Sye kissed him on the cheek. "Our intentions were good, please believe that. We wanted you to know your mother and all that she did for you. There was no way to show that to you without revealing who your father was."

He nodded. Compassion. Understanding.

"We didn't expect anything else from you, just that you got to know her," Jaxon ruffled Xander's hair. "Stay strong, kid."

A slight grin emerged. Perhaps, he was learning to accept his mother's memories, her past and his father.

"Take it easy on him," Ryder gently advised, as he gestured towards Servil. "She was as much his sister as she was your mother. He loved her dearly. We all did."

Xander approached Servil. "Uncle," he smiled.

"I see her in you," Servil grinned back. They embraced. Then he turned towards me. He placed a pouch much like the one Sye had given me the day before. "The dragons might be defiant at first when they see you. It's what happens when they've been oppressed for too long. Take this pouch. It's filled with dust that will freeze anything, even a dragon's breath. So if you want to be able to speak to them at all, you may need to summon the frost."

"Summon the frost," I repeated. It was familiar. I'd heard this expression before from Nellie." Thank you, Servil."

"Good luck," Sye and Ryder waved.

"Remember to go around the crater to Sutters Valley," Hyra called out after us. "Oh! And if you're feeling tired, don't rest at the-"

A screeching hawk flew overhead, and we ducked to avoid his talons.

"That was a close one," I breathed.

The fog was thick and the further we walked, the less we could see or hear of the fairy siblings.

"Did anyone hear what Hyra was trying to tell us?" I asked.

"Something about resting. She probably doesn't want us to rest at the bridge. We probably should find somewhere to stop just before," Nevel suggested. "I don't know about you, but I could barely sleep a wink last night."

"I think we can all agree yesterday was more than we bargained for," I said as I glimpsed at Xander. "You okay?"

"I can't say I've felt worse, but I'll survive."

We traveled in silence for hours. Night was nearing and the temperature had dropped considerably. Snow began to fall. At first the light dusting didn't bother us. We trudged on through, quickly moving to cover more distance. Within minutes, the storm peaked and we unexpectedly found ourselves in an entire valley covered in a thick white sheet. Snow flurries swarmed erratically around us, making it increasingly difficult to find our way.

"I see a house," Nevel shouted over the gusts of howling wind. I couldn't see what the home he'd pointed out, so I followed him as closely as I could. We trod as quickly as our legs could take us in the knee-high snow until we finally arrived at the door of the house. Nevel knocked frantically at the door. "Hello, is anyone home? We're travelers, and we mean no harm."

The door opened, and we were greeted with a blast of warm air from inside. "Come in. Come in. Hurry. You're letting out all the goodness."

Our eyes followed the voice downward. He held the door open and motioned for us to step inside. The mole man couldn't have been more than two and a half feet tall with spectacles as thick as shortbread cookies. He shut the door behind us as we melted in his living room. With the flurries out of our eyes, we could see a lot clearer. This was no ordinary home. It was more than a house, it was a mansion. The smell of smoldering hickory permeated the air. I spied the source – a large fireplace nestled within a flagstone wall. Its faint crackling could be heard echoing off of the generously wide wooden planks that lined the vaulted ceiling, coming to a peak in the center of the large room. A large chandelier fashioned from sets of massive antlers hung from the center beam, suspended by a thick black chain. We cautiously stepped further into the room.

The mole man carefully examined us from head to toe, as he pushed up his spectacles for a clearer view. It was then that I noticed the thick, black mole on the back of his hand. Three coarse black hairs sprouted from it. "You kids are not from around here," he finally declared.

"What gave that away?" Nevel grinned. He seemed amused by our little host.

"Well, for starters, you're not dressed for the weather."

"It all happened so fast," I said, as my teeth chattered.

"It can get that way here in the valley, warm one minute and then snowy blizzard the next. Everything here seems to change, nothing ever stays the same for long." He scratched his bald head, as he reflected. After a while, he suddenly perked up, "Oh, forgive me. I'm not being such a good host. The name's Varian."

"I'm Astrid, and these are my friends, Nevel and Xander."

"Astrid, Nevel and Xander," he exclaimed as he shook our hands enthusiastically. "I've heard about you. There's word all across the land of three warriors just like you. Lots of people looking for you, especially the king."

I shifted, uneasy about the prospect that our newfound resting place would turn into a prison. Or worse yet, a battleground if he was hungry enough to turn us in to the fenova.

"We wouldn't want to put you in harm's way. Please, forgive us for dripping all over your floor. We've been through much worse than this storm. I'm sure we could handle it. It may not be much further to the bridge."

"I can see your hesitation, but I can assure you this will be the best place for you wait out the weather. The storm is only growing worse out there. Plus, I have no desire ever to deal with those fenova. They are traitors of the worse kind. Wouldn't associate with them. You have my word," Varian insisted.

I glanced at Nevel. He appeared worn and exhausted. Xander touched my elbow and nodded reassuringly. "I've never heard of a mole you couldn't trust," he grinned.

"I suppose we could all use a good night's rest in something other than a boat or a tree," I said.

"Wonderful," Varian clasped his hands together. "I haven't had overnight guests in ages. Please, come. Follow me. I have rooms, lots of rooms. Feel free to use the fireplaces to dry your clothes. You can find a room that suits you best, each of you if you wish unless you all like to camp out in a single room."

"Oh, no. No, thank you," the three of us said in unison.

"We mean," I explained, a little flushed, "thank you for your hospitality on such short notice. A room for each of us is very generous of you. I'm sure, with this beautiful home, you have plenty of chores that need to be done. We'll be glad to take some up. It'll allow us to earn our stay."

"No worries, dear. It's just me in this house, nobody else. Not much mess to be made when it's just me. You're welcome to stay for as long as you wish. I have been expecting company, but with the storm I don't think he'll make it in time," he assured. Then he sighed, "Three guests are better than one anyway. The more the merrier. Follow me, and I'll show you around."

With every turn, the mansion proved to be a labyrinth of short hallways and doors. We followed our host as he led us around a corner and down an expansive hallway, its roughly carved wooden floorboards stretching impossibly forward. The flames from the candle holders mounted along the walls danced and cast a warm glow down the corridor. Wooden doors were spaced ten feet apart on each side of the hall.

"Choose as many as you'd like," Varian gleamed. "I'm sure you're plenty tired from your trip. We can talk in the morning. Make yourself at home. I'll be just around the corner if you need anything."

The mole hobbled down the hallway that appeared to stretch on forever. Xander took to the first door handle he could grab.

"I wonder if these rooms are as grand as the rest of this house," he said. "But I guess it doesn't matter because I'm beat. Any place out of the snow sounds great to me. See you guys in the morning. Shall we say, just before the first sunrise?"

We agreed and said our good nights, as he disappeared into the room he'd chosen. Nevel gestured towards the line of other doors. "So many rooms. Which one will you pick?"

"The one with a bed and no fenova," I yawned.

"Good choice. Good night, Astrid."

I turned the polished bronze handle of the nearest oak door and pushed it forward. It creaked softly, revealing the room before me, bathed in a warm glow. A small fire was smoldering in the far corner. It flickered off of the golden colored walls. In awe of the grandeur, I stepped inside and closed the door behind me. Beneath, my feet felt the cushion of a woven rug that covered most of the floor. It was maroon with a golden vine pattern that extended from the center out to the edges. The furniture in the room all seemed like it had been carved from the same tree, with grain that swirled fancifully and glimmered in the firelight. I sat down on the large sleigh bed at the far end of the room. It felt like I was sitting on a haystack of feathers, nothing like my flattened, old mattress at the castle. After setting aside my weapons, I crawled under the luxury duvet and sunk my head into the pillow. I wondered how Nevel and Xander were finding their living quarters. It felt amazing and wrong all at the same time.

That night, I dreamt of a beautiful amber sunset. A younger version of me was in a London park with my parents. We'd just finished eating the sandwiches my mother had packed for our picnic. As the sun began its decent, we decided to pack up and head on home. I felt a raindrop on my forehead. One. Then two. It was slow and steady at first, and my mother laughed as she gently wiped my face. At once, a sudden downpour of rain was falling upon us. My father grabbed the picnic sheet and placed it over our heads. It was no use, the raindrops crashed down, each one larger and heavier than the first. A strong gust of wind knocked the sheet from my father's grasp. The rain pelted my skin hard, but it seemed to hit my parents even harder. They crouched in pain beside me, and there was nothing I could do to stop the torture. The rain grew louder, hitting their backs like a hammer against a wall. I turned my head to the sky, the raindrops pelted as I stared into them eyes wide open. Before a massive drop could do more damage, I woke. A knock at the door that seemed to grow louder with every passing second finally caught my attention. I clumsily grabbed my weapons and slipped them into my holster. For a moment, I was in a haze. Nothing seemed familiar. Perhaps I'd forgotten where I was. I'd been so vividly transported to London in my dream, I couldn't discern what was real at first. I took a quick glimpse around the room to remind myself of where I was. That was odd. The fireplace in the far corner of the room was nowhere to be found. I shrugged it off. Perhaps I was too tired before I climbed into bed and didn't observe the room very well the first time around. Whoever was at my door continued to knock. I forced myself out of bed with the feeling of being disoriented still. Finally, I got to the door and cracked it open.

"Xander," I sighed, relieved.

"Can I come in?"

I swung the door open and motioned for him to come inside. He sat on a wooden stool in the middle of the room. It was way too short for him, and his legs sprawled out. I wondered if he was comfortable.

"Can't sleep?" I asked drowsily, as I plopped onto the bed.

"Astrid, my father's Haggin. Do you think that's something I can wrap their mind around in one evening?"

"I'm sorry," I guiltily forced myself to sit up.

"No, I'm sorry. I didn't mean to wake you up and put all this on you." He stood and headed towards the door, but I was faster.

I grabbed his hand and turned him to face me. "Wait. This is crazy. You can't go through this alone."

"Remember when you said looking at my mother's memories won't change me? Well, I'm not sure you could've guessed what secrets the memories were going to reveal, but I think it's inevitable. I can never be who I was before. I'm no longer just an orphan raised by a witch in a cave. I know that doesn't sound very simple, either but... Now I'm half fairy and the son of a king who's in the process of destroying our planet. I'm not sure what to do now."

I hesitated. It was complicated, he was right. Then I placed my hands on his chest and said, "I don't see you any differently now than I did before you opened that chrysalis. Whatever you are in here, is the same Xander who is my friend that I care deeply for. Your plight may be different, perhaps even more meaningful. But your heart will never change."

He took my hand in his and leaned in towards me. I adjusted my chin down, thinking he wanted to place a kiss on my forehead. Then he tapped my chin up and caught me off guard as he hovered his lips over mine. I tensed.

A hard knock on the door stopped Xander short in his plight, and a wave of relief washed over me. Our gaze turned towards the door that I didn't think I'd need to shut. Nevel stood at the doorway with a cheerless expression on his face.

"I was coming to wake you, Astrid, but I guess Xander beat me to it."

I broke away from Xander's arms and headed to the door. "Thank you, Nevel," was all I could think of to say. Before I could reach him, he pulled at the door and shut it closed.

"Don't worry about him," Xander placed his hand on my shoulder. He gently turned me around to face him. "Maybe it's best if we stayed back while he continued on to Kasus. It's too dangerous out there. Together, it wouldn't matter who was in control of Alderek. We're not warriors like everyone thinks we are, Astrid. Let me protect you. Come back home with me, away from all this evil and destruction."

"What about my parents?"

"Astrid, I hate to be the one to bring this up, but what makes you think Haggin hasn't already...you know," he hesitated.

"No, I don't know, Xander. I know they're alive and on that mountain. I'm not ready to give up. And I'm not going to let you give up so easily either."

His hand caressed my cheek, as I stared at him with sorrowful eyes. Who was this person before me? Where was the compassionate, selfless person I'd grown to know? Had I gotten him all wrong? I placed my hand over his, and I knew immediately something was not the same. I fashioned my other hand over my bullwhip.

"Xander," I began cautiously, "did you notice if I had a fireplace in my room when you entered?"

"Of course, you have a fireplace," he chortled. "It's there in the center of that wall over there."

I glanced beyond his shoulder. There, in the center of the wall was a grand fireplace. The mantle was carved intricately out of marble. It was nothing close to the small fireplace I'd noted in the far corner when I first stepped into the room.

"I'm not sure about this place. Everything seems to keep changing."

"You've been under a lot of stress lately. Maybe you should get more rest."

I pulled his hand from my cheek and continued, "You have a mole on the back of your hand."

"I guess I do," he shrugged, as he stared at the mole.

"It's funny because I don't remember you having any significant markings like this on your hands."

"Perhaps it grew overnight," he raised his eyebrow.

In one swift motion, I pulled my bullwhip from the holster and wrapped it around his wrists. "Nice try, Varian. What are you? And who are you working for?" I demanded.

In a matter of seconds, he shape shifted from the image of Xander to Colonel Bojra. "Remember me?" he rasped.

"It can't be. You're dead," I gasped.

"Oh, my mistake." He shape shifted into an image of a girl with black hair and her head down. Varian looked up, and I was face to face with a splitting image of myself. "Is this better?"

"Who are you?" I demanded again, tightening my grip on the bullwhip.

"I'm Astrid Noble, of course."

"Don't try my patience," I scowled.

"Nevel seemed to believe me last night when we talked for hours. I think I helped your situation with him move forward quite a bit. Just a tip. Maybe you should relax a little bit when you're talking to him. I'd go as far as to say he liked 'this side of you' better," the shape shifter pointed to itself and grinned. "You should be thanking me. Of course, you had to blow it when he saw you with imitation Xander."

"What kind of monster are you?" I grimaced.

"I'm just as I had told you before. I'm Varian, master shape shifter. I am everything I've ever touched and their most recent memories, yet I am nothing."

He disappeared suddenly, and the end of my bullwhip fell to the floor. My eyes were drawn to movement on the rug. Headed towards the door was a hissing roach. He escaped under the crack of the door and into the hallway. I cracked my whip after him, but he was too fast. Nevel bolted out of his room, weapon drawn and flustered. "What's going on? What did he do to you?"

"Who?" I shouted.

"Xander. Isn't that who you're trying to fry with your whip?"

"No, of course not!" I pointed to the hissing roach, as he made his way down the hallway. "It's Varian. He's a shape shifter. It was never Xander."

"Are you okay?"

I nodded. Then I gasped, "Nevel, where's Xander?"

"I'll get the roach, Varian. You go find him."

I watched as he transformed into a fox before I made my way to what I remembered would be Xander's room. Instead of a door, that entire side of the hallway was a wall. I pounded the wall with my fists, as I searched for a sign of a door.

"Xander?" I kept calling out as I hit the wall. No answer. I turned to the other side of the hallway and ran to the first door I could get to. Nobody was in the room. I turned back to the side of the wall, when my eye caught sight of a door that wasn't there before. I rushed to it. As I went to grab for the handle, the door vanished. It reappeared a few feet to my right. Again, I rushed to open it, but before I could get there the door disappeared once again. This time, it didn't reappear. Frustrated, I kicked the wall. Panic was beginning to settle in.

"Xander, where are you?" I said under my breath. Then, as if to answer my request, I heard a stifled cry. It came from beyond the wall. I grabbed my machete and held it back, ready to tear down the wall. A door appeared in front of me, where there was none before. Did the house surrender under the threat of destruction? There was no time to lose, I grabbed the handle and pushed the door in. There he was, sprawled out on the bed, wrapped tightly within the coils of the vines that protruded from the design on the rug. The vines were thick and strong. They covered him significantly, exposing only his eyes and nose.

With my machete, I began to chop at the vines. I had to work quickly. For every two vines I'd chopped, one more would snap at me. When it finally realized I could hack it faster than it could grab me, the vines retreated. I helped Xander from off the bed, carefully inspecting his hands for any suspicious markings.

"What are you doing?" he asked.

"You can't be too careful," I warned. "Do you still want to go all the way to Mt. Iris?"

"You'd better believe it."

I grinned. "Let's get out of here."

"Which way out?" he asked when we hit a dead end.

The hallways continued to shift in this constantly changing labyrinth. It seemed futile to keep on trying. The house would never let us pass. Xander gripped the curved horn hilt of his weapon and activated the spring-loaded triple blades. He buried the blades deep into the wall that appeared out of nowhere in front of us.

"Let us through, or you leave us no other choice but to hack our way out," he warned the house.I held my machete to the wall to let the house know we were serious. In a sign of surrender, the wall dissipated and the hallways ceased to change.

"Good work."

"Anytime," he saluted and winked.

We finally made our way to the living room where we'd first arrived the night before. Nevel stood proudly, displaying a glass case in his hand. Inside, a roach hissed at us as we peered in.

"What are we going to do with him?" Xander asked.

"I don't know. Crush him like a bug, I guess," Nevel said.

"No," I jumped in. "He's like any other creature on Alderek. We have to put him down and get off his property immediately." I turned to the glass case and stared into the eyes of the roach inside. Then said to him, "Let us leave, Varian, and we won't hurt you. I promise."

I took the glass and set it on the floor. I turned to my friends, "All right. Let's get out of here."

Before we could get to the door, we heard a CLINK! We turned our heads around to where the glass case had been on the floor. It was turned over and the roach was exposed. He doubled in size, then tripled and so forth. As he expanded, his body transformed. His arms spread out into purple and blue speckled tentacles and his head elongated. He glowered upon us with yellow eyes dusted with flecks of red.

"Run," was all that could escape from my mouth before I felt the strong tug on my arm, Nevel urging me to go.

The giant octopus lifted a tentacle above our heads. We raced out the door as it rammed onto the spot we once stood.

"Nevel was right. We should've crushed the little roach when we could," Xander panted.

"Well, it doesn't help to dwell on the past," I said.

I glanced back and noticed Varian easily squeezing through the doorframe. Once out, his long arms alternated forward as he thrust himself closer to us. He gained speed with every forward motion.

"How long until we're off his property?" Nevel shouted.

"The bridge," I hollered. I pointed to the wooden bridge a hundred yards in the distance.

The arms of the octopus slammed the ground. We could feel the ground tremble below us as he got nearer. At long last, we were at the bridge, and Xander motioned for us to cross before following after us. Almost to the other end, Varian placed his first tentacle on the bridge. He shook it violently, as we struggled to maintain our balance. Nevel and I finally made it off the bridge, but Xander still fought to make his way.

I reached out my hand to his. "Hurry, Xander," I urged.

Varian crept dangerously close behind him. The octopus reached his tentacle out and grazed Xander's leg before grabbing it. Nevel threw his tri-blade baton and severed the arm that gripped his leg. Varian emitted a high-pitched, shrill cry. Xander reached down to retrieve the baton. He took my hand and safely returned to land. The shape shifter didn't give up. He raced towards us, snapping his beak repeatedly. I took out my machete and began to hack away at the ropes that held the bridge on our end. Varian flung himself at me, his beak nearly reaching my face when finally, with one last hack, the ropes finally broke. The bridge swung to the other side, as Varian gripped onto it. We watched as he pulled himself to safety, and glared his yellow eyes at us. We turned our backs to him and ventured into the fog ahead.

CHAPTER 16

It was nearly impossible to see beyond the noses on our faces. We carefully navigated through the opaque swirls of dense fog. At any point below our feet, the cliff could drop and we would all plunge to our deaths.

"I don't know if we're headed in the right-" Nevel began but was cut off before he could finish. The sound of loose rocks and gravel crumbling from the side of the cliff permeated through the thick, moist air.

"Nevel," I gasped. "Where are you?"

"Don't move, or you'll fall," he warned cautiously.

I dropped to my hands and knees. I felt around for the edge of the cliff. When I finally found it, my hands searched for Nevel.

"Xander, feel for the edge of the cliff with your hands. Nevel, keep talking. We need to hear you if we're going to find you."

"We talked a lot last night. I'm not sure I have much more to say," he said.

"That wasn't me, silly. You were flirting with a master shape shifter."

"What makes you think I was flirting?"

"I don't. I mean," I said befuddled. "What did we, uh, you two talking about?"

"Weapons and fighting techniques, of course."

Grateful to the fog for once, I could feel my cheeks redden.

"Gottcha," Xander proclaimed.

"Actually, Xander," I said. "That's my hand."

"Sorry."

I heard more rocks loosen and slip off the cliff's edge. "Nevel? Are you still there?" I asked, trying not to sound too worried.

"I'm fine. Doing great, actually. I'm climbing down towards the bottom. I figured, we have to get down there anyway, and I was already in a good position." His voice sounded more distant as he migrated further away from us. "I'll meet you guys down below."

I carefully swung my legs over the edge of the cliff and climbed downward. It was surprisingly not as difficult as I'd expected. The further I descended, the less dense the fog was until I was out in the clear. I saw the dirt below and Xander quickly emerging from the fog above me. In no time at all, we were both on flat ground and sauntered over to where Nevel waited.

"That's one time I wished my fairy genes were a bit more dominant. Would've been great to have had a pair of real wings," said Xander, as he wiped sweat from his face.

"It was a cinch for me," Nevel chimed in.

Xander flexed his arm and patted on the obvious muscle that protruded. "A little more work climbing down when you've got a bit of an extra load to haul down with you, I suppose."

Nevel was about to say something, but I beat him to it. "The doors," I exclaimed. "Just as Queen Pavia had mentioned would be here."

I rushed past Nevel and Xander to get a closer look. I ran my hand against the intricately carved wood of the first door. They were each remarkable in their own right. All displayed a different scene etched into the wood. They were surrounded by stone doorframes set into the side of a mountain.

"It's absolutely beautiful, such craftsmanship. These images," I said. "I wonder what they mean."

"Myrilla would know," said Nevel. "How are we going to know which one to open without her?"

"Couldn't we open them all?" asked Xander.

"No," Nevel shook his head. "Only one leads to Kasus. The others, if opened, are portals to other worlds. Only a few know how to travel those portals and return anywhere they're welcomed back on Alderek, like Willox."

"Or the tall agent with the grey eyes," I said under my breath.

"Who?"

"Someone," I said, as I broke out of my deep thought. "When I was in London, Haggin had sent someone to find me. I never found out who he was, but he must've traveled one of these portals."

"So, let me get this straight," Xander said. "If we opened the wrong door and end up in another strange world, we may never come back?"

"Right," said Nevel.

"Well, how hard is it to travel through one of these portals anyway? What prevents you from coming back?"

"I'm not sure, but I'm not willing to find out either. You've got one chance to go through and make it back. If you aren't knowledgeable about how to do that, then you're stuck. Would that be a chance you'd be willing to take?"

Xander shook his head, "I guess not."

"I didn't think so."

"Could I use the portal to get back home?" I said.

"Home?"

"Yes, London."

"Of course, but like I said, you'd have to know how."

"Who can show me?"

"Astrid," Xander dropped his voice. "You aren't thinking of leaving us, are you?"

I turned away, torn between reuniting with Pike and the orphans who relied me at the castle and the life I could possibly have with my parents in a new Alderek. It was tempting to go back. The opportunity to travel to London was at my fingertips, but, at the same time, I had a commitment to fulfill here. So many had placed their trust in me to bring back Alderek. Would it be wise to abandon them now that we've gotten this far at the door of Kasus? *Focus*, I reminded myself. I gazed up and shook my head, "No, just curious. So what do we do?"

"I think we're all as clueless as the next person," said Nevel.

I walked to each door and examined the intricate carvings. "The clues must be in the details," I thought aloud. I ran my hands along the lines of each design.

Each door appeared to have a different warriors carved into the wood. The first bore a large cypress tree as tall and as wide as the door itself. The flattened leaves fanned out and decorated the branches like the feathers of a bird. Underneath the tree, an armored knight leaned against the trunk for support. The second door bore the image of another armored warrior. This time, he was as tall as the cypress tree in the first door. The belt of his armor resembled the head of a fierce dragon with horns atop its head and a serpent-like tongue that hung from its mouth. Carved on the last door was a caped warrior standing with his head cast down in a somber gaze. His hands were clasping the hilt of his downturned sword, and a winged helmet adorned his head. Behind him, the setting double suns aligned with his head and the horizon aligned with his shoulders.

"I honestly have absolutely no clue what this all means," Nevel said, as he gazed upon the doors. "Just to let you know, if we all get stuck in another world and food is scarce, you have my permission to eat me in fox form. I feel like this journey has really brought us all very close together. Just don't try it here in Alderek, okay? Not here, no way."

"I'm not sure how to take that, buddy, but thanks," Xander replied awkwardly.

"No one is going to get stuck in any world without food unless we let Haggin continue to destroy our resources the way he's been doing," I assured them. "Anyway, I think I may know which door leads to Kasus."

"Wonderful, Astrid. Which one?" Xander asked.

"That one," I said, pointing to the door with the somber gazing warrior.

"Are you sure?" Nevel seemed concerned.

"I'm fairly certain."

"Are you *sure*?"

"Yes, I'm pretty sure."

"Fairly certain and pretty sure don't sound so certain to me, that's for sure," Nevel crossed his arms.

"Would you like to open the door you think is the one? Go in, come back, and let us know," I said.

He scratched his head. "I haven't a clue. I'm sure your guess is much better than any of ours could ever be."

"I'm sure she has a good reason for selecting that door. If you'd let her explain her reasoning, you might feel a little more comfortable with the decision," Xander said. Then he turned to me, "Go ahead, Astrid."

"Of course," I began. "You see, in the first door, the cypress tree takes up most of the size of the door. Its dominance is apparent, especially since the warrior is leaning against the tree for support. Nature over man. The second door displays a huge warrior. No nature is present. The image of the dragon is on his belt, signifying man is the dominant player. Man over nature. And, finally, the last door, the door I've chosen. You can see the warrior's head is bowed in what I'm interpreting as respect. His head and shoulders are at the exact same level as the twin suns and the horizon. Man *with* nature. They're equal, which is why I chose this door."

"You made that all up in your head just now, didn't you?" Xander grinned.

"Sounds good, though, doesn't it?" I winked.

"Good enough," said Nevel. "Looks like Argon's about to set, so we'd better hurry up. Something tells me it won't be as much fun to meet the dragons in the dark as it would during the day."

The three of us pushed the massive door forward and stepped inside. The door shut immediately behind us, and the possibility that we were truly in another world didn't escape me. The temperature was significantly colder than where we were on the other side of the door. We could see our breaths, puffs of air in the form of miniature clouds. As we ventured further from the door and out of the shadows, we quickly realized we were in a cave. Pristine water flowed through it, and all around were columns of crystal stalactites that formed archways overhead. The cave wall was carved just as the doors had been with intricate designs that spanned from the floor to ceiling.

"We're in some kind of ice world," Xander said.

I placed my hand on the wall. "This isn't ice. It's crystal."

"Where do we go from here?"

Nevel's eye widened as he pointed out into the distance. "I think we have company."

A swiftly moving, erratic tuft of cloud rushed towards us. When it got closer, I could make out its the s-curve motion, as if it had a tail like a serpent. Until, finally, I saw it for what it really was.

"A dragon," I gasped.

Except for the embellished golden spade on its tail, the dragon was all white and as transparent as the crystals around us. As it flew closer to the walls of the cave, it almost seemed to vanish and then reappear as it moved away. It stopped inches from our noses. It gazed upon us, sniffed Xander and Nevel, and then snorted as if to approve. Then it fixed its pale blue eyes on me and softened. I placed my hand on her head. For a moment, we stood there and communicated telepathically with words meant only for each other. When we were done, she surprised me with a lick. Her tongue was dry and sticky, but tickled as it ran along my neck and face.

"She says they're expecting us, and she's here to take us to Kasus," I explained.

"It's a she?" asked Nevel, as he petted her between the nostrils and received a snort in response.

I laughed. "Her name is Aolani. She's been waiting here for us for days ever since they heard my first calling. All of the dragons have already come out of hibernation, except for Merrek."

"Merrek?" asked Nevel. "I'm guessing he's the baby of the dragon clan?"

Aolani snorted in Nevel's ear.

"Hey! Okay, I didn't mean to offend. I'm sorry. What did I say?" he said, wiping the dragon mucus.

I stifled another bout of laughter. "He's their elder. Essentially, the alpha dragon, the grandfather to all the dragons. All their bloodlines can be traced back to him."

"Why is he still in hibernation then?" asked Xander.

I shifted legs, as I listened to Aolani's explanation. It wasn't good news. Then I said, "Merrek's opposed to living amongst humans again after what they'd done to the dragons. He stays in hibernation to avoid having to kill us."

"Oh, great," Nevel sighed. "The granddaddy of them all is protesting. Please, tell me he's the only dragon who'll attack us if we go out there to Kasus."

Aolani nudged me.

I took a deep breath. "There are others, but they'll only fight if Merrek tells them to."

Xander put his arms over our shoulders and smiled, "So, what are we waiting for? It's freezing down here."

Aolani tucked her legs under her belly and lowered her wings. We climbed onto her back. In one rapid motion, she sprung up and lifted off the ground. Her wings were glorious and strong. They pushed the air beneath them, and we soared through the crystal cave like a bullet on the loose. We came to the end of the cave where the mouth opened up to what appeared to be an endless sky. Instead of the vast blue skies, it was a crystal dome that protected the city from the sea above it. The water that flowed through the cave dropped below us into a magnificent waterfall, where the beginning of a rainbow was born out of its frothy mist. The city of Kasus was breathtaking. It was a mystical land of rocks, rivers, flat topped trees and misty rivers at every corner. Aolani ducked into a tunnel made of arching trees and decorated with hanging flowers actively blooming before our eyes. Petite waterfalls dribbled between every other set of arches. I leaned over and caught some water in my hand and took a sip. Sweet and pure, it was delicious. In the distance, I could make out a stone fortress. It stood out amongst all the natural splendor. Nothing about it besides the rock it was made out of seemed natural. It was largely out of place, dark and seemingly isolated from the life outside.

  Aolani soared through the gates that opened when it heard her dragon call. Once inside and safely on the ground, we got an idea of how truly expansive the perimeter of the stone fortress really was and how it barely resembled the land we saw beyond its border. It was a different world within the walls of Kasus' fortress. The land desolate, flat, and dry. Nothing in particular stood out except random boulders and the occasional flat-topped tree. It was quiet, but I had the sense that something was out there.

Aolani snorted loudly. She thumped her hand against the ground. The gentle vibrations almost made me lose my balance, but not before Xander caught my fall.

"She's calling the others," I told him.

Then, as if on cue, from behind the boulder nearest us, a pair of emerald green eyes peeked out and then disappeared. Further ahead, a head and a long neck craned out from behind a wide tree trunk. It was definitely a dragon. Some flew from out of the leafy flat-topped trees, displaying the ease with which they could lift their heavy bodies in flight and land as carefully and as lightly as feathers. One by one they started to emerge, slowly and gracefully, until everywhere we looked, dragons of every color came forth and gathered together. I felt a gentle tug on my shirt and my eyes wandered downward. An olive green, baby dragon no taller than my knees gamboled around me. She tilted her head and offered a tender smile before making her way back to a dragoness I presumed to be her mother. Hundreds of pairs of eyes were promptly on us, the visitors from the land above. Would they welcome our presence or urge us to leave them in peace as Merrek would wish them to do?

Aolani addressed her clan. She made several grunts and vocalized sounds from the back of her throat. Then she stepped back, kneeled over her front legs, and bowed her head down before us. The others followed suit, and I knew these dragons wished to restore the freedom they once had on Alderek, living amongst the other creatures.

"This is a good sign," I said.

"That there's a good possibility they won't char us for dinner?" Nevel said. "Yes, I believe it is a good sign."

Just then, a group of four dragons swooped in low from above. I ducked, nearly avoiding an impact with the sharp claws of one of them. The other dragons lifted their heads and backed away, making room for the four to land before us. One of them stepped forward, his neck branched out towards me. I could feel the warmth of his fire-breathing breath. It sent chills down my spine as I watched his steamy breath escape from his nose. He was a currant red dragon with a silver belly and steely blue eyes that focused on me alone.

"Why have you come?" he asked, telepathically as he grunted aloud.

"Are you Merrek?" I inquired aloud.

"My father sleeps in the cavern below. I am Leif," he answered. Then he repeated, "Why have you come?"

"I've come to seek the help of the dragons against King Haggin," I said.

He lifted front legs off the ground and his head to the sky, as he let out a high-frequency cry. Then his eyes found mine again. "I can't help you. None of us can. If you think the fate of Alderek can be saved if we dragons band together once again with you humans, you're sadly mistaken. Move on and live your life the best you can before all the world is inevitably lost."

"I want to see Merrek," I replied.

"Dragon watcher, Merrek will not help you. He will destroy you. You're lucky I refused to carry out his bidding for him."

"Why didn't you?"

"What good would come of it if I did?" he asked rhetorically in return. "Aolani will take you back to the crystal cave. Go home to your family. There isn't much time left."

He turned, and we watched as he dragged his tail behind him and his entourage followed. The other dragons made way as Leif passed through the crowd. This couldn't be it. We'd traveled so long and so far to get to the dragons. I couldn't accept his refusal to help us, especially since there were so many other dragons in the clan that were willing to assist.

"I still want to see Merrek," I blurted.

Leif slowly turned to face me. He approached until he got close once again so I could feel his warm breath.

"Please," I said, standing my ground.

With Leif and Aolani leading the way, we descended down the steps that led into the dank cavern. It smelled of citrus and lamb shanks, and I could vaguely feel the rumble within my stomach. We traveled down a long corridor that eventually led us to the end of the cavern.

"You're on your own from here," Leif said. He and Aolani parted to the sides of the cavern and my friends and I stepped forward. Then we saw him, the sleeping black dragon. His horned frill adorned partly down his neck and gray horns swept back from his brow. Thick black whiskers embellished on the underside of his chin like a beard. He rested his long slender jaws on his immense clawed hands. Although he was asleep, his furrowed face was plagued with tension. His massive size alone was already intimidating. More than thrice the size of Leif, it was apparent why the others in the clan wouldn't freely join in alliance with me without the support of Merrek. I suddenly felt puzzled. How did a creature so large and powerful become so afraid of confronting a human like Haggin? Haggin's army of fenova couldn't have been as large in numbers then as they are now. Why was Merrek so afraid?

"Stay here," I prompted the others.

Nevel grabbed my hand. "Are you sure, Astrid?"

I nodded and squeezed his hand to reassure him. I approached Merrek, making sure to leave several feet between us. Then I dropped to one knee and pulled out the pouch that Servil had given me. I held it between my hands as I bowed my head and spoke to Merrek so only he could hear my thoughts.

"My name is Astrid. Astrid Noble. I'm a dragon watcher by blood, the one who woke the others from their slumber. I'm here to ask for your help. Alderek is suffering, much greater than it has been before your hibernation. Villages, lands, families. So many have been destroyed. Burned. Separated. I believe, together we can restore the peace you once knew in this world. Humans and dragons, all creatures, living in harmony. I can sense it's what many in the clan want, but they won't act without you. I see Kasus is a beautiful city. It's glorious. But you can't let the rest of the dragons hide behind the fortress for all eternity while you stay here and hibernate. We need you. You are the key to a better future for all creatures. Please, wake," I said.

There was no response, not even a flinch or a breath. It was like talking to a statue. I would have to try another approach.

I stood tall and elevated my head so I could look directly into the face of the sleeping dragon. "You don't have to be afraid of Haggin anymore," I said aloud.

Just as I expected, he opened his anger-infused, golden eyes. He lifted his head and threw back his neck as he let out a painfully, screeching roar. His lower jaw dropped and flames escaped from his throat and out his mouth, as it scorched the cavern ceiling. Then, without warning, he craned back down again so his face was level with mine. For a moment, we held our gazes. He was filled with fury. I was struck with fascination. He was bold and strong, yet stubborn and full of hostility. He dropped his jaw.

"Astrid," I heard Xander holler.

I felt the temperature rise and the heat escape from his mouth. I emptied the entire content of the pouch into my hand. The orange glow at the back of his throat was the first sign of flames I could see. I threw the dust into Merrek's mouth as the flames shot out. I felt my body thrown to the ground, uncertain if I had been burnt to a crisp. When I opened my eyes, Xander was laying over me.

"Sorry, I had to tackle you," he panted as he helped me back to my feet. "Don't do that again."

"Do what again?" I asked breathlessly.

"Get so dangerously close to death."

Nevel rushed over. "Are you all right?"

I nodded. Then I turned my attention to Merrek, who continuously opened and closed his jaw, unable to spew his fire. He craned his neck over me and gagged.

"Don't worry," I said. "It'll wear off." Although I wasn't quite sure that it would, I certainly hoped the dust would last long enough for me to convince him to join forces with us.

He noticed Leif behind us and raised his leg. With great force, he slammed it into the ground. "She wasn't supposed to get this far. I told you to remove her from our city."

"She wouldn't leave," Leif said.

"Obviously," huffed Merrek. Then he turned to me, "If you desire the Alderek that once was before the Great Divide, you'll have to attain it without the help of my clan."

"But the dragons are our last resort. You've worked before as peacekeepers alongside humans. No other creatures could have achieve that peace," I explained.

"You'll find another way."

"There is no other way. There's no time left either," I pleaded. "Haggin has an army of fenova and minotaur that keeps on growing. Thousands of creatures are kept as prisoners to work in the fields with little or no food and water. Land everywhere, villages and forests, are burning up there and no one can stop them. No one is strong enough or fast enough to even slow them down. But with the dragons, we have a chance."

"It has taken centuries to build our clan in numbers. We were lucky the first time that Haggin didn't wipe out our entire species. He'll do far worse than force us into hibernation next time. I can't take that chance."

"But if you don't take any chances at all, we'll all surely die. Every one of us."

Merrek shook his head. "The dragons have survived centuries below the ground while man, beasts, and creatures have warred on land. We can sustain our species. I can't help it," he pointed a claw upward, "if they can't."

I didn't know what else to say. What more was there when Merrek was clear he couldn't care less about the others that shared his world. I remembered the butcher in the marketplace. Even with the daily thievery of his goods, he gave an orphan a chance to redeem herself for the sake of the other children. There was hope in that marketplace for a better life, to somehow help each other. Perhaps because Alderek was on the brink of extinction, compassion was an endangered species better saved for no one.

The lump in my throat swelled, and I hung my head low. Overwhelming sorrow made me tremble. I buried my face in my hands and dropped to my knees. I panged for a free Alderek, but I wept for my parents. They had risked their lives to save me from this world. Now, the tables were turned, and my parents were the ones in danger. The only problem was, I didn't know if I could do the same and save them from this world. Without the strength of the dragons, even with the help of every remaining creature, we were small in numbers and mostly untrained.

I felt a hand on my shoulder. Nevel said, "Astrid, are you all right? Do you need more time?"

"We all need more time, Nevel," I said as I wiped my tears with the back of my hands. Then I rose from the ground and lifted my chin high. We were already in close proximity to Merrek, but I decided to take a few steps closer. I looked him in the eyes and said, "My great, great grandfather, Arturo, fought alongside you and your dragon clan once before to free this world from King Ganic. He didn't doubt your abilities or give up trying to become your ally, and neither did I. For a few days, I believed I could be a dragon watcher like my mother and the others in my family before her. I wasn't born into this world. I didn't grow up here either. But this is where the roots of my family stem. This is where our history began, but I'm not going to let it die here. I'm sorry your faith in mankind and this world had to end like this. I truly hoped we could've fought together side by side, so we could once again live together side by side." I bowed and took a few steps backwards as I continued, "Good bye, Merrek. I'm sorry if I wasted any of your time. I know there's not much left."

I turned and motioned my friends to follow me. "Come on, guys. It's time to climb that mountain on our own. If we can at least get my parents, Willox, and the others out, they'll know how to start a rebellion, with or without dragons."

Our footsteps echoed as we left the cavern, resonating against the walls. Yet with each step that took us further away from Merrek, the more they sounded like nails that drove deep into my heart. They were nails of doubt and apprehension. But all I could do was walk and hope no one would see me bleed.

CHAPTER 17

Don't give up hope. Those were Aolani's last words to us before she flew away through the crystal cave and disappeared into the distance.

We walked through the door and found ourselves above ground once again. After hours of moving forward in silence, we reached the entrance to the forest. A shallow pond guarded it, with only the trunk of a single fallen tree providing a path across. A wispy fog lazily danced over the water, which shone bright green with algae blooms in the early evening sun. Stepping carefully, we traversed the log, slippery with patches of moss. The branches of the trees were draped in long veils of moss that hung like tapestries, embellished with pink and blue flowers that grew on vines weaving their way through the strands. We reached the other end of the log and felt the crunch of dry brown leaves that carpeted the ground, contrasted by the bright green ferns that glistened in the mist. We journeyed deeper into the forest, minding the roots of the massive silent giants that loomed over our heads. When finally, we came upon a small clearing that lay before what must have been the tallest of them all. Its branches extended out and interlaced with the trees surrounding it, the moss enveloping them and making it hard to tell where one ended and the next began.

"Time to rest," Xander declared, as he leaned against the trunk before gradually slumping down.

"What if there is no other way," I wrung my hands, while I paced. "The further we get from Kasus, the more I worry and wonder. Are we giving up our only chance to survive?"

"It'll be a lot easier if we had the dragons with us, that's for sure. But, unfortunately, we don't. We can't be wasting time that can be spent building up a rebellion," Xander said.

"I hate to say it, Astrid, but Xander's right," chimed in Nevel. "Merrek seems like he isn't willing to budge. There's no telling how long it may take, if ever, to convince him to fight alongside us. Besides, you said so yourself, with the help of Willox and your parents, we may not need the dragons to start and win a rebellion."

I parked myself onto a tree stump and sighed. "I just wished I could've done more."

Nevel cocked his head and stood before me, "More? I don't know that any one of us could've done as much as you have combined."

I shook my head, "Willox and Queen Pavia brought me here to wake the dragons. They had faith I'd be able to convince Merrek. You were right, Nevel. I'm just a girl. I'm no dragon watcher."

Xander came up next to Nevel and raised an eyebrow, "You really told her that? She's *just a girl*?"

"Well, not in those exact words," Nevel shrugged, his cheeks flushed. "But I didn't mean it, and you immediately proved me wrong, Astrid. If I hadn't been traveling with you, I'd have been pushing up daisies at least three times already."

"He's right," Xander said. "I can absolutely attest to that. Only I'd probably bumped the number to about half a dozen or more times."

"Sometimes I wonder if we're friends," Nevel turned to Xander and joshed before returning to me, "Point is, we wouldn't have gotten this far in the first place if it wasn't for you. It may be a lot harder to defeat Haggin without the dragons, but it'll be nearly impossible to do it without you."

"Well said, buddy," Xander embraced him unexpectedly.

Overcome with laughter, I didn't realize when, almost immediately, I was lifted off the tree stump. Xander held me in his arms, and Nevel joined in without hesitation. Although this suffocating display of affection wasn't something I was used to, I felt grateful for it. I allowed myself to relax and closed my eyes in what I was convinced was the safest place on the planet.

Serenity didn't stay for very long when my trance was broken by sudden removal of Nevel's arms. My eyes burst open, but he was already gone. I pulled away from Xander and turned my gaze upwards. Vines wrapped around his body from his mouth to his knees as he was pulled higher towards the branches.

"The tree," I exclaimed, "it has Nevel."

Vines dropped from the top of the tree and writhed like snakes in search of prey. Xander activated the spring-loaded triple blades and slashed at the vines that grabbed for us. I reached for my bullwhip. The vine hadn't reeled Nevel in high enough that I couldn't reach him. I cracked the whip and sliced the vine above his head. Like an apple falling from the tree, he came crashing down. He transformed into a fox, and I quickly caught him before he hit the ground.

I set him down, and he transformed into his human form. "You see? What would we ever do without you?"

"Die," Xander blurted, as he continued to hack away at the reaching vines.

"Or you could run," I said. A vine swung towards my head, and I ducked in time to avoid strangulation. This time I took it as a hint to take some action. I shouted, "Run!"

Vines continued to swoop down, grabbing at us like hungry claws. We dipped and dodged, uncertain if we'd ever make it to a clearing. I felt my heart rapidly beating in my chest. The growing side stitch ache warned me I was running too fast and too much. Then I saw her, what appeared to be a dwarf rabbit of some kind. She was a tiny, butterscotch-shaded creature, no larger than my cupped palms. Her rounded ears rested atop her shaggy face with cheeks that protruded as if forever stuffed with leafy greens. She stood as tall as she possibly could on her hind legs, and with her puffy, little paws, she frantically waved me over.

I steered myself in her direction, and she immediately turned to run. She was fast, but when I fell behind, she stopped in her tracks and waited for me to catch up. Before long, the rabbit darted into the hollow at the base of a massive tree. I stooped low and crawled into the vast space with her. Nevel and Xander followed closely behind. We watched as the confused vines tangled against each other and retreated to the tops of the trees that surrounded us.

A giggle immediately caught our attention as we looked back at the rabbit that led us to safety. "That was quite an adventure," she said. Still in the process of catching our breaths, we stared at her amused. She cleared her throat, "Sorry. Not much happens around here. Humans rarely visit, and it's a largely uninhabited forest. I think you can guess why. You have to be small, quick, or live underground if you want to survive around here. But even the small *and* the quick avoid living here if they can. The trees have a rather voracious appetite."

"What are you doing here, then?" I managed to finally catch my breath.

"The trees don't bother with me. I eat the weeds. I used to live in the Valley of Mintz until the fenova started to march through it on a daily basis. This place is like a paradise for me. Plenty of food, privacy, and no fenova. They wouldn't dream of entering here. The trees won't let them get very far."

"Are you a shape shifter by any chance?" Nevel panted.

She looked at us with delighted brown eyes that hardly shown any white. "Not a shape shifter. Just me. Ordinary me," she grinned. "I'm Bun-Bun."

"Well, thank you, Bun-Bun, for coming to our rescue. I'm not sure how much longer I could've run out there," I said. "I'm Astrid No-"

"Astrid Noble," she interrupted gleefully, as she patted her paws together in a silent clap. "Yes, I know. And these are Nevel and Xander, the ones you helped escape from the collection compound. I know everything."

"You do? But how?"

"Friends I haven't seen for ages have been showing up. They've been laborers at the compounds for months, and now they're free because you gave them the key. A rebellion has begun. Nothing huge, but it's something nonetheless. Most everyone who was once held captive is now on the run, helping to plan and recruit."

"What about the fenova? I can't imagine they're sitting on their hands and allowing all this to happen," said Xander.

"Oh, no. They're furious," she said. Her ears twitched. "King Haggin has ordered more land destroyed, homes smoked out, and no prisoners taken. Entire villages, families, even the old are on the run. Nowhere is safe, and everyone is on the move."

"That doesn't sound any better," I muttered.

"No, but it is," Bun-Bun's eyes lit up. "Don't you see? The oppressed are free, and the rebellion has started. Many of us may be losing the homes we have now, but regaining all of Alderek back is just on the horizon. It's only a matter of time."

She was small and her voice squeaked, but somehow Bun-Bun seemed much taller when she spoke. I looked out of the cavity we were in and back into the forest. The giant trees loomed, deceivingly innocuous and still.

"Bun-Bun," I said, "how do we get to Mt. Iris from here without becoming plant food?"

"Simple. You're in luck, because you came at the right time. Some of my friends are the best diggers around, and they've come to visit me. It's a good thing they haven't left yet. Actually, they were the ones who brought me the news about the rebellion and informed me about the infamous dragon watcher and her friends," she gestured at us. She continued perkily, obviously eager to assist, "I'll go fetch them now." Bun-Bun disappeared into another hole in the ground.

Nevel glanced over at each of us, his face full of consternation and anxiety. "Are we going to wait for that thing to come back?"

"You mean the bunny?" Xander asked, amused. "Bun-Bun, was it?"

"Yes, the *bunny*, if it really is a *bunny*."

"What makes you think she's not?" I inquired curiously.

"Well, maybe she *is* a bunny, but the friends she's going to fetch may be fenova or some other monster creatures."

"I don't know. She seems genuine, Nevel."

"Are you afraid of her?" Xander chuckled. "Didn't you used to eat rabbits?"

"I'm not afraid," Nevel shrugged. "It's just, we never can be too cautious. That's all. Remember mole man, Varian? He didn't turn out to be very cute in the end either."

"She's a bunny, Nevel," Xander said flatly. "I'd rather wait for the bunny than get mauled by man-eating trees out there."

Nevel nodded. "Okay, point taken. But if her friends turn out to be man-eating rabbits, don't say I didn't warn you."

The soil shook beneath us, and we immediately moved away from the center where the ground began to rupture. A geyser of dirt erupted into the air in front of us. As the spray settled, out popped three furry faces with cheeks that protruded, one wore glasses and a huge grin.

"Uncle Nevel," the three squirrels exclaimed in unison. They leapt from the opening in the ground and trampled into his arms.

"Benny, Tasha, Annie," he said, a huge smile planted on his face. He held the girls in his arms as Benny clung onto his neck from behind.

"Something tells me these aren't man-eating bunnies, Uncle Nevel," Xander quipped.

"Argh..." Benny playfully ruffled Nevel's hair.

Nevel shrugged. "Guess I can't be right all the time."

The baby squirrels' mother, Nellie, was the next to exit from the ground hole carrying a torch. Bun-Bun rapidly poked her head from the hole, followed by a male squirrel with glasses that closely resembled Benny. Nellie came forth and embraced me.

"Thank you for bringing back my Hubert to our family. Without you, who knows how long it'd be before we were all reunited again, if ever," she said.

Hubert approached and took my hand in gratitude. It wasn't until I got a closer look did I recognize him as the one at the collection compound that caught the key. It all made sense now. Each of his shoulders bore a branded serial of numbers that I guessed corresponded to each of his offenses. "Thank you, dragon watcher," he repeated, the same words he'd mouthed at the compound.

"Please, it is I who should be thanking you," I said. "You got everyone out of that compound and now there's hope of a growing rebellion. It's the step we so desperately needed to move forward."

"Just know, we are forever in your debt, me, Nellie, our whole family. Haggin has taken so much away from us already. What can we do to help you remove him and restore the peace we once had under the watch of the dragon watchers?"

"We need to get to the base of Mt. Iris without having to deal with the trees," I said. "Do you know a way?"

"The best way out is in that direction." He pointed towards the entrance of the tree from which we came. Then he dropped his hand and pointed to the ground, "From under here."

"Perfect. What are we waiting for?" I grinned.

"Nellie. Bun-Bun. Kids," Hubert instructed. "It's time to make history."

Nellie handed me the torch. Xander, Nevel and I did as much as we could to break through the soil, but our work was nothing compared to that of the giant squirrels and the dwarf rabbit as they burrowed effortlessly. The tunnel ran under a good few miles stretch of the forest. We navigated around the scattered roots of the trees above, careful not to disturb them in the process. After a few hours, the three little ones stowed away on the limbs of their Uncle Nevel. My arms grew sore as we continued to trudge through, eventually using sticks and rocks to scrape the dirt. Before our arms could turn to jelly, Hubert finally announced we'd hit rock.

"Mt. Iris," he shuddered. Then he pointed upwards, "Just a few feet more and you'll be in a different kind of danger's zone. Shall we see what's on the other side?"

Hubert raise his paws, ready to claw the dirt above him. I held my hand out before he could break through. "Wait," I said. "Please, take your family and Bun-Bun. We don't know what's on the other side, and I can't risk you being here to find out."

Nevel handed the children over to Nellie. They'd fallen asleep and were limp in her arms. "Be safe, Astrid. We won't stop believing in you. In all of you," she said.

"Thank you, Nellie. Stay safe. Keep spreading the word to everyone. Together we can take back Alderek and finally go home." I planted a tender kiss on the foreheads of each the sleeping children. We watched as the squirrels made their way down the tunnel they helped create.

I felt a gentle weight over my boots. "I can stay, Astrid. You might need me," Bun-Bun said, as she sat on my feet. Her brown eyes awaited my answer, and she appeared as innocent and young as slumbering squirrel babies.

"It's too dangerous. There's no telling who or what Haggin has guarding the mountain," Xander said.

"I'm small. When you break the surface, I can get out there and survey the area. It's quiet up there right now. They'll detect you in an instant unless you know how to get around."

"If they found you, you won't stand a chance," Nevel responded. Then he turned to me, "We can't let her stay, Astrid. Tell her she can't stay. It's too risky. I'm with Xander on this." Bun-Bun innocuously hopped towards Nevel. Her nose twitched, and she sniffed his shoes. He bent over to give her a pat between the floppy ears, and, before any of us could register how it happened, she bounced off the walls like a wild bunny on fire. In an instant, as quickly as it had started, she froze and faced us. In between her teeth, she held his baton with the tri-blade stars.

"There's a reason those trees leave me alone," she murmured with the baton in her mouth. She spit it out, "I'm fast."

"Okay, she's in," Xander blurted.

"Me, too, I second," said Nevel.

"I'm glad you agree," Bun-Bun smiled broadly. "I can dig a hole right through the top. Want to see?"

"Slow down, Bun-Bun. We'll break to the surface tomorrow. You can stay with us until you've surveyed the land on top. Once it's clear, we'll have to go our separate ways," I said, settling against the tunnel wall and staking the torch into the dirt. I picked up a stone, pulled out my machete, and began to sharpen its edges. When I was done, I wiped the machete over my pant leg to remove the steel burrs from the blade.

"But, Astrid, you might need me when you get to Haggin."

"It's too much of a risk. There's a reason why Merrek won't allow the dragons to fight, and it's because he's afraid. He's afraid of Haggin. I'm not sure why he believes Haggin is powerful enough to wipe out his species. But I have a feeling we're going to need to be at our best because we're going to find out for ourselves really soon."

I closed my eyes, hoping to find some solitude. It had been a long day, and I didn't expect tomorrow to be any shorter. I shuddered, uncertain of what I was afraid of more, facing the nefarious king of Alderek or meeting my parents for the first time in over a decade. Part of me knew the answer to that. I pulled my knees in and tucked myself into a tight ball, as I waited for sleep to claim my restless mind.

"Astrid, are you awake?" Xander whispered close to my ear.

Sleep hadn't come for me yet, and I opened my eyes. Xander sat against the wall wringing his hands. I propped myself up next to him.

"I hope I didn't wake you," he said apologetically.

"Don't worry. I'm exhausted, but I can't seem to relax enough," I assured him.

Xander nodded his head in the direction of where Nevel slept. He laid on the ground with Bun-Bun curled under one arm. "I don't think I've seen a more unlikely friendship than that one."

"How about the son of a greedy, evil king befriending the daughter of his enemies, the peacekeepers?"

"Life has never been so interesting as it is now. Unfortunately, the situation can only get more dire," he sighed. "One of us will eventually have to kill him, and it probably should be me."

"Xander, there are other ways. Maybe if he sees you, finds out who you are, he'll give up everything."

He shook his head and chuckled slightly. "My father's track record for putting family first isn't exactly perfect. My mother died. Whether or not it was at his hands, he was the reason she's not here today. If he cared anything at all about us, about me, he wouldn't have stopped looking. Finding his child would've been his mission, not world domination. But he had to go one step further. Not only did he tear apart our family, but he's destroyed hundreds of thousands of others. That's no small feat, Astrid. If there are other ways to stop him from wreaking more havoc, he doesn't deserve it. He has to pay for his crimes, and I'll make sure he does."

I hung my head low and nodded. It was a sorry situation he was in, but he was not alone. "Haggin is everyone's problem, not only your own. We'll do this together," I said as wrung my hands.

"I've never doubted you, Astrid," he breathed.

"Whatever happens, I'll always be here for you," I promised. The words came out naturally, but a part of me was uneasy for possibly implying too much. Unable to think of what to do next, I turned to offer a friendly kiss on the cheek. I didn't notice his face was already turned towards me until it was too late. My lips planted over his, and, for a moment, I froze. I pulled away, and quickly turned my gaze back to my hands. Perhaps he saw me blush under the golden light of the burning torch, but he didn't force me to explain. Even if he did, I couldn't. I was grateful for his silence. He wrapped his arm around me and nuzzled his cheek atop my head. I rested my head on his shoulder. Once my redness from my cheeks cooled, I allowed myself to relax until I finally felt safe.

CHAPTER 18

"I hate to be the bearer of bad news, but it's time to rise and shine," Bun-Bun said in her usual sprightly voice. "Today's the day you kick the king out and take back the planet."

"Oh, another one of *those* days," I sighed. I stretched, as Xander fetched us some dried serpent jerky and rolls from our satchels. I scanned the tunnel. "Where's Nevel?"

"He went to collect some roots to eat," she began. "I think he needed some extra time to think after waking up and finding himself snuggling with a bunny. Bun-Bun is cute and all, but still his natural food source."

I chuckled.

"I bet he would've preferred to have woken up to something less furry and more pretty," she continued. Then added, "Like you."

Her nose twitched and a smile slowly stretched along her face. Before I could think of what to say, Xander returned with the food.

"You are lucky, Mr. Xander, very lucky," she said before she hopped away.

Xander tilted his head. "What was that all about?"

I bit into the stale piece of bread in my hands and shrugged. The truth was, I knew exactly what she could see was happening, but I didn't know how to make it stop. So I decided to ignore it. I had to remind myself of what I'd told Eden before. There were more important agendas that I needed to focus on than this emotional conflict that I couldn't quite shake off. I didn't want to lose sight of our mission. It was a priority, as well as a distraction. If I knew anything at all for certain, I knew how to physically fight. Emotions were never my thing, and I wasn't about to let them be.

"Xander, about last night-" I began.

"Don't worry, Astrid. I care about you, too," he muttered, staring only at his food. With brave eyes, he turned his gaze over to me. "I may even love you. But I know how things are right now, and I don't want to complicate things any more than they already are. I'm hoping, in our own time, you'll find the answers for yourself. Maybe, I might even be one of them."

It was difficult, but I forced myself to swallow the food in my mouth. I could hardly move, as he held my gaze. Tenderly, he wiped the crumbs from my lips and caressed my chin.

"Breathe, Astrid," he whispered sorrowfully into my ear. "That was the only thing that got me through when I found out, too."

He wandered off to another part of the tunnel. When I was certain he was out of earshot, I breathed in deeply, unaware I'd been holding my breath. The sound of thumping by my feet nearly made my heart stop. I looked down and noticed the pile of large, cut roots on the ground.

"Time to eat," Nevel grinned. He helped himself to my machete and began to shave off the skin of the roots. "Here, try this."

I took a bite of the thick yellow root that resembled a carrot. It was crunchy at first, but quickly grew gummy and bitter in my mouth. "It's disgusting," I said, as I spat it out. I guzzled water from my canteen to wash the pungent flavor from my mouth.

He took the root and shoved the remainder into his mouth. "Really? I think it's quite interesting. I've been snacking on these all morning."

"Must be an acquired taste," I grimaced, watching him peel another root.

Bun-Bun hopped over and sniffed the roots at my feet. "Those are raggard roots, otherwise known as aviary plunges."

"What an odd name. Do the birds drop the seeds that make them grow here?" I asked.

"Oh, no. Not the birds," she said. "Actually, the dragons used to eat the raggard fruits. Their droppings are what make the roots taste so bitter."

Nevel gagged in mid swallow. He looked about ready to faint. I tried my best, but my attempt to contain my laughter was unsuccessful.

Xander returned. He spotted the raggard root and took the one in Nevel's grip. "Great, you found raggard roots. I love these." He chomped on the root and elbowed Nevel in a thankful gesture. "I don't know about you guys, but I'm eager to get this over with. This may be the beginning of the end after today."

"Or the end of the beginning," Nevel coughed.

"Nevel, I want you to know I've always enjoyed your company. I've never always understood you, but I've always tried to enjoy you."

"Thanks, Xander."

I caught myself holding my breath, as I watched Xander munch on the raggard root. My focus was clouded and my mind wandered to our conversation this morning. It took a simple gesture on his part to realize the tension was my own creation. His blue eyes caught mine, and he smiled tenderly. I returned a reassuring smile.

"Are you ready to find your parents, Astrid?" he said.

I took in a deep breath and nodded. "As ready as I'll ever be." I turned to Bun-Bun, "It's time to put your skills to the test, Bun-Bun."

"I'm on it," she replied enthusiastically. Nevel held her up to the ceiling as she dug her way out. She was small, but she was fast and efficient. Before we knew it, she'd broken through the ground and scurried to the outer surface.

The minutes stretched, and it began to feel like an eternity before we heard her tiny voice again. "All clear. Move out of the way down there. I'll dig a hole from here big enough for you to come out one at a time."

In no time at all, the hole had tripled in size. We climbed up to the surface, and I scanned around quickly to make sure we were alone. No one was in sight, and I didn't see any structures, let alone a castle, anywhere in view. A thick forest stood before us. Behind us, a steep cliff wall extended upward, Mt. Iris. I craned my neck to look skyward and that's when I saw the castle. It was at the same time hauntingly alluring yet dauntingly intimidating. Nothing at all like the old abandoned factory back in London but a genuine stone castle that reached towards the heavens. The castle was carved into the rock at its base, appearing as if the structure had sprouted from the cliff. Its spire-topped towers and battlements jutted into the greyish-blue clouds that swarmed around it. The grey stone walls with narrow windows stretched at least six stories tall. As stark and beautiful as the mountain from which it had been carved, the castle loomed formidably over everything below. A tall, cylindrical guard tower rose from one side another four stories, providing an unmatched vantage of the rest of the mountain range. Had we not come underground, we likely would have been spotted.

I lifted Bun-Bun into my arms. "Thank you, good friend. We would've never made it this far without you."

"Does that mean I can stay?" she stared at me with eyes wide.

I shook my head and patted her affectionately. After we'd said our goodbyes to Bun-Bun and covered the hole from which we came, we turned to the mountain. The cliff was steep, but had many crevices from which rugged plants had grown.

"Only one way to get up there from here without wings," I said under my breath.

"It may take us a whole day," Xander said.

"Then a whole day we'll go. I'm not stopping until we find Willox, my parents and the others."

"Well, then. What are we waiting for?" Nevel said.

In a fluid motion, we made our ascent up the mountain. It felt like minutes when only seconds passed, hours when only minutes passed. Nearly halfway up, I spotted a ledge for us to take refuge. I moved my left foot to the next foothold and reached for the next crevice for a stable holding.

"Astrid, look out," Xander bellowed from several feet below me.

I felt the sharp end of a spear graze my shoulder and watched as blood spilled down my arm. As quickly as I could, I made my way to the ledge. Stealing glances at the attacker above, I noticed he was not alone. A garrison of minotaur glowered fiercely at us. They gathered their spears and aimed, hoping for more bloodshed.

"Nevel! Xander!" I called out. "Hurry to the ledge. Follow me."

Iron spears fell straight down, as if the dark clouds were given permission to rain weapons. Many of the spears struck rocks jutting from the cliff that acted like natural shields and barriers. I drew my machete and did my best to swipe at the crashing spears. Finally at the ledge, I pulled myself onto it. Once I gained my footing, I swiftly went back to wielding my machete to block the spears from hitting the others. Nevel and Xander pulled themselves onto the ledge, and we all pressed against the mountainside under the protection of a slender, rocky overhang above.

"Are you okay?" Xander panted, gently touching my injured shoulder.

Nevel ripped the sleeve from his shirt. He pressed it firmly against my bleeding shoulder and fastened it tightly around. He ripped his other sleeve and stuffed it into his satchel.

"There. Now it's even," he said. Then he kissed his biceps and added, "May not be much to look at, but they got me this far up."

"What do we do now?" Xander asked. Spears continued to tailspin downward passed us. "We can't stay here forever. I'm sure once they run out of spears to throw, they'll find something else." At that exact moment, a minotaur fell into view, narrowly missing our ledge.

"Did that just happen?" Nevel gasped.

"I think they've run out of spears," I said in disbelief.

Another minotaur plummeted from the castle. This time he was able to grab hold onto the ledge. Before he could pull himself up, we all together pushed him over and returned to seeking coverage under the overhang. It wasn't long before the next minotaur made a perfect landing onto our ledge. He snorted and twirled a mace over his head, as he flashed a wicked grin.

"It's three against one, mister," I addressed the minotaur. "Maybe you should think about laying down your arms before we do some permanent damage."

Just my luck, another minotaur safely landed on the ledge. He spun a double ax.

"Like I was telling your friend over here," I said to the newcomer, "three against *two*. Surrendering may be your only option."

Two more minotaur planted a perfect landing onto the ledge. They positioned their spears at us.

"I'm not sure if being diplomatic is helping any, Astrid," Nevel said.

The minotaur glared at us and approached closer, pushing us back until we could no longer press against the wall behind us any further.

"Well, then. How about this?" I swiftly drew my bullwhip and snapped it overhead. The end wrapped around the minotaur's mace, and I jerked it out of his hand and onto the ground. Before he could react, I swooped low to grab the chain attached to the mace. One of other minotaur next to him pointed the spear at us, ready to jab. With no time to lose, I swung the mace and knocked the disarmed minotaur in the chest as he lunged towards me. Faltering backwards, he lost his footing, and, like a domino effect bumped into the spear wielding minotaur next to him. They both fell off the ledge to sudden doom. The other spear possessing minotaur and the one with the double ax charged and directed their weapons toward me at once. Nevel and Xander used their weapons to block the minotaur in front of me.

"I would leave the lady alone if I were you," Xander warned them through clenched teeth. The sweat dripped from his temples and his arms shook as he pushed against the minotaur.

The minotaur with the ax snorted. "That is no lady," he grunted, amused.

"Okay. But don't say I didn't warn you."

As if on cue, Xander and Nevel released their hold against them but not without giving them a shove back a few feet. A clear path was made between the minotaur and me. I turned my back towards them and ran up the mountain wall into a flip. When I landed, I was behind them, near the rim of the ledge.

"You're right," I grinned. "I'm no lady."

With his spear held horizontally out in front of him like a bar, one of the minotaur charged at me. His goal was perhaps to shove me off the ledge with the spear. I snapped my bullwhip. It wrapped around the spear, as I swung the bullwhip upward. The minotaur, still holding onto the spear was tossed up and over me, following the arc of the bullwhip over my head. When I flung the bullwhip back forward, the minotaur was gone.

"Catch and release," I said.

The last minotaur twirled his double ax between his two hands in an impressive display of control. He drew his arm back, ready to toss the weapon at me when finally he was knocked to the ground by Nevel in fox form. Nevel growled and bared his teeth. The minotaur clutched his ax. Xander placed his foot over the minotaur's wrist before he could swing at the fox. He bent down to pick up the ax.

"I could use one of these," Xander said, admiring the craftsmanship of the double ax.

I hovered over the minotaur and demanded, "Is there another way into the castle besides climbing this mountain?"

He snarled and snapped at Nevel, who reacted quickly to avoid a bite and immediately growled more fiercely in return.

"You can cooperate and answer my questions, for which you will be rewarded," I said, "Or, continue the way you've been acting, and you'll be sent on a skydive to the foothill of this mountain without a parachute. The choice is yours."

He grunted. Perhaps it was a minotaur's way of groaning. Then he said, "There is no way to the get to the entrance but climb. The king made sure no one could reach the castle without extreme hardship. Even the fenova have no way to enter. The height of the mountain discourages them."

"Then how do you leave?"

"Once we are brought to the castle to guard it, no one leaves."

"And the king?"

The minotaur chortled. "The king is a different beast. Some believe he's not all human."

"What do you mean?"

"He can create things, magical things like portals," he said, lowering his voice as if afraid someone else would hear him. "And, he possesses the power to destroy anything or anyone with the simple twitch of his finger."

"He twitches his finger?" Xander asked, confused.

The minotaur nodded.

"There's no time to waste," I said. "We have to keep moving. Nevel, bind his arms and legs and set him against the mountain."

Nevel transformed back into his human form. After he bound the minotaur, Xander assisted in dragging him out of the way. I leaned back to glance beyond the hangover and to the castle above. Dozens more minotaur had gathered on the parapet walk. Arrows were aimed in our direction from behind the battlements. The moment they spotted me peek from below, the arrows came flying towards me. Without delay, I ducked under the cover of the overhang as arrows continued to pour down.

"Now what?" Nevel asked.

"We wait it out," Xander suggested, uncertainty in his voice.

I turned to our captive, "How much ammunition does the fort hold?"

"There are several rooms that are dedicated to weaponry alone. We can fight for years," he grumbled. "You guys have no chance."

"Perfect," Nevel forced a smile.

We had traveled so far and gone through so much. I refused to believe it was over. There had to be another way. Then I heard the answer, a distant rumble and the powerful reverberation of something extraordinary like the slowed movement of sails thrashing in the wind. I gazed out into the grey skies beyond the sheet of falling arrows.

"What is it, Astrid?" Xander inquired.

"They're here," I proclaimed in disbelief, not taking my eyes away from the distant sky.

"Who?" Nevel asked.

I pointed off into the distance. There they were. Three magnificent dragons led by a fourth, their currant red leader with a silver belly and steely blue eyes.

"You've come," I said to Leif, in a way only the dragon could hear.

"What would a dragon watcher be without her dragons?" Leif answered. "Looks like you've gotten yourselves into quite a predicament."

"Can you get us out and to the top of the castle?"

"I'll see what we can do."

The dragons rapidly swooped in, dodging and striking arrows in their path. They soared over the garrison of minotaur that hid behind the parapet of the battlement. Fire spewed from the back of Leif's throat. Crouched down low, the minotaur held their shields up to block the flames. Many of them fled and dashed back into the castle. Other began to load catapults with heavy rocks. They aimed them at the dragons, striking an orange dragon with a yellow belly on the lower jaw. In response, the dragon swooped towards the perpetrators. With feet sprawled open and sharp talons fully extended, it clutched the catapult and lifted into the air. The minotaur watched as the dragon drifted further and further above them with the catapult still in his grasp. Without warning, he let go of the catapult, sending it straight down towards the minotaur below. They scrambled to get out of harm's way just in time, as the catapult shattered into numerous pieces where they once stood. The remaining minotaur retreated back into the castle avoiding confrontation with the four dragons that landed on the parapet walk.

A grey dragon with an amber belly flew down to retrieve us from the side of the mountain. Her wings had a turquoise gradient that reminded me of the waters that flowed around the crater's basin near the collection compound. She tucked her nose under the ledge and closed her eyes and she waited for us to climb onto her. She held steady, as she beat her wings slowly to keep her in place.

I turned to Nevel and Xander who seemed in awe at the docile behavior of such a majestic creature. "Her name is Teanna. She wants us to make our way over her neck and onto her back."

After settling onto Teanna's back, she took flight, pumping the air below her wings in a smooth and rhythmic pattern.

"As amazing as this is, I'm not sure I'll ever get used to this," Nevel said as he wrapped his arms around Teanna's neck as much as he could. Xander held his arms in the air and hooted excitedly.

Once at the parapet walk, we dismounted her and came face to face again with Leif. He bowed his head and spoke, his words clear in my head.

"My father wants to acknowledge his wrongful act. He sent you away when he shouldn't have. For generations, our families have worked together, lived together, until Haggin rose to power. He made us forget what it was like to live with the humans. When the dragons were banished underground, sent to hibernate for years, we were unaware of what was happening to our world above. For us, the dragon watchers could never have made it under Haggin's ruthless tyranny. If they did survive, they had abandoned us. Little did we know, the truth was far from what we'd expected. When you brought news of your parents and their captivity, Merrek knew what he'd done. He'd expected the worst out of humans and abandoned our allies in their time of need. Now he," Leif hesitated. With much thought, he continued, "*We* want to rectify it and ask for your forgiveness."

I placed my forehead against his, ready to move on and focus on freeing my parents and friends with the help of our dragon allies.

"What did he say?" Xander inquired.

"I think our rebellion may have a standing chance after all," I smiled. Without delay I added, "Not that I didn't believe we didn't before but-"

"We need to hurry, Astrid," Nevel urged. "Haggin knows we're here by now. There's no telling what he'll do to the prisoners."

The sky darkened, and thunder clasped loudly overhead. A lone jackal bird flew over the castle, and I thought it strange for such a bird to be flying so far from home. Dense droplets of rain fell from the grey clouds above. They began to descend few and far in between but that didn't last long. In a matter of a few seconds, we were all nearly half drenched.

"We'll meet you in the courtyard after we free my parents and the others," I informed the dragons. Before making our way into the castle, I turned back to them and uttered, "Thank you."

Xander pulled me closer beneath the shelter of the castle doorway, as we watched the dragons effortlessly lift from the ground and depart over the curtain wall. They were finally here to fight beside us in this rebellion. They would be a source of strength alongside the determination and loyalty of the citizens of Alderek. Still, I couldn't shake off this feeling in the pit of my stomach that cast a shade of doubt. The idea that it didn't matter how strong in numbers or physical strength we were. This sense of imminent danger that lingered in the back of my mind that made me suspect, even for a moment, nothing and no one was as powerful as King Haggin.

CHAPTER 19

The rain pelted into the doorways and open windows of the first tower. As the wind picked up and blew harshly against the castle, the heady smell of wet stone and rain filled our noses. Further into the castle, we made our way through a covered parapet and directly into a corner tower. With the dragons at the exterior of the castle, we thought it odd we had yet to encounter minotaur in our path headed for the battle outside.

"Get ready for anything," I warned, drawing my bullwhip into my hand. "I don't have a good feeling about this."

We descended the uneven coiled steps of the tower. It was dangerously long and narrow, much like every other part of the castle we ventured through so far. The feeling of claustrophobia seeped in. Nonetheless, it didn't take long before my impression would dramatically change. At the bottom of the tower was a door that opened up into a grand and expansive hallway. The black and copper textured walls stretched endlessly as it reached upwards towards the intricately carved wooden panels on the ceiling. The dark grey rugs draped over the stone floor. If it had been an attempt to add warmth amongst the vastly sinister ambience, it was a failed one. Through the narrow slivers of windows that lined the stone walls, streams of sunlight barely made its way in, a sign that the rain had stopped. Two-tiered lighting minstrels hung from the carved stone arches that repeated all along the length of the hall. Halfway through the expansive hall, we'd already past a few arched wooden doors with decorative wrought iron hinges. All were locked and no signs of life could be heard.

"Where do you suppose we go from here?" Nevel wondered aloud.

At the end of the hall was an atrium with three archways, each leading to stone double doors. The stone door in the center creaked slightly open, as if to answer Nevel's inquiry. I gripped my bullwhip until my knuckles turned white, and we made our way to the opened room. Once we were all in, the door shut itself behind us.

"I have a feeling we're not alone anymore," said Nevel.

"I'm not sure we were ever alone," Xander remarked. "Haggin could've had us attacked at any moment in the other parts of the castle. There's a reason he let us live. He wanted us here, in this room, but why?"

"He wants something from us," I said, realizing we were stepping into a trap.

"But he wants you dead to prevent the prophecy," Nevel said.

"I'm not sure about that anymore."

Daggers of yellowish light beamed down into the chamber from a set of high, narrow windows. The room was still very dark, but more and more, outlines of the carvings in the stone walls were coming into view. I could make out the faint silhouettes of dragons, swooping gracefully downward, their clawed feet extended forward, fire streaming from their opened jaws. Venturing further, I could see centered along the far wall of the room, was a throne. Its jagged edges and points were barely visible, but definitely there. Something was positively sinister about this place, I could feel it begin to radiate throughout my body. Axes and swords suspended from a long chain decorated the side walls, but too far out of our reach to be of any use. This was a room of dark victories, with the stale stench of death permeating the stagnant air. The bare stone floor amplified each step we took, perforating the otherwise gloomy silence. As I approached nearer the throne, the dim light began to reveal its grisly secret. Intertwined bones formed the frame of the chair. Long foot bones were used at the bottom of each leg, and massive wing bones were arranged to form the tall seatback. But, crowning the throne, just above where Haggin's head would rest, was an enormous skull that could only have belonged to one creature.

"A dragon," I gasped, as I felt my stomach turn queasy just looking at it. A virulent mixture of fury and disgust rose from within. "Let's get out of here. The others must be-"

"Right here," a low, rich voice came from behind us. A dark, oversized hooded robe covered most of his face and figure. With his head lowered, he sauntered past us towards the throne of dragon bones. As he sat tall in his seat, he lifted his head and the hood fell back revealing his long sandy brown hair and chiseled face. A long scar crossed his left cheek, and I wondered how it was placed there. I stepped forward, unafraid of the stormy grey eyes that stared back at me. "We meet again," he said, dubiously.

"I've been hoping to meet you face to face wihout the ski mask," I said.

A sly smile came across his lips. "I was hoping you'd die on the way over here," he casually uttered. "But I suppose this could make things a little more interesting."

"Where are you keeping them, Haggin? Where are my parents and the others?"

His eyebrows raised, "In a rush, are we?"

"I don't have time for games," I warned.

"Then where will the fun be?" He grinned, as he narrowed his eyes. "Really, Astrid. Did you think you could storm my castle and make demands without consequences? The prophecy is real, and you will eventually die. But, you see, my dear girl, it's much more complicated than that. There is something I need you to do that could potentially prolong your life while ensuring me absolute power over Alderek."

"You could never have absolute power over anything."

"Oh, but I can. You see, I spent years trying to convince your mother to call on the dragons. I even offered to spare your life if she could bring them over to my side. So I suppose you can say it's your mother's fault I came to kill you."

I shook my head, "My mother did what was right for all of us. She knew I could take care of myself."

"However you want to see it. But I need you to bring the dragons to me. If I can alter them the way I created the fenova, there would be no end to my greatness."

"They're a stronger species than you can ever imagine."

"Which is why I've altered my plans from annihilating them to converting them. After years of research, I've perfected the potion for their conversion," Haggin said, frankly.

"Conversion?"

"You've heard of the dark fairies of Alderek, haven't you? The only one thing I regret about creating the fenova is I didn't beat the idea of loyalty hard enough into after their memories were wiped. With the dragons, there will be no question who their master is."

"Do what you will to me to make your prophecy end, but I can't promise you the dragons. In turn, I ask that you free my parents and the others."

Xander grabbed my arms and turned me towards him. "Astrid, are you crazy? Don't you know what you're getting yourself into?"

"It's the best chance we've got to saving them," I said. "Please, Xander, trust me."

"I don't think so," he shook his head. "There are other ways that include your safety, as well."

"What is this? A lover's quarrel? Interesting," Haggin tilted his head, amused. "Don't stand in her way, Xander. You'll only end up dead trying to save her."

Xander turned to Haggin with hate in his eyes, "You would know so much, wouldn't you? Zahra lost her life because of you."

Haggin's eyes grew with resentment. He rose from the dragon throne and approached Xander until the two were only inches apart. Without warning, he wrapped his hand over Xander's neck and squeezed, lifting him off the ground. Nevel transformed into his fox form and sprinted towards them, baring all of his teeth. Not taking his eyes off of Xander as he struggled to breathe, Haggin held his other hand out. A blue ball of energy formed in his palm and he aimed it at Nevel. It flew from his hand and struck Nevel on the nose, causing him to sail across the room until colliding into a pillar. I cracked my bullwhip, and it wrapped around Haggin's free hand. The electrical shock from the whip coursed up his arm, and he clenched his teeth in noticeable pain. It didn't take long, however, for him to recover and he wrapped the end of my whip more around his arm for a better grip. He yanked it hard and swung me over his head, and I flailed to the ground.

My head was sore from the impact on the stone floor, and it took a moment for my blurred vision to clear. I looked over at Nevel back in human form, gradually shifting to consciousness on the ground after his own impact. Then, as quickly as I'd forgotten, I remembered Xander. Haggin gripped him higher and higher as he squeezed out every last breath.

"No, Haggin!" I pleaded.

"It'll be your turn soon enough, dragon watcher," he proclaimed. "Be patient."

Unable to get to my feet soon enough, I reached out and implored, "Don't do it. He's your son!"

"Impossible," Haggin gritted his teeth and tightened his hold. "My son, Finn, was murdered by a witch when he was only three."

"Let him go! I have proof. He wears your wife's pendant," I bellowed, desperation in my voice. "Mirdeth didn't kill him. She raised him. She's alive. *He's* alive if you let him go!"

In an instant, he released his clutch on Xander's throat. Xander fell to the ground, his body limp and still.

Nevel scrambled over to me and helped me to my feet. "How's your head?" he said as he wiped a spot of blood from my forehead.

"It could be worse," I said. "And you?"

"There's nothing like getting splayed against a stone pillar every once in a while."

Haggin hovered over his son, and then fell despondently to his knees beside him. "I never wanted to believe that he was dead, so I searched countless, endless days for him. Those days turned into weeks, then to months, and quickly into years. It was a very long time before I came to realize I would never get him back."

He reached for the string of vine just behind his shirt and pulled out the pendant. For a moment, we observed as King Haggin's shoulders appeared to tremble. Would this be his turning point? Would the discovery of his long lost son be the answer to saving Alderek?

Just then, five minotaur bombarded the double doors. The marched halfway into the room when they suddenly stopped. One of them stepped forward and announced, "Your Majesty, we've detained dragons in the bailey. What would you like for us to do with them?"

Haggin peered at me over his shoulder. At this point, deep inside, I hoped Haggin was more human than I'd been led to believe. I prepared to witness a softened demeanor or an acknowledgement of the wrong path he'd taken. Instead, I was met with a wry smile that materialized at the corner of his lips. It was at that moment that I realized, nothing meant anything to this monster, not even his own flesh and blood. "Thank you for leading them right to me. It looks like I won't be needing your assistance with the dragons after all." He immediately turned to the minotaur and inquired, "How many are there?"

"There are three."

Three dragons? I thought. Were they attacked? Did one of them get away or was he dead?

"Perfect. That'll be enough to run my tests and still have room for error," he said to himself with an undertone of malicious pleasure. He ordered the minotaur, "Take the dragons to the dungeon and lock them down."

"Right away, Your Majesty," he bowed obediently.

When the minotaur turned to leave, Haggin said to them in an austere manner, "Only one of you needs to inform the rest of the garrison. The others need to stay and kill these two intruders."

Nevel drew his sword, and I my machete. As the minotaur neared us, I quickly glanced over to Xander. Haggin lifted him into his arms and began to carry him away.

"Xander," I hollered, as I started towards him.

"Astrid, watch out behind you," Nevel hollered.

A minotaur grabbed onto my shoulder pulling me back slightly. Able to keep my balance, I swiftly turned and chopped with my hand into the crook of his elbow. When a second minotaur ran towards me, I shoved the first one into him, sending them down like dominoes. After Nevel had taken down one other minotaur, he wrestled with the last one on the ground. His sword had fallen a few feet away from him. The huge minotaur seized one of Nevel's wrists and held it against the stone floor. He pulled back his other arm, ready to knock my friend out cold. I flung myself to the sword on the ground and slid it hilt first to Nevel's reaching hand. Before the minotaur could do any damage, Nevel struck him with the sword.

"We need to find Xander," I said and turned to the direction Haggin took him.

Nevel gently grabbed my wrist. "Astrid, it's probably best to find and free the others first while Haggin is occupied."

I knew he was right, but I couldn't help but worry about Xander. He was at the hands of a psychopathic lunatic. Would he be all right? Had Haggin choked him so hard he would never regain consciousness? What did Haggin plan to do with him? Part of me ached not knowing what would become of him. Still, time was running out, and we needed to find the others before any more orders were carried out that would stop the rebellion.

"I'll be the first to admit, I was never too happy about him tagging along with us in the first place," Nevel continued. "But I don't wish him any harm either. He'll be all right, Astrid. You've seen him fight. He'll make it, and we won't forget to come back for him after we find the others. I promise."

I nodded, uncertain about what the lump in my throat meant. I closed my eyes and focused. We'd come to free my parents, Willox and the others. Now, we had to free the three captured dragons, as well. They would all lead the rebellion, and I would finally be able to return to the orphans in London. I took a deep breath. When I opened them again, I knew I was ready. "Let's move," I declared.

Nevel rested his sword on the chest of one of the injured minotaur that had fallen onto the ground. "Which way to the dungeon?" he demanded.

The minotaur pointed towards the atrium that led to the three double doors. He said, "The doors to the right."

"Thanks," Nevel said. Then he cautioned, "Don't even bother to get up and warn the others. If you do, you'll be the first one I seek out."

The minotaur nodded, too tired and intimidated to fight us off alone.

"Wonderful. Take a nap," Nevel suggested. He reached down and pulled something from the minotaur's belt. When he came back up, he dangled a set of iron keys on a ring in front of me.

"Keys," I said, impressed. "Good thinking."

We made our way to the atrium and pushed through the bulky double doors to the right of Haggin's throne room. It opened up to a narrow hallway, which was lit from the meager sunlight shining through narrow windows above our heads. I could feel the stone floor sloping downward and steadily curving to the right. There was no sound other than the hollow echoes of our footsteps. The corridor seemed to wind down endlessly without any doors in sight. Then, up ahead, I noticed that the ceiling began to sharply angle downward. As we approached, I could see that we were about to reach a staircase. It was narrower than the hall, and Nevel and I cautiously descended the sometimes loose blocks that formed the steps. Gas lanterns mounted on the walls shone dimly. There were no windows in sight. An air of mustiness grew stronger as we traveled lower. I remembered looking at the castle from outside and seeing how it seemed to sprout from the rock cliff. We must have entered the part below the walls, into the solid foundation under the castle. A faint but steady dripping could be heard coming from somewhere down below. I knew that we had to be getting closer to the place we were seeking – the dungeon.

We came to the first iron gate and peered through. It was clear, and I was surprised no one guarded the area. Nevel's first attempt with the keys was a success, and we were in almost immediately. He headed down the corridor and I followed behind, picking up the pace in a quick jog. Suddenly, Nevel raised his arms and stopped. I tripped over myself, careful not to bump into him and force him into the spearhead that nearly pierced his belly.

"Holy smokes, what has he done," I gasped.

Around the corner appeared, on the other end of the spear, a beast I'd never encountered before. His blackened curved horns framed his bulging forehead. His wide chest was like that of a minotaur and his frayed, blackened wings were characteristic of the dark fairy. He possessed fangs and teeth possibly an inch in diameter. They jutted out of his mouth, too large to fit within the confines of his jaws. If this was the game that Haggin played, he was taking on the role of God.

"He's gone and created a new species," Nevel said. "What do you think? Minova? Fenotaur?"

"I'm not sure naming it is such a good idea right now, Nevel."

"Fenotaur. It's definitely a fenotaur."

"Okay, whatever," I said. Without warning, I wrapped my hands around Nevel's shoulders and flung him to the side. I kicked the spear from the fenotaur's grasp.

The beast opened his mouth and let out a high-pitched scream. He fluttered his wings just enough to lift him from the ground slightly and then drop over me. I ducked but not before his sharp claws scraped along my shoulder blades. I winced in pain. Nevel drew his sword as the fenotaur dove towards him, right into his blade. Although the beast was impaled, he continued to flail and drove Nevel into a wall. As he stood dying, he snapped his jaws unrelentingly until his last breath.

"Did he hurt you?" I asked, running over to Nevel.

He drew his sword back and the fenotaur fell to the ground. "I'm not too bad. Probably a bruise or two in the shoulder after you slammed me into the wall."

"I'm sorry. I wasn't planning on doing that, but you kept rattling on and on. I'm surprised that monster waited that long for you to finish out your thoughts without sticking you with his spear."

"Thank goodness for that," he said. "Don't want to learn the hard way that I need to shut my trap."

I smiled, grateful for Nevel's ability to turn a dire situation into something lighter. "We better get moving before we encounter any more of those creatures."

He nodded. I turned to lead the way when he remarked, "Your shoulders, are they all right? Looks like he left some pretty deep gashes."

"I'll be fine."

We made it to the end of the corridor where the path split into two directions.

"Which way?" he inquired. "Left or right?"

I glanced to the left. I couldn't make out much in the darkness besides a faint light at the end. Then I glanced to the right and noticed the three fenotaur headed our way. It was a no brainer. I knew which way my parents were held captive.

I pointed towards the approaching fenotaur. "That way," I declared.

"Why did I have a feeling you were going to say that?" Nevel sighed. "Okay, what's our strategy?"

I cocked my head to the side and thought. "Attack, kick butt, win."

"You've got to be kidding me. What would Xander say if he were here right now?"

"I think he'd add, 'And don't get killed.'"

"I think that ties into the whole 'win' part of the strategy," he said, facetiously.

The fenotaur ran in a triangle formation. Each wielded a spear aimed directly at us. I gripped my machete in front of me and readied for battle. As they neared, the first fenotaur took a giant leap. He flapped his wings to gain a greater distance and landed in front of me. We faced each other and, without hesitation, entered into combat. I took a fleeting look over at Nevel and noticed the second fenotaur already dead on the ground. The third appeared fiercer and was perhaps the bulkiest of the three. Hopefully, Nevel would be able to handle him or hold him off until I could clear my plate. I turned my attention back to my opponent. He was nearly twice my size and intimidating in every way. Each of the blows he delivered with his spear, I blocked with my machete. The force of his strike radiated through my arms, into my shoulders and down my spine. I imagined I was a nail he was sending into the ground, as he pounded away. After several strikes, the machete's blade cracked and dropped to the ground. I narrowly blocked his next blow with the hilt before flinging it and hitting him across the forehead. He paused only long enough to snarl at me. Then he lifted off the ground and came back down with full force and every intention to hammer me in with the handle of his spear. Acting quickly, I drew my bullwhip and cracked it against the spear. It wrapped around the rod but not before sending an electric bolt through it. The shock burned the fenotaur's hand, and he released the spear. Just as I grabbed the fallen weapon, he kicked me under the chin and sent me soaring until I landed hard on the stone floor. He picked up his spear and maneuvered towards me, prepared to pierce me when in range. I scooted backwards with my legs as he approached closer. When he practically hovered over me, he struck with his spear to my left as I rolled swiftly to my right. He tried to jab me on the right, but I rolled to the left. I could see the frustration building in his face. He was so close to finishing me off, and I was prolonging this satisfaction. He lifted the spear high over his head right before he sent it straight down again towards my heart. Before the spear could reach me, I thrust my body forward and slammed into his belly. The force caught him by surprise, and he dropped his spear. He was too heavy to topple over, and I didn't have my next move planned after hugging his belly. The fenotaur did, however, and he lifted me up, his extra large hands crushing me around my waist. I could feel the pressure on my spine, and I winced in pain. If I couldn't get out of his grasp, I would be squeezed to death like a wet rag. He brought my face to his level, and I could see the reflection of my dying self in his black eyes. With my bullwhip still in my hand, I managed to draw back my arm without him noticing until I could crack the whip. It wrapped his neck, choking him as I pulled. An electrical current coursed through the whip and through his neck. His grip around me loosened until I fell to the ground. A few seconds later, the fenotaur fell, too. I found the strength to get to my feet. Fortunately for me, I couldn't say the same about my opponent. My ribs and back were sore but intact. I scanned the corridor for signs of Nevel, but neither he nor the last fenotaur could be found.

    I tucked away my bullwhip and claimed the spear of my fallen opponent. Cautiously, I headed down the corridor from which the three fenotaur appeared.

    "Nevel," I called out.

    No answer. The corridor was eerily silent. My stomach knotted, fearing the worst. The blood-curdling screech of a fenotaur echoed throughout the stone corridor.

    "Nevel!" I shrieked, and bolted towards the sound. I turned corner after corner following what sounded like the magnified screeches of a bird of prey. When the noise ceased, I stopped in my tracks, uncertain where to turn next. I was lost. The feeling of helplessness sunk in. Where was Nevel, and how could I get to him in this labyrinth dungeon?

I closed my eyes and concentrated on connecting with the dragons that were held captive. The walls were thick and heavy, making it difficult to make contact. I was about ready to give up and resume figuring out the labyrinth through trial and error when I heard someone.

"Leif," I said aloud. I listened to his faint voice, barely audible in my head but still there. "I know where you are. I'm on my way."

I was only able to run a few more feet when a steel cage fell over me, knocking the spear from my hands and trapping me in my tracks. I turned my gaze upwards and noticed a wooden door dangling open from above. Ever so slowly, out appeared a large, rounded forehead and two beady black eyes magnified by the thickest spectacles I'd ever seen. It was the mole man or, rather, Varian, the master shape shifter. He sneered when he caught my stare. I pushed against the cage, hoping it would fall over, but it didn't budge. Ramming the side of my body only made the wounds in my shoulder blades ache some more. It didn't take long for Varian to demonstrate his abilities, as he transformed into a snake, a deadly rattlesnake. Slithering down upon the cage and through the bars, he curled around my shoulders. I turned away as he waved his forked tongue near my face and hissed.

"Varian, I should've known you were a Haggin sympathizer. Everything about you is vile," I said through gritted teeth.

"Why, thank you, dragon watcher. You make it very difficult for me to kill you when you say things like that."

He reached for the cage and slithered down the bar to the outside. I drew my bullwhip, and, at once, he transformed into an innocent looking girl, perhaps about the same age as Pike. She wore a white dress with blue petals along the trim, and a matching blue bonnet over her curly, long blonde hair.

"You wouldn't hurt a little girl, would you?" she pouted and looked up at me with watery blue eyes.

I lowered my bullwhip and kneeled down so I was eye level with the girl. "How ever did you get so close to someone so innocent?"

"Easy," the girl said, matter-of-factly. "I killed her mother. She was a trespasser."

"And the girl?" I asked, appalled.

"I don't know," she shrugged. "I let her run away into the valley. It amuses me to think of all the possible outcomes for that child."

"You're demented."

"You're sweet," she sneered. "I'm thinking I may be nice since you've been so full of compliments lately. I'll let you live a little longer instead of the original plan of killing you in a jiffy. Torture it shall be."

I cracked my whip and it wrapped around the girl's ankles, bringing her to the ground. She screamed in pain when the bolts of electricity shimmered through her lower legs. Varian transformed into a rat and crawled into the cage with me. I snapped my whip at him, but he scurried too quickly before shape shifting into a slick, dark scorpion as large as my hand. Stomping my feet, I attempted to crush him, but he proved to be stealthy even with his thick and stocky legs. With remarkable speed, he crawled up my leg and torso until he got to my shoulder. Before I could brush him off and sent him sailing into the air, his stinger pierced my left arm. He crash landed on the ground outside of the cage and scuttled away in a flash. At the same time, I leaned against the bars of the cage and slid to the floor. I could feel a welt form where Varian had stung me. There was a localized burning sensation that throbbed, and I could barely lift my arm without a shooting pain to my neck.

The gradual echo of someone's footsteps as they approached distracted my focus off my shoulder. I gripped the bars and pulled myself to my feet in preparation for another confrontation. Then I saw him in his black gambeson and grey tights. His fiery red hair was all out of sorts as usual as he rushed over to my cage.

"Astrid, thank goodness I found you," Nevel rushed to the cage. "I thought that fenotaur was going to do me in for good. He was brutally relentless. He chased me into every single corner of this place. I'm amazed I made it out alive."

He found the lock and, using the set of iron keys, was able to open the cage door. Lunging himself at me still inside the cage, he gave me a squeeze. I groaned as the pain swelled in my shoulder, and he let me go at once.

"Are you all right? What happened?" he said, examining the damage Varian had left on my arm.

"Wait," I said, taking a step away. "Prove to me you aren't a master shape shifter."

"I'm a shape shifter, but nothing more than a fox to human and back. What's going on?" he asked, notably concerned and confused.

"Varian is here. He transformed into a scorpion and stung me before he got away," I explained. "Tell me something that only you and I would know. Nothing from recent memory."

Nevel was silent. He furrowed his brows as he concentrated on remembering. He said, "I'll forever regret that I didn't believe in you right away the way Xander did. He's probably a lot more than I could ever be. But, when this is all over, I hope you'll take the time to find the two bright stars I showed you that night in my old village. I hope you'll continue to see the heavens and remember the plain old fox boy that was never a prince but always a true friend."

I raised an eyebrow, surprised by his unanticipated sappiness and slightly embarrassed by what it possibly meant. Was he aware of my growing affections for Xander? Did I have growing affections for Xander? Were they that obvious to everyone else but me? I took a step closer to where he stood in the cage with me, confident he was no shape shifting mole man. "Are we having a moment?

Because I just wanted to make sure you weren't a wicked master shape shifter," I said, timidly nudging him.

"I know," he said, with a forced grin.

"Thanks for getting me out, old fox boy. Now let's get out of here before someone locks us in and throws away the keys," I said, as I exited the cage. "Follow me. I think I know where Leif and the other dragons may be."

"Hey, that's *plain* old fox boy to you," he called after me.

"You'll end up just plain lost if you don't keep up," I said.

I massaged the soreness in the shoulder that Varian had bitten. The bump felt harder now, as if a small rock was placed under my skin. I decided to quit rubbing on it so much. The more attention I gave to it, the more irritation it seemed to develop. Navigating through the channels of the labyrinth, I focused on the calls of the dragon to find my way. We arrived at a dead end, and faced nothing but grey rock walls.

"I'm not sure we're even close to where they are, Astrid," Nevel said with noticeable uneasiness. "The dragons are obviously too gigantic to fit between these narrow walls. I doubt the minotaur took them to the dungeon through this crazy maze."

I motioned for him to be quiet. The dragons were telling me something I needed to know. "They weren't taken through this labyrinth," I explained. "They were taken through an underground passageway from the bailey."

"So how do we get to the bailey from here?"

"We don't," I answered. "We're exactly where we need to be."

"I don't know that I'm quite following you," he said, eyeing the stone barriers in front of us.

I began to push on the individual rocks that made up the wall in front of us. I leaned and pushed, but they were all too heavy.

"Not sure if we can move these walls," Nevel said, concerned.

"I'm not trying to move walls," I said, pushing on different spots on the wall.

He tilted his head to the side, as he observed me. "No. By the look of things, I think you really are trying to move walls."

"I'm trying to find the right rock," I said, irritation building in my voice, "that will open up the-"

Suddenly the ground fell open from under us, and our fall was broken as we landed on the fleshy, scaly back of a dragon.

"-trap door," I smiled.

We slid ourselves off the smallest of Leif's entourage, a green dragon with a grey belly. His name was Tourage, the son of Teanna, the other captured dragon. They appeared lifeless in front of us, their limbs shackled to the walls on short chains. Muzzles trapped their mouths shut, and iron collars around their necks kept their heads locked to the ground. There was barely enough light left from a dim, fading lantern hung on the stone wall. No windows would have provided them any relief of light in the morning because there were none. The dragons were basically left in a stone tomb, left to die or worse, fall victim to Haggin's latest experimental creature project.

"Quick, Nevel," I urged.

He took out the set of keys he'd collected from the minotaur in the throne room and used the them on the shackles, collars, and muzzles of the dragons. All failed to turn.

"They don't work," he said, anxiously. "What do we do now?"

Tired and defeated, Leif looked up with me with discouraged eyes. I placed my hand on his head and said, "We'll get you out of here. I promise." I grabbed the handle of Nevel's sword from his belt. "Can I borrow this?"

Stunned, Nevel replied, "I think you already did."

I pulled back with the sword over my head and came down hard repeatedly between the chain links of Leif's shackles. After a few hits, the chain broke apart. I swung again, coming in contact with the chain that connected his collar to the wall until that too broke. Finally, with a single mighty blow to the lock on the muzzle, it split open. Leif shook his head, and the muzzle clanked onto the ground. After freeing Teanna and Tourage, the dragons bound to their feet. They stretched their necks and tails, as if waking first thing in the morning like giant fire-breathing cats. Teanna and Leif crouched down and lowered their shoulders.

"They want us to climb on," I told Nevel. "Leif knows the tower where my parents are being held captive."

I could tell he was nervous about flying on a dragon again, but he simply nodded. I climbed onto Leif and motioned for Nevel to get onto Teanna. He gulped and bravely climbed onto her back. Tourage turned his back to the wall and used his hind legs to hit knock down a hidden door. The dragons took us through a wide, underground barrel vaulted passageway that inclined steadily until we hit yet another door. Again, Tourage slammed his hind legs into the door and it burst open. The suns were on their way down towards the horizon and the sky blazed a blood orange and amber hue, as the dragons took flight.

I looked back at Nevel, only to find him laying low on Teanna's back. He caught my eye and lifted his head slightly. "Not what I expected to be doing when I signed on for this mission," he said.

We flew to the farthest end of the castle where the dragons landed safely on the parapet wall. A tower, tall and narrow, stood before us. We dismounted the dragons.

"Leif says he can hear my mother inside here," I told Nevel.

"That's wonderful," he said. "That means she's alive. And the others, are they with her? Are they all right?"

I shook my head. "He doesn't know. My mother's not well, so her communication isn't the best." A lump formed in my throat, and I fought my best to swallow it down. We'd gotten so far, and I wasn't about to let my emotions take over.

Unexpectedly, Nevel took my hand into his. "It's okay to feel worried. It doesn't make you any less brave."

As much as I tried to blink back the tears, a rogue teardrop escaped from the ducts of my eyes. I wiped it away quickly, hoping no one caught sight of it. "I never asked to care for anyone," I murmured.

"We never do," he answered simply.

Suddenly, a swarm of minotaur and fenotaur rushed towards us on the parapet wall.

"Get in the tower and free the others," Leif urged, as he came between us and the Haggin's henchmen. "We'll handle these brutes until you get back."

"We won't take long," I called out to him.

"Take as long as you need, as long as everyone is brought back safe and alive."

I nodded, then looked up to see two minotaur on the top of the tower. They held a net directly over us. "Leif," I warned, as I pointed upwards. "Look out!"

The net dropped down just as Leif looked up. He took in a gulp of air, then expelled a burst of fire. The net disintegrated in mid air. What was left were ashes and sparks that fizzled out before hitting the ground. Tourage took flight and grabbed the minotaur on the tower, one curled under each foot. After several feet, he dropped them from his hold. Teanna stationed herself in the middle of the wall walk and swiveled her tail as fenotaur dashed towards her. She batted at the arrows that targeted her, until it was all too overwhelming. Turning to face her attackers, she let out a loud screech. When that didn't deter them all, flames spewed from her mouth sending all those that remained jumping off the walls in a desperate act to escape.

Taking the opportunity to duck into a doorway, Nevel and I hurriedly maneuvered through the tower. The stairs were uneven and plentiful as we climbed to the end, eventually leading to a corridor with three solid, wooden doors. After a couple of failed attempts to use the iron set of keys to unlock the first, Nevel tossed them over his head. Without hesitation, he grabbed his multi-blades baton and chopped furiously through the lock. The door opened, and the blood drained from my face. The enclosure was incredibly tight, but the vaulted ceiling was so high and the single window so unreachable, it presented the effect of being trapped in a pit. Nevel handed me his sword. I could barely feel my body move as I ambled into the dank prison cell. My mind was too occupied and overwhelmed with what I saw. The fear of meeting my parents after so many years dissipated, as I realized there was something much greater in my life that needed fearing. Sitting against the wall with their hands shackled above their heads were two figures, malnourished beyond recognition. It didn't take long for the shock to dissipate, replaced by complete and utter rage.

"What did he do to you?" I exclaimed through gritted teeth. The anger within me boiled, and I took it out on the locks on their shackles. When their arms came down and the shackles fell to the floor, I collapsed to my knees between them. For the first time, I didn't care to contain my emotions. I allowed the woman to sweep her thin arms around me, as I buried my head against her bony chest.

I could hear her heart, fast and alive. I allowed my tears to flow into pools that soaked into her clothes. For the first time, I didn't care who saw me, meager and weak with emotion. None of it mattered, for I was finally in the arms of my mother.

CHAPTER 20

Her hands were merely fragments of bones held in place by a sheet of skin. She could barely open her tired eyes. Her long, blonde hair was dry, brittle, and white. Everything about her seemed aged, frail and broken, as if life was literally seeping and escaping uncontrollably from her pores.

My father sat beside her, tall and lanky. With his head drooped in exhaustion, he too seemed drained and devoid of life. His hair was slick with oil, resulting from the lack of washing. His clothes, which may have once fit him perfectly, were now much too large for his weakened frame. When he lifted his head, I immediately recognized his blue eyes, although dulled and sunken, as those I'd seen through the amulet.

"Astrid," my father whispered, almost inaudibly. "I always knew you'd come." His lips were chapped and his throat sounded parched.

I grabbed my canteen and brought it to his lips to drink. Then I lifted the fragile head of my mother's and replenished her slowly with sips of water. I held her bony hand and stroked my thumb against her rubbery skin.

"Astrid," Nevel said. "There's something else you should see."

"We'll get you out of here," I reassured my parents. I opened up my satchel with the leftover food I'd been carrying. "Eat as much as you can hold down. I'll be back." I joined Nevel in the corridor.

"It's the other dragon watchers," he said. "I was able to unlock the door to the adjoining cell."

"Wonderful," I said, my eyes lit up. "They can help us get my parents to the dragons, and we can leave at once."

I started to head past him through the next opened door. He grabbed my hand, and avoiding eye contact, he warned, "Astrid, I'm not sure if you want to go in there. There's something-"

"Don't be silly," I interrupted and waved him off.

"-you should know first," his words trailed, and it was too late.

I set foot into the much larger and expansive room, expecting to find thirsty and hungry people. There would be the dragon watchers my parents had trained to work and fly with the dragons. These were peacekeepers, the heroes of our past and the answer to Alderek's future. When I walked into the room, there were no thirsty people. There were no hungry dragon watchers waiting to be rescued so they could join our rebellion against their perpetrator.

Instead, I entered into a room not filled with the flesh of the living but the skeletons of the dead.

They were laid out neatly in rows of five. There couldn't have been more than fifteen bodies. Stripped of everything but their dignity, their tattered clothes were piled in the far corner of the room. The only thing the skeletons wore were the dragon-shaped pendants around their necks that signified what I assumed were their ranks as dragon watcher.

"Haggin must've had them killed some time ago," Nevel said. "He obviously wanted you to find them like this."

"Whatever barbaric message he was trying to send," I seethed, "I got it. He was looking for the girl in the prophecy, he's found her. I'll be the one. He shouldn't expect anything less from me when I kill him."

Just then we heard a large crash from the outside. A screech from one of the dragons let us know the fighting outside was escalating.

"There's one more chamber we haven't opened," Nevel said.

"Willox and the fairies," I gasped.

Rushing back to the corridor, Nevel worked on breaking the lock of the last door. When it finally broke, we pushed our way through. Three separate metal cages hung from bars that jutted out of the stone walls. Inside each one, Ecson, Maddux, and Myrilla sprawled wearily. The moment they heard us enter, Myrilla sprung to her feet. She gripped the bars and shook them with excitement.

"Astrid," she managed to exclaim, through tired breaths. "Thank goodness you're here. I'm so happy to see you."

Maddux held his hand out from his cage as if to ask for mine. I offered it to him, and he planted on it a gentle kiss. "I, too, am grateful you're here. We never gave up hope you'd make it here." Then he turned his attention to Nevel and said, "You too, Nevel. I never thought I'd be relieved to see your wild head of red hair again, but I am. I truly am."

"Thanks, Maddux," Nevel said. "I may consider never eating you one day if you keep this attitude up."

"It's a deal, fox boy. Now, I don't suppose you have a plan to get us out, do you?"

Ecson rubbed his belly. "You wouldn't by any chance have anything to eat either, would you?"

"Yes," I answered Maddux.

"And, yes," said Nevel, as he pulled an apple from his satchel.

"You may want to stand back," I advised Myrilla. Using Nevel's sword, I broke the lock to the cages, one after the other until all fairies were free. Myrilla and Maddux fluttered around, stretching their wings and offering hugs, while Ecson attacked the apple in Nevel's hand.

"We have one more unaccounted for," I said. "Please, tell me you know where Willox is."

"They took him to the oubliette on the lowest level of this tower," Myrilla began. "It was terrible, Astrid, you should've seen him. Haggin treated him the worst out of all of us. Nobody realized the kind of magic the king possessed, and Willox didn't stand a chance. He had to back down and let them take him away before Haggin blew him to bits or fried him up. Either way, it would've been absolutely mortifying."

I shifted legs and bit my lip. There wasn't much time left, and the dragons could only hold off Haggin's army for so long. After a while, I made a decision. "Nevel," I said, "I'm going to find Willox. Can you take my parents out of this tower and lead them somewhere safe until we can all fly out?"

"Will do, but are you sure you won't need me to come with you?" Nevel inquired.

"I'll be just fine. I hope you don't mind if I took your sword with me."

"Whatever it takes," he winked.

"Thanks," I smiled. Then I turned to the fairies, "Myrilla, Ecson, Maddux. The dragons are out there fighting some pretty crazy creatures. I'm sure you've already encountered some. Do you think you can offer them some backup?"

The three fairies hovered in a line and saluted. Maddux answered for them, "You can count on us."

"We're on it," Ecson added.

They flew upward and out the tower through the sliver of window. I started out the chamber door when Nevel grabbed my hand.

"Be careful," he said.

I turned back to him. "Always," I said.

I raced down the stairwell wondering if Haggin really did place Willox in the oubliette. If he did, how long did he keep him there? I tried my best to concentrate on descending the uneven steps safely, afraid my mind would wander back to the images of the skeletal remains of the other dragon watchers. Were we the last ones, my parents and myself? The stairs appeared never ending, as if I was coming from a tower in the sky.

"There she is." I heard the grunt of a minotaur.

With Nevel's sword in my hand, I was ready for combat. There were two minotaur approaching. It was a wonder how their large feet could balance on the narrow and uneven steps. When they got near, the first blocked my sword's swipe by holding his spear horizontally in front of him. He laughed, thinking I wasn't quick enough. Distracted by his ego, I surprised him with a kick to the chest that sent him off his balance. He fell backwards and toppled over the other minotaur behind him. One after another, they tumbled downward until they were sprawled out on a lower step, most likely harboring concussions or worse. I skipped past them and continued down the stairwell.

At the bottom of the stairs, there was a door. The lock was opened, as if someone else was here. I entered and, immediately, my eyes were drawn to the iron grates on the ground.

"Willox?" I rushed to it and pulled the grate from the ground.

It was dark below, but I could make out his bushy, white eyebrows and long beard. "Astrid," he said, his voice hoarse. "You mustn't stay. It's a trap."

"A trap?"

"How many times do you have to repeat yourself before the young people listen nowadays? Yes, it's a trap. *A trap.*" Hearing his low, rich voice made me shudder. I turned and stood to face him. His eyes narrowed but his lips formed into a wicked grin I wanted to rip from his face.

I dragged the sword by my side and approached him with great disdain. "Where did you take Xander?"

"He should be of no concern to you anymore," he said rather calmly.

"What does that mean?"

"It means," he said, stepping closer until I could feel his breath on my face, "stay away. But that should be fairly easy for you once you're dead."

The scorpion's puncture in my shoulder intensified, and I doubled up in pain. Blood seeped through my clothing and covered my arm. I felt the poison course through my veins, sending spikes of electric shocks to my heart.

Haggin cocked his head to the side as he watched me grip my heart. "How does it feel to die like the other dragon watchers? Slowly but surely, reduced to nothing but bones. I suppose even the best of Omaans can get prophetic visions wrong now and then."

Behind Haggin, Willox rose from out of the oubliette in falcon form. He hovered high above to the ceiling. Haggin turned to see what caught my attention behind him. As he looked up, Willox swooped down with his talons and scratched at his face. Haggin swatted furiously, his arm coming into contact with the bird and sending him across the room. Willox hit his head against the stone wall, and fell to the ground. Haggin stormed out of the room, and I rushed over to the injured falcon.

"Willox," I cried out, picking up the falcon into my hands.

A glow radiated from the falcon, and I set him on the ground. He transformed back into his human form, rubbing the back of his head. I clutched my heart after a moment of pain, but it quickly subsided.

"I've bumped into worse than a stone wall," he said. "But it looks like you're in a more serious condition than I am."

"It's nothing. Just a minor bug bite." I brushed it off. There was something more than my injury that I wanted to discuss. "Willox, I know you have your reasons, and I'm sure it's a good one, but you could've used your powers to stop him from getting away just now. Why didn't you?"

Willox shook his head, and I wondered if he felt ashamed. "I have no powers that could possibly stop him. He is as strong as I was at his age, perhaps even more. If I used my magic against him, it would've only put you in more danger."

"What do you mean?"

He hesitated, but I knew there was no time to wait for his answer.

"We have to get out of here," I said. "The dragons are waiting for us outside, and I still need to find Xander."

"The dragons?" he asked, impressed.

I nodded.

"Well done," he said.

I helped him to his feet and turned to leave when Willox stopped me. "I'm sorry, Astrid. I haven't been completely honest."

"I don't know what you mean," I said.

He continued, "Haggin is my nephew, the son of my brother, Lazarius. My brother was sent away with the other wizards and witches because they didn't agree with Haggin's rise to power. I had a sister, as well, who was supposed to leave. But she escaped, no thanks to me."

"But he kept you. You were the last of the wizards, and he kept you. Why?"

"Because I stood by him. I didn't reject his earlier ideas. He was like a son that I couldn't abandon. Little did I know he would go too far, and it would come to this. By then, it was too late."

"Too late?"

"I'd given him all the secrets to the power of wizardry to be used for good when he became king. He was supposed to send the our brother and the others somewhere far so they couldn't interfere with the rebellion against King Ganic. He wanted to prove himself a worthy king and wizard. In the end, they weren't brought back. I'm afraid he never intended for them to come back from the very beginning. All that time, he'd deceived me."

"Just like the dragon watchers. He annihilated all of them," I said.

"He must be destroyed."

"But before we can do that, I need him to give me some answer. He's the only one who knows where Xander is."

"Xander?" Willox asked.

"Yes. Haggin's son," I answered.

"Finn. He's alive," he said in wonderment to himself.

"Willox, we have to get out of here," I urged.

With little time to lose, he transformed into a falcon and we dashed up the stairwell. When we reached the wall walk where I last saw the dragons, there was still plenty of action left for us to handle. I looked over the wall and into the bailey where Teanna was overwhelmed with fenotaur at all sides. She thrashed around, trying to shake off the ones that pounced onto her back as they avoided the flames she spewed out. They jabbed her with their spears and horns, and she yelped in pain as she bled.

"Tourage," I called out. He flew over to me, and I climbed onto his back. We swooped downward towards the fenotaur in the bailey. Tourage breathed fire over their heads, forcing them to abandon Teanna's back to seek lower ground. I jumped onto the grassy courtyard, immediately swinging around to kick an approaching fenotaur. He fell to the ground.

"Thanks," I said, taking his bow and arrows.

More fenotaur streamed out from the castle towards us. I took aim and struck one right after the other before they could get closer.

I noticed Nevel cornered in the bailey as he shielded my parents from the fenotaur's spear's. Realizing he only had his bladed baton to protect them, I drew his sword from my belt. Quickly, I slipped an arrow through the knuckle guard and placed the arrow on the bow.

"Let's hope this works," I muttered to myself.

Lifting the bow, I pulled back on the string. I aimed the bow and lined it up to the center of my target.

"Don't move so much, buddy," I mumbled, directing my comment to Nevel who was erratically jabbing and dodging the fenotaur's blows. He constantly came into my line of sight, and I felt my stomach knot. A bead of sweat formed and slid down my temple. I was ready, confident I had a clear shot of my target, a hefty fenotaur closest to Nevel. I breathed easy, as the string fell out of my fingers and the arrow was released. It struck the fenotaur in the neck, a mere inches from Nevel's face. The fenotaur fell to the ground, and he pulled the arrow from his neck to release the sword. He waved it in my direction as a sign of thanks and began to fend off the rest of the fenotaur.

I directed the rest of my arrows to the others that were coming from the castle to attack Teanna. Running out of arrows in the quiver, I began to worry we would quickly be outnumbered. Working alongside Leif, the fairies did what they could to distract the garrisons so Leif could whip them with his tail from behind. His flames were growing weaker, and so were the flames of the other dragons the longer they fought. We were an army of nine against hundreds of well equipped fenotaur and minotaur. It was obvious we were wearing down rapidly, and collapse would soon be inevitable. I caught glimpses of the destruction around me, and watched as our efforts slowly came to an end. The fairies and Willox were trapped by a net overhead, while Leif could no longer breath out a spark of fire. The fenotaur stormed over him like a colony of ants feasting on its prey. Tourage was nowhere to be seen, and Nevel had been seized by his attackers as well. I held the last arrow in my hand and drew it back on my bow. I aimed it at one of many fenotaur that advanced toward me. Before I let go, the already darkened sky grew darker. The moonlight was smothered above, and the magnified sounds of sails fluttering in the wind overpowered anything else. Everyone stopped to turn to the sky. The moon slowly revealed itself once again, backlighting the clan of dragons that were swooping down onto the castle. The first one to approach was a massive black dragon with a silver belly and steely blue eyes that reflected the moonlight. Tourage flew by his side.

"Merrek," I cried out.

The dragons dove in, sending constant flames through the doorways to prevent more garrison from coming out. They came to the aid of the others, freeing the fairies and Willox from the net and Nevel from his attackers. Merrek landed beside me and Teanna. He torched the grass around us, creating a flaming border from our attackers. With the last bow still drawn in my bow, I scanned the bailey. Then I saw him, his stormy grey eyes glaring directly through the fire at me. I narrowed in on my target and let the string go. The arrow sliced through the burning wall and struck him in the side as he tried to run away.

"Merrek, I need to get out. Haggin's getting away," I said.

The enchanting dragon nudged me onto his head and reached his neck safely over the flaming border. He gently placed me onto the ground.

"I'm glad you've decided to take a chance on us," I said. "Thank you."

"I was very selfish," he said, bowing his head. "Your ancestors have saved my children from certain destruction for generations. It would be ungrateful and unfaithful of me to forget this and not return the favor at least once."

I nodded. It took a tremendous amount of courage for someone so prominent to admit his mistakes. Flames broke out far and wide around us. Enemies were falling from the castle walls to their deaths. Rogue arrows took to the sky but were diverted to the ground by thick tails or the wind gusts from wings. Chaos was everywhere, except in this moment I had with the dragon leader. I embraced him around his snout, as he puffed warm air through his nostrils.

"Be strong, Astrid Noble, dragon watcher," Merrek said.

"Take care of my parents and the others," I told him.

"You have my word."

I darted towards the entrance of the castle keep where I last saw Haggin enter. Glimpsing back briefly into the bailey, I caught sight of Nevel. He pressed forward towards me with a look of consternation on his face. He must have noticed the determined look in my eyes, as he slowed to an eventual stop. For a moment, we stared at each other, as if we understood what needed to happen to fulfill the prophecy. For a moment, I longed for a different life in a different world. I hesitated as I watched his mouth open to say something. Afraid of what I would hear, I turned away before his words could reach me.

It wasn't difficult to guess which direction Haggin had wandered. The injury he sustained from the arrow caused him to leave a trail of blood on the cold, stone floor. The drops meandered up the spiraling stone stairs which wound their way along the wall of the keep. It appeared he'd slowed down, as the droplets became closer in distance. They trailed off into the doorway of a large hall. The door was ajar just enough for someone to squeeze through. I entered cautiously, knowing that Haggin could be anywhere, waiting to attack regardless of his injury. The room was massive, with stone arches that sprouted from the walls and met in the center. A round metal chandelier lit with candles hung high in the hall, its flickering glow glinting off of the many suits of armor that lined the walls. Above them, shiny broadswords, spears, and colorful shields were arrayed in grand fashion, contrasting the stark grey bricks behind them. It was utterly silent. My racing heartbeat pounded in my ears as I scanned the darker spaces. The blood had stopped. There was nowhere else he could go, no other doors that led out of the room. I felt for my bullwhip, prepared to use it at a moment's notice.

"Show yourself, Haggin," I said. "Let's finish this once and for all."

A sudden loud crash made me turn towards its direction. The iron helmet fell off one of the armored suits. It swayed on the ground for a moment before coming to a stop. I bent down and picked it up, turning it around between my hands. It was intricately designed, with two wing-shaped horns and a center spike that sprouted from the top. The large almond-shaped slits were embedded for the eyes, while protective side pieces extended low enough to guard the neck and nape. I heard something rattle from the inside. When I reached my hand into the helmet, I felt something familiar between my fingers. I pulled it out and saw Xander's pendant, the wings outstretched and magnificent. What was Haggin trying to tell me about Xander? I stuffed it into my pocket and cautiously surveyed the room. Another crash of metal on the ground. Drawing my bullwhip, I spun around to find an entire suit of armor dismantled on the stone. An innocuous mouse scurried from the mess and across the room. I let go of a breath I wasn't aware I was holding. As I neared the fallen armor, I clutched the pendant in my pocket. Then, the voice of evil finally revealed itself.

"He spoke highly of you," he said, rather calmly.

I held still in my tracks, feeling the hairs behind my neck raise slightly. I was afraid to ask, "Spoke? Does that mean he's not alive?"

"It means he *spoke* to me about *you*. That's all."

Slowly, I turned around to face him. He was closer than I realized, gripping a small, double-edged knife drawn back over his head. He plunged the knife down towards my heart, but I shifted just in time, getting myself out of harm's way. I cracked my whip, and it coiled around his knife-wielding wrist and sent electric pulses through his arm. The shocks didn't appear to faze him. I yanked on the whip to tighten my hold, hoping he would drop the knife. Instead, he hauled in the length of my whip, drawing me to him. When we were close enough, I released my hold. He stumbled back slightly and shook off the whip from his wrist. After he regained his balance, he sprinted towards me. I spun to gain momentum and kicked the knife out of his hand right before he tackled mc to the ground. His fingers curled around my neck, and his hollow grey eyes pierced right through me. My arms searched frantically for something on the ground, something heavy. Finally, my fingers reached the iron helmet that once contained Xander's pendant. With whatever life I still had left in me, I thrust the helmet with the winged- horns against Haggin's head and knocked him off. With one hand over his injury, he strolled even closer until I could hear his strained breath. I, too, gasped for air. The blood seeped from between his fingers and down his temple. He held his bloody palm up for himself to observe.

"Life can be so interesting at times, can't it?" he chuckled, cryptically. "The son I'd lost so long ago, an illegitimate heir to King

Ganic's throne, the throne I fought so hard for him to receive, is madly in love with the girl who was brought over to assassinate me."

"Where is Xander, Haggin?" I pressed, as I got to my feet.

"How do you think that made me feel when I discovered this tragic information?" he sulked. "I can tell you, it didn't make me all that happy."

"What did you do to him?" I seethed.

He leaned in so his lips were near my ear. Then he whispered, "There are some secrets I'd rather take with me to the grave."

When he pulled back, he drew out from within his brown robe another small dagger. Without hesitation, he held it between his two hands and pierced it through his heart.

"No!" I cried out.

As he fell to his knees, the castle walls began to rumble. Debris steadily rained from the ceiling. A small piece of stone hit my shoulder where Varian had delivered his poisonous venom. The pain resonated through my body, as I felt the poison flow through my blood. I crumpled to the ground next to Haggin's dead body, the castle falling apart all around us. Noticing my bullwhip nearby, I crawled to it and tucked it safely onto my belt. I winced in pain and brought myself into a sitting position. I couldn't tell if it was my head that caused the incredibly dizziness, or if the ground was truly swaying back and forth. Getting myself to my feet was a major accomplishment when I realized it was a little of both. I darted to the door, but stopped just short of nearly getting crushed by a large chunk of the ceiling that crashed down. It was the only exit I could take to evacuate. There were no windows or other doors that led to the room I was in. I was trapped.

Suddenly, a section of the wall on the far end of the room caved inward, exposing the darkened sky outside. A giant crimson eye peeked inside, then pulled away. Another crash against the exterior and the more of the wall caved in. There he was, a green dragon with crimson eyes carrying Nevel on his back. The castle jolted, and I lost my footing and fell to the ground.

"Astrid," Nevel called out.

Disoriented, I struggled to pick myself up again. I watched as the dust came in streams from the ceiling and onto my sweating body. The sound of rock against rock reverberated through my ears, and I trembled uncontrollably from the poison as it spread erratically through my body. Fighting against the nausea and temptation to pass out, I managed to make my way to the opening in the wall. The dragon flew down closer, and Nevel reached out his hand. Our fingertips brushed briefly, until the dragon swiftly moved further away to avoid the falling stones of the castle. The floor in the room behind me began to fall through as the castle imploded. Seeing no other way, I drew my bullwhip. Carefully, I sidearm cracked it to wrap around the leg of the dragon. I felt my body raise from the ground as the dragon lifted higher. I watched the castle disintegrate from a distance as we drifted further away into the cover of the night. Hauling myself up the whip, I slumped against the leg of the dragon. Compassionate arms scooped me onto the back of the dragon.

The voice of a familiar friend coaxed me in my ear and stroked my hair comforting me. "You're safe now, Astrid. Your parents should be with Queen Pavia by now with the fairies and Willox. Everything will be okay. Don't worry, I have you."

With eyes closed, I smiled as I relaxed in the warmth of his arms. "Xander. I knew you'd find me," I whispered.

"I'm sorry, Astrid, it's only me," I heard Nevel respond dismally. "We couldn't find Xander either. We searched everywhere we could on the castle grounds. If he was somewhere in there, he most likely didn't survive."

I opened my eyes slowly and gazed up at him. "I'm not sure if I'll ever stop looking for him, Nevel, even if he is gone."

"Don't worry. You won't have to look alone. I'll do whatever it takes to help you find him. I promise," he reassured. I didn't doubt his loyalty.

I heard the gentle fluttering of a dragon's wings. As my dizziness waned, I soon realized that the sound hadn't belong to a single pair of dragon's wings but dozens of others with us in the sky. I glanced back at the castle that once stood atop Mount Iris. What was once a grand extension of the mountain, was now fragmented and littered. Somewhere within the muddled debris laid the body of a feared king and his lost secrets. Our dragon continued on while the others veered away in the direction of Kasus, where they would join their leader, Merrek, to the safety of their underground city once again. Perhaps their fortress walls will crumble as well, and the future generation of dragons will wander and explore the never ending beauty of Kasus without the fear of King Haggin looming.

We approached a forest with thorny branches that shielded many secrets. Willox met us at the entrance, and with his help, the branches parted and soon was revealed a passageway. We dismounted the green dragon, whose name we came to know as Savant, and said our goodbyes. His size was too large to safely enter and would damage the pathway. Once we arrived at the cleverly disguised boulder home, my wizard friend tended to the poison injected into my body by the master shape shifter. He used an animal that resembled a leech of some kind to extract the poison. It hurt when it latched on and injected its own poison to counter the scorpion's. Like tiny liquid fire bombs, it discharged within my body and detonated in several sections where the poison did the most damage as I writhed in astonishing pain. When all was done and I was healed, we ventured onward. Beyond the wizard's enchanted dwelling stood a tall, thick forest, the hidden forest where Queen Pavia resided with her colony of fairies. When the fairies caught a glimpse of us, there was a silence unlike the first time I'd encountered them. They advanced towards us as one group in wonder, then bowed their heads. The fairies parted down the center, as they made way for a captivating couple. The woman wore her blonde hair long down her back, and he had his black hair parted neatly to the side. She wore a stunning, flowing yellow dress, and he dressed to match her perfectly. Their appearance was a stark contrast to how I remembered seeing them the first time, frail and thin, barely holding on. They were remarkably returned to health and now stood before me.

The fairy queen followed behind them, her skin radiating a light blue halo around her. My parents moved over to the side to let her pass. Nevel discreetly stepped back leaving me in the presence of Queen Pavia with everyone else looking on. She took my hands into hers.

"We are forever grateful for your honor and your loyalty. You have truly shown bravery in the face of danger." she said. Then she tenderly placed her hand on my shoulder. I bowed my head in respect. "On behalf of all that are present and every person and creature of Alderek, we bestow upon you honorary citizenship for life and the official title of Dragon Watcher, peacekeeper and protector to all."

Myrilla came forward, her cheeks rosy and her smile contagious. With little difficulty, she carried a pendant on a silver chain almost as long as she was. Queen Pavia took the chain from the fairy and fastened it around my neck. The pendant hung on my chest where I finally got the chance to observe it. It was in the form of a strong, black dragon much like Merrek with dazzling golden eyes and blood orange flames that spewed from his mouth and encircled his body, framing him.

"Thank you," I said, swallowing the hard lump that formed in my throat.

Queen Pavia smiled. She threw her arms in the air and turned to her colony, as she proclaimed, "Let the festivities begin!"

Music and cheers filled the air. Maddux and Ecson took turns spinning Myrilla. Caught up in the excitement, my parents drew me into their arms but my mind wandered elsewhere. For a fleeting moment, I remembered the orphans in London and the apple-cheeked child that stole my heart. I knew I needed to get back to them, but now wasn't the time. I couldn't abandon this world when there was still more danger in the wings. Although we celebrated the downfall of a cruel and oppressive king, I was well aware the rebellion was far from over as long as the dark fairies still roamed the land. When that time came, I told myself I would be ready with my parents, Nevel, and the dragons by my side. Maybe one day also, whether in another time or another world, my path with Xander will cross once again. Until then, reunited with my mother and father, I knew I was home in Alderek.

EPILOGUE

Covered in debris from the waist down, the body of Haggin lay buried underneath the rubble. His pale face was showered in a chalky dust that made him appear as if he was a part of the stone. A piece of a broken statue, a casualty of the implosion. It could be that this was what it appeared to be, if not for the peculiar spasms that twitched the muscles in his face. The spasms happened at random, at first. Look away and the occurrence would be missed. As time progressed, so did the frequency of the spasms until they became unambiguous, blending together between different sections of the face. They grew larger, more intense, with each passing convulsion. When they finally stopped, Haggin's face was just a mere memory. In its place was no longer the image of the king of Alderek but of a hairless man with a large, rounded forehead and two beady black eyes that stared into the void of the universe. Protruding from the rubble, his stubby fingers still clasped the dagger used to pierce his own heart. On the back of his hand was a thick, black mole from which three coarse black hairs sprouted. Nobody knew it, but Varian was dead. The master shape shifter had died at his own hands and laid trapped in the ruins of the castle.

###

He could hear the destruction of the castle above, massive heaps of stone crashing to the ground. The tragedy of his castle and most loyal follower was a massive loss, but he could only hope it was worth it. The demise of the girl would make it all worth it.

Covered in his brown robe with his hood turned over his head, he pushed the stone into the wall that opened a hidden door. It led to the stairs that would take him deeper than he already was within the mountain. He followed the stairway where it curved to the other side of the mountain, all the way to the very bottom. He pushed through another door that blended into the surrounding rock and soon found himself outside. The fog was dense, too thick for anyone in the sky to notice his wooden boat at the water's edge.

Slumped in the boat was the body of a man, tall and muscular. His wavy, light brown hair hung disheveled over his closed eyes. The robed man pushed the boat into the water, then climbed in. He removed the hood from over his head, and with his stormy grey eyes, stared off into the limited, hazy distance. He turned to his unconscious companion and held his hand just below the man's chin. An illuminated blue mist rose from his palm and swirled into the man's nostrils and out his ears.

"Wake, my son," he commanded.

The man woke, his eyes under the spell of the blue mist.

"I will teach you everything I know. From now on, we will be indestructible. Do you understand?"

The mist cleared, and the man blinked and rubbed his head. When he looked up into the face of the his captor, his head cleared. "Yes, I understand," he nodded. Then with little hesitation, he added, "Father."

"Very good, Finn."

From the Author:

Thank you so much for reading my book. I truly hope you enjoyed it! If you feel compelled, please leave a review on Amazon.com for *Astrid Noble and the Dragon Watchers*. I would greatly appreciate it!

Coming soon in 2016, the second installation of the Astrid Noble trilogy, *Astrid Noble and the Wizard Prince*.

With warmest of wishes,

E. M. Ritter

@authorEMRitter

Printed in Great Britain
by Amazon